Kirby Williams

RAGE in PARIS

a novel

ISBN: 978-1-888889-76-5

Published by Pushcart Press
P.O. Box 380
Wainscott, New York 11975

Distributed by W.W. Norton Co.
500 Fifth Avenue
New York, New York 10110

PRINTED IN THE UNITED STATES OF AMERICA

Note to the Reader

The novel includes a number of terms relating to African-American ethnicity which were in wide use in the period (1895-1936) in which the novel is set, but may be unfamiliar to today's reader. For example, the term "African-American" had not yet been conceived. "Colored" was considered a polite form of address for referring to African-Americans and did not bear the derogatory connotations associated with it by some today.

Similarly, a number of terms for ethnicity used in the context of the novel's time period may be unfamiliar to the present day reader. These include:

"mulatto"(for a person of half-African and half[white]European ancestry);

"quadroon"(for a person of one-fourth African and three quarters[white]European ancestry); and

"octoroon" (for a person of one-eighth African and seven-eighths [white]European ancestry).

To Liz

"Those who cannot remember the past are condemned to repeat it."

- George Santayana, *The Life of Reason: Reason in Common Sense*

PART I

CHAPTER 1

Paris, Tuesday, February 6, 1934

I was drinking a snifter of calvados at the bar at Chez Red Tops in Montmartre near Place Pigalle in the early evening, listening to Stanley Bontemps drip honey from his soprano saxophone. Time seemed to stop when Stanley played. But I knew that was an illusion. Like thinking that spring was around the corner just because, this afternoon, a little sunlight brightened up the gray skies of a cold, early February day in Paris.

The owner of the nightclub, a red-headed lesbian mulatto named Redtop, was biting her lavender fingernails as she listened to Stanley.

She had served me my drink herself. Her regular bartender had called in sick, frightened off by the growing street violence as left- and right-wing agitators squared off in the streets of Paris, fighting for political control of France.

Redtop took a glass of water to an enormous, black-skinned youngster sitting alone at a corner table in the half-empty club, scribbling furiously in a notebook. He was an admirer of Stanley's named Darius Swilley. Everyone called him Baby Langston. The story was that Baby got the nickname after the famous colored poet, Langston Hughes, heard him recite one of his poems at La Belle Princesse, the Montmartre nightclub owned by Baby's uncle. Hughes proclaimed that Baby was a poetic genius and the next Walt Whitman, whoever that was.

Stanley's sweet sounds were a counterpoint to the raging schemes swirling through my brain about how to make some fast cash to keep my private investigation agency, Détective Privé Domino, in business by bribing some people in the Prefecture of Police to renew my temporary working papers. Any day now, I was expecting a deportation notice from the police to leave France as "an indigent person without French nationality"(or any visible means of support) and with "bad frequentations." That would mean going back to America, and I wanted to avoid that at all costs.

The police kept me under "discreet surveillance" because I used to be a big-time clarinetist in a New Orleans Creole jazz band and the owner of a nightclub in Montmartre, Urby's Masked Ball. They figured that I was using my private eye agency as a cover while I made money by playing jazz illegally on the side, but they were wrong. I had run my club for ten years with the woman I loved, Hannah Korngold. When she finally got fed up with my ways and left me to go back to America two years ago, my music left me too.

Being a private eye in Paris these days was a dirtier job than being a French politician. Still, it was just as well that I'd found another line of work when my music shriveled up. "Hot black jazz in Montmartre," which had been all the rage in Paris since the end of the Great War, had started dying out soon after Hannah had headed back to New York.

The French musicians' union, jealous of the stranglehold that colored American musicians had on jazz in Paris, finally succeeded in pressuring the Prefect of Police into enforcing an old law limiting to 10 percent the number of non-French musicians employed in a jazz band or orchestra.

Whenever club owners stuck to the law, their businesses went belly-up. The Parisian public wanted to see colored American jazz musicians, not French ones, playing music Made in the USA by "les noirs américains." Stanley was one of the few of us the police never hassled. The club owners made so much money off him that they paid the Prefecture a huge bribe to leave him be.

I used the meager savings left from selling my nightclub to set up a private investigation agency and get the necessary work permits. But the savings and the permits have run out, and my business has kept shrinking as increasing numbers of Americans—white and colored—have dragged their tails back to the States, with this Depression snapping at their heels.

I didn't take notice of the man who sat down next to me at the bar at Chez Red Tops until he tapped me on the shoulder.

"Ah you Uhby Brown?" he asked. "Private investigations?"

"Maybe," I answered, sipping my calvados.

The man looked around as if he was afraid someone was tailing him. He was a big, ruddy-faced fellow with pale blue eyes, about my age. He sounded like a Boston Yankee, saying "ah" for "are," and the way he said my name. He was dressed like spring was arriving early this year. The man was sporting a straw boater with an orange-and-black hat band. His white-striped seersucker suit was rumpled, as were his white shirt and orange-and-black tie. His brown-and-white two-toned shoes were polished to a high sheen. As a concession to reality, he carried a raccoon coat draped over one arm, to protect himself against the cold and the biting winds that whipped up from the Seine.

"I have a proposition for you, Mr. Brown. Some quiet place we can go to speak?"

"Sure," I said. "Let's go to my office; it's right around the corner, a few minutes on foot."

I donned my Homburg hat and my double-breasted gray Harris tweed overcoat and waved at Stanley as we left Chez Red Tops. Bent over his horn but watching everything, he raised his eyebrows in a question, and I shook my head no. Redtop and Baby Langston eyed our every move as we left.

My office was in the rue Houdon, a rundown street off Place Pigalle. To get there from Chez Red Tops at night, even on a Tuesday, you had to make your way past wildly careering taxis and buses, horse-drawn carts and wagons, crowds of beggars pushing their war wounds in your face; past street musicians, mainly accordion players, with crowds around them singing from the sheet music that the musicians sell them for a few sous; past swarms of prostitutes selling themselves to the slumming American tourists. In some places, you had to scan the ground to sidestep the trash and smelly filth littering the sidewalks and streets.

The rich Americans, who could still afford to make the Grand Tour with a Paris stopover, tended to be bossy and tried to call the tune, even with a proud people like the French. Worst of all, many of them were doing their utmost to make the French bring Jim Crow to Paris just like back home in the States. If you were dark or yellow-skinned and sat in a café next to a table of them, they gave you their chilly stares.

A number of the colored folks who had settled in Paris after the war were war veterans, like me. Some of the musicians had come to France to play in army bands led by James Reese Europe and ended up as part of the all-black Harlem Hellfighters, the American troops most decorated by the French for their bravery against the Germans and their allies.

This war-tested breed of Harlem-in-Paris coloreds, the sons and grandsons of slaves, weren't about to let US rednecks turn Montmartre into Mississippi on the Seine without a fight.

The dangerous Corsican pimps at Place Pigalle buzzed around the whores and the rich Americans. My neighborhood felt safe to me; I knew those pimps and whores on a first-name basis.

The big Yankee lumbered along behind me, looking like a giant bear in his raccoon coat. He huffed and puffed his way up a flight of stairs and into my office. Once inside, he took off his straw hat and his overcoat and wiped his brow with a big white handkerchief that he pulled from the sleeve of his jacket. Then he took off his jacket, exposing orange and black suspenders over his white shirt.

The walk from Chez Red Tops looked like it had given him the fright of his life. I slid one of my beaten-up office chairs in front of the desk, and he flopped down into it, gasping for breath, his eyes closed. I took off my Homburg and overcoat but kept my jacket on. The radiator was keeping the office just warm enough for us to keep our overcoats off, but I wondered when they would shut down the heating. The bill was long overdue, and it looked like the cold weather was going to hang around for a while.

When the Yankee opened his eyes, he looked around as if in a daze. I took an unlabeled bottle of farmhouse calvados and two shot glasses out of my desk and waved them in front of his glassy peepers. He nodded and I poured; he knocked it back and then sputtered most of the moonshine onto my fine Moroccan rug. He kept coughing and choking, his face turning even redder. Slowly, he regained his composure and put his empty glass back on my desk warily, as if it contained nitroglycerin.

"Thank you," he said. "I'll pay to get the rug cleaned. That's some drink you've got. What the hell is it?"

"Calvados. This kind's brewed up by farmers in Normandy. From apples mainly." I held up the bottle. "But you won't find it in any café or liquor store."

He looked around my shabby office as if it was what he was expecting. Then he fixed his pale eyes on the bottle of calvados. I poured him another glass, and he handled it more gingerly this time. A sip came with a crooked smile.

"Really swell neighborhood you live in, Mr. Brown," Robinson lied.

"Yeah," I said, deadpan. "It's nice...and real safe. That's what I like about it."

He stared at me for a while, studying my face, and then started wheezing with tears flooding from his eyes. He banged on the desk so hard that I thought its flimsy top would collapse. I realized that the man was laughing.

"Very good, Mr. Brown," he wheezed. "Safe." His laughing stopped as suddenly as it had begun. "How safe ah *you*, Mr. Brown?"

He riffled through the pages of a small notebook he pulled from his pocket and then handed it to me. I read the words, written in a spidery scrawl:

"You can trust Barnet Robinson, Urby.
I vouch for him. Help him if you can, pal.
Sean James O'Toole."

The note was dated October 16, 1933, just four months ago. It was from Tex O'Toole, my buddy from the Lafayette Flying Corps.

"I suppose you're Mr. Barnet Robinson," I said, handing back the notebook.

He nodded. "Bahnet Robinson III, in fact."

"How come you know Tex? He's from another part of the country. You're from Boston or thereabouts, aren't you?"

"He's a good friend of a Princeton classmate. When I told him I had a problem to deal with in Paris, he put me in touch with Mr. O'Toole. O'Toole said to look for you in the jazz spots around Pigalle because, if you were still alive, you were the best man to handle my problem."

That made me smile. Tex was the best person to handle any problem anywhere.

He went on. "To answer your other question, yes, I'm originally from Cambridge, near Boston, but I went to Princeton and settled nearby when I graduated. In a place called Hopewell, New Jersey. You know it?"

"No. I never went to New Jersey when I lived in New York," I said. Then I asked casually, "How's Tex O'Toole doing?"

What I really wanted to know was why Tex had not come to deal with Robinson III's problem himself.

"Badly, I'm afraid. He suffered a stroke a while back. They saved him, but he's going to need a long convalescence."

I couldn't imagine that giant of a man lying in a hospital bed with doctors and nurses fussing over him. Barnet Robinson III had a big problem indeed if Tex was asking me to help him. I hadn't seen hide or hair of him since the end of the war. I also knew how hard it was for Tex to ask for help.

"Sorry to hear it. What size problem have you got, Mr. Robinson? I don't know if I can help you." I gave him the once-over again. My gut was yelling at me to walk away, despite Tex's note and my need for cash. "I can give you the names of some private eyes who'd be more useful to you…in the circles you travel in."

"No, I need the services of a private eye," he said slowly, searching for words, "of your…persuasion."

I puzzled out his meaning for a while and then blurted out, "You mean you need a *colored* private eye?"

"Yes."

That really surprised me. I couldn't imagine what kind of problem Barnet Robinson could have that involved colored people.

As if reading my mind, he said, "It's not what you think. I don't want you to shadow some dusky Delilah." He smiled sheepishly at his awkward words.

"Look, Mr. Robinson. Tex has vouched for you, and I'll help you if I can. But you have to level with me before we go any further. White and colored Americans together usually spells trouble, and the same crap's starting up here. I don't need any more problems right now."

He studied me intently, mulling over my words.

"By the way," I continued, "the reason I never went to New Jersey is that people in Harlem say that the Jim Crow South starts when you cross the Hudson River."

"You're right, Mr. Brown. It's a bad state of affairs for you people in America. But I'm only taking yours and O'Toole's word for your race because you say so. You look as white as the driven snow to me," he said with a smarmy smile. He probably thought that I would be flattered, but I was enraged. But for Tex, I would have socked him in the face and kicked his smug, bigoted ass out of my office, however much I needed his money.

He must have sensed my rage. He drew back, looked up at the ceiling, closed his eyes, and said, "All right, Mr. Brown. I'll level with you. I'm looking for my dawtah, Daphne. She's going to be twenty-one in July." He bowed his head to stare at the rug. "She's got mixed up with… a negro musician. She sent one cable saying they were planning to live the good life in Paris. Then she sent another that was an SOS. She asked me to hole up at the Ritz until she could escape from the man. I got your name from O'Toole and cabled her that I was on my way and that I was engaging you to track her down.

"If the word gets out," he continued, "her life will be ruined. She'll be kicked out of Smith College, miss getting her diploma. I'm on the Board of Trustees, too."

"I guess her mother must be mighty upset, too," I put in, not feeling any sympathy for them at all.

"My wife died on the *Lusitania* with her parents when it was torpedoed by the Germans in 1915. Daphne wasn't two yet."

"Sorry to hear that."

He waved off my try at genuine sympathy.

We eyed each other for a while, and I poured us more calvados. Now I felt sorry for him, but I took the musician's side. I had been there myself—on the run with a white woman. Without hearing Robinson's story, I could guess what had happened because it was a cliché:

A sheltered, rich white girl goes out on a date in Manhattan with a rich male with a background just like hers. He's told her that he knows the scene in Harlem, the hotspots where they do the Charleston and the Black Bottom like it's supposed to be done. Hotspots where real black folks go, not white-only preserves like the Cotton

Club. She sits in a dark speakeasy, overwhelmed by the music, the musky smell of the wild dancers, the black laughter. It's like nothing she's experienced before. When her escort orders her another glass of rye and Canada Dry, she starts really looking at the virile musicians, noticing how handsome and alive the drummer is. Then she thinks about the clean, safe banker in her future as a high society woman with a perfect family and the right friends. The drummer is looking right at her, flashing his pearly whites. She blushes, hides her face behind her black velvet gloves, smooths back an errant lock of her hair. He is playing for her. She feels her heart beating in time with his drums.

Robinson and I finished the bottle without saying another word. I kept thinking about Sean James O'Toole, from Galveston, Texas, who took on those flyboys in the Lafayette Flying Corps on my behalf, knocking their teeth down their throats if they even looked at me sideways. Tex knew that I was the second best pilot, and he wanted me backing him up when he flew the point.

When the Air Service of the US Army refused to let me fly for Woodrow Wilson's air force in the war, Tex threatened to quit. Then they upped the ante and swore they'd ruin him.

I rejoined the French Foreign Legion and saw out the war killing Germans in the mud in the slaughters in northern France. The last time Tex and I met up was on Bastille Day in 1919, before the allies' victory parade down the Champs-Elysées. The US Army had banned its colored soldiers from marching in the parade. But, as a French Foreign Legionnaire, I was going to march in it. I ended up missing out, though, because a few minutes before it began, a drunken redneck doughboy walked up to Tex and me and a legionnaire from Senegal and called the African a dirty ape and ordered him to get his black butt out of there. I head-butted the fellow, mashing his nose into a bloody pulp. Tex held off a platoon of enraged doughboys single-handedly while the African and I ran for our lives down side streets.

It came back on me, though. The US Army made an international incident out of the affair. The French Army kicked me out of the legion without a good conduct certificate, so I lost my chance at French nationality. They were going to deport me until my French boss from the Lafayette Flying Corps, Captain Lacroix, moved heaven and earth and they let me stay in France. Tex led a successful campaign to square me with the Americans.

Now, Tex wanted me to help Barnet Robinson III because Tex was too sick to handle the business himself. The more I remembered how he'd stuck by me, the more I knew that there was no way for me to refuse Tex's request.

Barnet Robinson was staring at me expectantly, all traces of fatigue and moonshine calvados gone from his eyes. "Ah you going to help me, Mr. Brown?"

"It won't come cheap. I hope you didn't get caught up in that Wall Street crash stuff."

"I've never dabbled in stocks and bonds, Mr. Brown. Too risky. I'm a metals man, gold mostly. Don't worry about the money. Matter of fact, I'll double your fee. I need your utmost discretion."

He took a wallet out of his jacket pocket, fanned out some banknotes, and handed me five strange-looking, gold-tinged twenty dollar bills. He grinned as I scrutinized them.

"Seen banknotes like those? Gold certificates, as good as gold. You won't go bankrupt with them. They'll buy you a lot of francs on the black mahket."

I knew all about that market. I folded the bills, slipped them into my pocket, and then asked Barnet Robinson straight out: "It was the drummer, wasn't it? The one your daughter ran off with?" He looked really surprised and nodded.

"Photograph of your daughter?" I asked.

He stared at me as if I had offended him.

"I'm not the drummer, Mr. Robinson. I'm your detective. I have to know what she looks like."

He cooled right down. "Of course you do." Pulling the photograph from an envelope in his jacket, he smiled at it. He was a man who loved his daughter; there was nothing phony about that. He handed the photo to me and then studied my reaction.

The photographer had taken a great photo of Daphne Robinson, but he had a lot to work with. Blonde and beautiful, she seemed to shine from the black and white image as if lit by klieg lights.

"She looks familiar," I said.

"Everyone says she looks like Greta Gahbo, only a lot more beautiful."

"Yeah," I said. "That's about the size of it." It was not my place to comment on her beauty to him, but I was awestruck by the photo. I held onto it a bit too long, and he held out his hand. I was about to hand it back to him as he searched my face, an icy look in his eyes, but I had my poker face on. When he seemed satisfied that I knew my place, I pulled the photo back and said, "Sorry, Mr. Robinson, I'm going to have to keep this for a while. I have to show it around to find out if anyone's seen her." I could see that he did not like the idea of my holding onto the photo of his daughter and "showing it around," but finally he nodded his assent.

"Be careful with it. I only have two more photographs of her with me."

"You know the drummer's name?" I asked.

He wiped his brow, as if searching for a name. But I sensed he already knew everything there was to know about the man, except where he had gone with his daughter.

"Thigpen…something Thigpen," he said uncertainly.

"You mean Buster Thigpen?" I asked, surprised.

He snapped his fingers. "That's right. You know the man?"

"Sure do. Me and Buster go way back to New Orleans as young sprouts, and then we played jazz music together in Harlem."

Barnet Robinson only nodded, not at all surprised, I thought. He must have learned a lot about me from Tex O'Toole.

Damn it, I said to myself, the heavenly Daphne Robinson must like her men rough and roving if she's hooked up with Buster T. He was one of the best drummers who ever came out of New Orleans and the best I ever played with—when he was sober. He grew up rough in the Battlefield, the most dangerous neighborhood in New Orleans, maybe the whole world, with a straight-edge razor and a switchblade as his saviors.

But his true savior was Father Gohegan, the head of St. Vincent's Colored Waifs' Home, who convinced the police to release Buster into his custody instead of bundling him off to the Louisiana State Penitentiary, nicknamed "Angola," to raise cash crops for the politicians until another inmate raped or killed him within a few days, weeks, or months.

Under Father Gohegan's musical guidance, Buster turned into a great drummer. He told me all about it on a rare good day for him, when he was clearheaded and sober and could string more than three words together. There weren't many days like that for Buster before or after he left St. Vincent's.

We didn't get along there. He was two years older and a lot bigger than me until my growth caught up to his. He was the newcomer, but he had decided to make my life a living hell because he thought I was "too white" to be at St. Vincent's. That was rich coming from him; he was a light-skinned, straight-haired, yellow–green-eyed quadroon who could have "passed" as a Spaniard, Italian, or another Latin-race person.

He was a good actor, too. Despite being the worst bully in the Waifs' Home, he had convinced Father Gohegan that he was pious and upright. He had become Father Gohegan's right-hand boy for enforcing discipline, and he directed most of his efforts at me.

When I caught up with Buster in Harlem a few years later, I thought, at first, that a miracle had happened and that he had become one of the best and nicest musicianers I had ever worked with. He was funny as hell, great company, and the ladies couldn't keep their mitts off him.

But Buster had a giant-sized problem. When he got moody, he would turn into a whole different person, becoming again the boy who had stayed alive in the Battlefield, by dint of his fast feet and his skills at wielding a cutthroat razor and a switchblade.

He would try to get out of his "black moods" by snorting Happy Dust cocaine and smoking muggles reefers. Then he would turn as wild as a mustang with a catamount on its back. Once he got going, he would throw any kind of drug, liquor, or pill he could buy, beg, borrow, or steal down his chops to keep flying higher and higher.

When he was like that, Buster turned into a monster from *Ripley's Believe it or Not!* and played the drums worse than your great-grandmother. The man couldn't keep a steady job when I left Harlem because he was out of his mind more often than not.

Finding him in Paris was not going to be easy because he looked like a "Mediterranean type," and there were plenty of such men in Paris.

I knew, though, that, sooner or later, Buster was going to need to feed that monkey jockey on his back, and my network of informants would tell me where he went to feed the beast.

Suddenly, I felt more at ease about the job. I was pretty sure that I could track Buster and Daphne down quickly, take lots more of Barnet Robinson's pretty-looking money and, as a clincher, settle my debt to Tex O'Toole.

Things were looking up for me. Thanks to the Boston Yankee, the threat of my electricity, water, and heat being cut off and, more importantly, of my receiving a deportation notice, was beginning to recede. His money would make things right.

I clinked my glass against his and said with confidence, "I'll find her for you, Mr. Robinson."

"I want you to bring Thigpen to me personally, Mr. Brown."

"What do you plan to do with the man? Give him some money to get him to stop seeing your daughter?"

A flicker of irritation iced over his eyes before he answered. "I won the Ivy-league heavyweight boxing championship as a senior at Princeton. I intend to teach Mr. Thigpen some civilized conduct."

I didn't want to be around to see that. Buster didn't box to the Marquess of Queensberry rules. He was a peerless knife-fighter who protected his drummer's hands by not using them to slug people. Any attempt to engage Buster in fisticuffs was likely to prove fatal...for Robinson.

I walked Robinson to the metro station for his return to the Ritz Hotel because the taxis were on strike. Then I spent a few hours wandering around in the bitter cold, checking out my Montmartre sources, starting at Chez Red Tops with Redtop herself. She had left Harlem to come to Paris with Josephine Baker and her Revue Nègre as a pretty 23-year-old singer and dancer in 1925; she had not returned to America with the others. She had not seen Buster in a long time, and she did not miss him at all, she said.

I showed her Daphne's photo. The effect on her was immediate: she smoothed down her unruly red hair with her chewed-up lavender fingernails and fanned her face with her beige-colored hand.

"Oooooo," Redtop moaned. "That's the most beautiful creature I ever seen on this here earth, and I done seen a lot of loveliness walk through these doors. Still, if she be with Buster, he be makin' her run like Man o' War to keep up with him 'cause that man attract womenfolk like honey attract bears."

I made the rounds of the dwindling number of colored-owned American bars and jazz clubs and liquor shops and drug dens in Harlem-Montmartre. I drew a blank each time I showed somebody the photograph of Daphne and explained her connection to Buster. Nobody was glad to hear that Buster Thigpen was in town. But they all wanted to see Daphne in the flesh and as soon as possible, please.

None of the drug dealers had sold Buster T. any dope in any way, shape, or form. With nothing coming down the Right Bank grapevine, I decided to do some investigating on the Left Bank in a few Latin Quarter bars that catered to musicians and the artistic set.

As I was going into the Nord-Sud Metro Station at Pigalle heading for the Saint-Germain-des-Près stop, I saw a stout, black-skinned war veteran busking on the sidewalk near the station entrance. Wearing the tattered remains of his US Army uniform, he sang in a bottom-of-the-well voice "Old Man River" from that musical *Showboat* that came out a few years ago. He was surrounded by a group of drunken American rednecks shouting at him to sing "Dixie" and "Old Black Joe." Instead, the big fellow kept on singing "Old Man River" so soulfully that a crowd of Frenchmen gathered around to listen and dropped coins into his begging beret. The Americans bayed at him more loudly, dangling big franc notes in front of him and snatching them away from his trembling black fingers. I walked down the steps into the metro station, remembering the Mississippi River and New Orleans and what brought me to Paris in the first place.

CHAPTER 2

It all started on July 4, 1895, on the front steps of St. Vincent's Colored Waifs' Home for Boys in Gentilly, New Orleans. The head of the school, an Irish-American priest, Father Gohegan, later told me that my mother, a quadroon Storyville whore named Josephine Dubois, had left me there. He found me at daybreak and took me in.

He was about to turn me over to a home for white foundlings, when he saw my mother pass by the Waifs' Home a few days later and peep through the window. He thought that she was a genteel white lady and, puzzled by her presence in the mostly colored neighborhood, invited her in for a chat. Then she told him her story and asked him to confess her.

During her confession, she told him that she worked in a bordello in Storyville and that I had been fathered by a rich Frenchman who had promised to take her back to Paris with him but had left her when she fell pregnant. She had another child, by a quadroon pimp, but the baby was being raised by the pimp's mother in the Battlefield, a neighborhood so violent that she was afraid to visit the child there.

Josephine Dubois pleaded with Father Gohegan to write to my French father right away and tell him to come for me and take me to France. Father Gohegan stubbornly refused her pleas. He told her that it would be a sin and blot on his conscience to let me "pass" as white, even in France, now that he had learned that I had "drops" of colored blood in me. A week after Father Gohegan heard Josephine Dubois's confession and refused for a final time to make the one dream keeping her alive come true, she hanged herself.

Father Gohegan also told me that, conscience-stricken by her suicide, he decided to protect me from the deadly world outside St. Vincent's walls for as long as he could. It was he who named me after my father, although "Brown" never sounded like a French moniker to me. Father Gohegan told me all of this on my eighteenth birthday, my next to last day at St. Vincent's. On that day, he begged me to leave New Orleans to save myself, the white girl I was in love with, and the Waifs' Home. In the end, nothing survived the hatred raging in the world outside St. Vincent's.

After Father Gohegan took me in that first day, he didn't know what to do with me. I was a blue-eyed, blonde baby, but the knowledge that I had some colored bloodlines in me trapped him—an "Upper South" Marylander assigned to pastoral duties in the Deep South—in a moral dilemma, and his conscience forbade him from placing me in an orphanage for white children. He decided instead to take personal charge of my education.

He would not teach me the catechism and the Catholic faith, though. They would be of little use to me in the world outside the Waifs' Home, where other teachings and prejudices would contend for my soul. He decided, he said, to "arm my mind" to enable me to withstand whatever harshness and hurt life threw my way. He resolved to hold me to an even higher learning standard than he would if I were a white student in the best schools New Orleans had to offer at the time.

What he was planning for my education could put me, the Colored Waifs' Home, and himself in physical jeopardy, but Josephine Dubois's suicide weighed on him more and more. He felt he caused the despair that made her take her life. He was also determined to help her other child living with her former pimp's mother in the Battlefield, but he did not have the time on that next to last day of his life to tell me whether he had found the child.

Father Gohegan discovered early on that I had musical ability and decided to teach me to play the clarinet. That did it for me. I played in the famous Waifs' Home Brass Band almost as soon as I started wearing knee pants, and the band became my life. Our idols were King Oliver on the cornet and, especially, Stanley Bontemps on the clarinet because he was a St. Vincent's waif like the rest of us.

Swearing me to secrecy, Father Gohegan taught me how to read, write, and develop a critical faculty. He was short-tempered with me when my mind wandered or if he thought I was slacking off in my concentration during lessons. Sometimes a sadness came over him, and he would let me lark off for a while. At those times, I had an inkling that he knew in his heart that the world outside his office, where he shaped my intelligence, would not let me use my education to develop my full potential.

Father Gohegan also discovered in me a love for language and literature, and he encouraged it by giving me books to read in his office for short periods. It was essential, he kept telling me, not to arouse the suspicions of the other colored waifs. These reading sessions began when I was around eight, he said, when he realized I was a quick learner and had a rage for learning akin to his own. He started me on works by Robert Louis Stevenson, such as *Treasure Island* and *Kidnapped*, and Rudyard Kipling's *Jungle Book* and *Kim*.

He also had me read translations of works by foreign authors. I read *The Three Musketeers* by Alexandre Dumas, *The Hunchback of Notre-Dame* by Victor Hugo, and *The Captain's Daughter* by Alexander Pushkin. Father Gohegan told me that Dumas and Pushkin would be considered colored by Louisiana standards, just like me, so I should never believe anyone—white or yellow or black—who said that colored people were naturally ignorant and fit only to live a life of bondage and servitude.

He reminded me after each session not to let on to the other waifs that he was giving me "special lessons." He warned me always to "hide my light under a bushel" from white and colored alike, for my own safety. I became a skilled dissembler, which had served me well in my work as a private investigator.

I honed my clarinet skills by sneaking away to play gigs with Creole jazz bands on the Mississippi River and Lake Pontchartrain riverboats. That's how I met Stanley Bontemps.

The first time I played with him, he taught me some of his riffs and listened, eyes shut like a blind man's, as I played them back to him. Years later, he told me he knew right away that I would outdo him on the clarinet, and he took up the soprano saxophone instead.

I fled New Orleans for New York the day after my eighteenth birthday, after I saw the Waifs' Home burned to the ground and Father Gohegan die in the flames. It was the work of the police, Klan lovers, and a mysterious foreigner. I thought, at the time, that the Klan supporters and the mystery man had come looking for me and burned the home down because I had fallen in love with a white Jewish girl named Hannah Korngold. Hannah was the daughter of my part-time employer, the rag-and-bone merchant Abe Korngold.

I thought that by fleeing to New York I would forever escape from the Klan lovers and Jim Crow, my feelings of guilt from the death of Father Gohegan, and the burning of St. Vincent's. I thought that I would find freedom and become a whole man. It probably would have worked out all right if I could have brought myself to assume a new identity as a white man and live out a life of obscurity in a big city like New York.

But something kept me from "passing" for white. Maybe it was my memories of Father Gohegan and everything he had done to make me value who I am. Or my friendship with Stanley and my awe of his genius. Or, it might have been my memory of the time I saw a colored man lynched by a mob as I watched, helplessly, nearby, pretending that I was white to save myself from being lynched.

My refusal to "pass" made for a strange life in New York: my white skin made colored musicians uncomfortable despite my clarinet's "from back down home" sound. Yet, I played the clarinet "too colored" to fit into the white jazz scene.

Then I hooked up with Stanley Bontemps again in one of the really hot colored-owned clubs where "blacks and tans" rubbed shoulders, Johnny Sutton's Blue Heaven Nightclub. Stanley and I fronted Johnny Sutton's band.

I learned that there was war brewing in Europe. I was itching to see more of the world, to discover a place where I would find freedom and become a whole man. Knowing that my natural father was a Frenchman, my thoughts turned to France. I booked passage to Le Havre, on the French-liner *France* in mid-July of 1914, nearly two weeks after I turned nineteen.

When the big guns opened up in Europe that August, I ditched my touring Creole jazz band in Marseilles and joined the French Foreign Legion.

For the next two years, I was just another legionnaire killing machine, no more, no less. My unit was cosmopolitan with some of the worst scum from every corner of the earth. But it didn't matter who you were in the Legion, just how well you could kill. The other members of my outfit wanted to fight by my side because I was a sharpshooter, and they believed, mistakenly, that I didn't fear death. But I was dissembling again; I feared death as much as any of them, and my two years mired in the mud and blood of battle were a nightmare.

When Captain Lacroix asked me if I wanted to kill the "Boches"—the derogatory French name for Germans—by shooting at them from a flying machine, I said, "Pourquoi Pas?" I would climb out of the muck and mire and into a clean cockpit and uniform.

I and the other chosen legionnaires were sent to a French airbase in Algeria for training. It didn't take them long to discover that I was good in the air and, me being an American, they assigned me to the Lafayette Flying Corps, American volunteers flying for France.

When a bunch of bigots in the outfit assaulted some North African Spahi light cavalry in a café and I stood up for the Arabs, they figured that I had to be colored not to side with them, and I told them my story.

After that they really attacked me. But Tex O'Toole, the best flyer and the toughest man in the Corps, knocked their heads together and put a stop to the race-baiting.

CHAPTER 3

When I came out of the metro station at Saint-Germain-des-Près, it was dark and cold and all hell had broken loose. People were sprinting past me on Boulevard Saint-Germain brandishing torches and carrying flashlights. They were heading toward the National Assembly building to defend it. I spotted workers wearing cloth caps and ragged overcoats, carrying bicycle chains, slingshots, hammers, and clubs. Well-dressed young men and women, probably students, marched shoulder-to-shoulder with them. Here were the heirs of the workers and intellectuals who, since the great French Revolution of 1789, had sparked three others—in 1830, 1848, and the Paris Commune of 1871.

Three days ago, the new Premier, Edouard Daladier, had dismissed the Paris Prefect of Police, Jean Chiappe, darling of the Fascists and monarchists, accusing him of slowing down the police investigation of a big-time swindler named Alexandre Stavisky who had "theoretically" committed suicide less than a month before by firing *two* bullets into his brain. Stavisky had pulled off some of the biggest swindles in a French history riddled with great ones. But the Fascists and monarchists were particularly incensed because Stavisky was a Jew.

They gave notice that nothing would satisfy them, short of dissolving the "corrupt and Jew-infested National Assembly" and replacing its members with right-thinking pro-Fascists. They had called upon their sympathizers to join them in an attempt to seize the building by force and chase out all of the deputies.

From the volume of the noise in the distance, I figured that they were attacking the French National Assembly building right now because, for once, both the workers and the mounted police were headed in the same direction: *toward* the building to keep it from being captured by the Fascists and monarchists.

Being caught up in the middle of the screaming, surging crowd was like being tossed around by a hurricane battering New Orleans. There was no way to turn back, and I was buoyed past the Deux Magots café, its windows aglow like a Christmas tree in hell. My feet barely touched the road.

I could keep my Homburg on only by lashing it to my head with its leather straps. The smell of rank sweat, French tobacco, and smoke from burning trash was stifling. Thousands of voices chanted the workers' anthem, "l'Internationale." Picks clanked on cobblestones as rioters prised and mounded them up to hurl at their opponents.

Coming toward us were thousands roaring out, "La Marseillaise," which meant the right-wing groups were closing in to cut off the throngs rushing to beat back the attack on the National Assembly building. I felt like a lone swimmer between two giant battleships about to collide in a fog-bound sea. I tried to figure out how to avoid being crushed in the collision.

Just then, I felt a tugging at my coat sleeve, and an imposing, square-jawed American woman of about my age named Jean Fletcher grabbed my arm to keep from stumbling and being crushed by the stampede. I had met Jean at Chez Red Tops a week ago. She was a reporter for a New York magazine. Her job was to provide information on anything happening in Paris of interest to American readers of her fortnightly "Paris Diary." In the course of a boozy evening, we became pals. I agreed to give her the lowdown on the jazz scene and life in the underbelly of Paris for her diary in exchange for useful tidbits. She kept telling me my face was familiar.

Jean was really struggling to stay on her feet, but her added weight helped to keep my feet on the road.

"We've got to get the hell out of here, Urby," she said. "If we get pushed as far as the National Assembly, we'll probably end up in the Seine." Jean was a really funny woman, but she wasn't joking now.

"Uh-oh," she whispered. I followed her eyes. Some workers were dragging, with long chains harnessed to their bodies, a giant metal cauldron on a tumbrel with a blazing fire underneath it. It was piled high with rivets glowing yellow-white like giant fireflies. Jean pointed to workers wearing chain metal-covered gloves and carrying metal-mesh slingshots.

"What the hell's going on?" I asked. At that moment, the crowd parted, and up ahead we could see a solid line of mounted mobile guards riot police and mounted gendarmes, some with their sabers drawn. We could hear the clanking of metal hammering against metal and the frenzied whinnying of horses.

Through a break in the wall of mobile guards, I saw a band of men in red, white, and black storm-trooper uniforms, the colors of the swastika flag of Hitler's bunch in Germany. I craned my neck to see a man holding a giant torch and could make out a red lightning bolt running through a white cross on the front of his red and black uniform jacket.

"Who are those boys?" I asked Jean.

"They're a monarchist, Fascist bunch of nuts called the 'Oriflamme du Roi,' 'the King's Battle Standard.'"

Jean said they were some of the nastiest of the French Nazi sympathizers, led by a Count named René d'Uribé-Lebrun. She stopped and looked at me and then fell silent, as if remembering something. Then she went on, "Rumor has it that Swindler Stavisky helped to bankroll his outfit."

Something else was bothering Jean. She was so engrossed in whatever it was that she tumbled to the ground. Fortunately, I had bent over to pull her to her feet because white-hot rivets, flung from the metal-mesh slingshots of workers right behind us, went whizzing over where my head would have been.

The glowing rivets flew over the mobile guards and gendarmes like tracer bullets and landed among the storm troopers of the Oriflamme, who surged forward trying to outflank the guards and get to grips with the workers. The guards charged into them, flailing at them with the flat of their saber blades and slashing at them with pikes and nightsticks.

Some of the mounted gendarmes had charged ahead too fast and were encircled by scores of Oriflamme, who swung at them with bicycle chains and brass knuckles. A mobile guard went down, blood spewing from a brass-knuckled punch to the mouth. Blood was flowing on the streets of Paris again, and it looked likely that a lot more would be spilled before the night was over.

I pulled Jean to her feet. "Lady, if we're going to get out of here, now's the time."

I had spotted some space off to the left where we could escape down the rue Saint Guillaume. I figured if we could get there, we could make our way to the Boulevard Raspail, head for Montparnasse, and hotfoot it away from the battle. That was figuring without Jean, who was a reporter through and through.

"Let's keep going a while, Urby. This is grand material."

"Material? Look, Jean, those Oriflamme people want to bust some skulls, ours included. Let's cut out now." Suddenly I saw something that bowled me over. We were close enough to the storm troopers to see that one of them was none other than Buster Thigpen. I wondered what the hell Buster T. was doing, dressed up like Adolf Hitler.

At that moment, a ringing clanged in the din of noise: it sounded like one of those handbells that rich folks use to summon servants to the dining table. A hush fell over the crowd. A man wearing a white uniform with an ivory walking stick in his left hand and what looked like a silver handbell in his right clanged the bell until his troopers released the mounted gendarmes they had surrounded and had at their mercy.

The man in white advanced to about ten yards away from us, braving the suddenly quiet throng of workers and students. He was tall, handsome, and brown-haired, almost blonde. He wore a gold-colored patch over his right eye, and he sported a silver and gold cape. He bowed to the relieved-looking gendarmes, to the crowds of workers, and then he executed a sharp about-face and marched back to his men. The fallen mobile guard was stretchered off by his comrades.

The man in white snapped another about-face and stood facing the crowd, holding his ivory walking stick like a fencing foil. Buster Thigpen was standing right next to him, looking at him like he was Jesus Christ come down to earth again. I was racking my brain, trying to figure out how I could get close enough to Buster T. to subdue him before he could draw his straight-edge razor to cut me. Jean nudged me.

"That fellow in the all-white duds is Count d'Uribé-Lebrun, the man I told you about, the leader of the Oriflamme du Roi. Now I know what was bothering me. Did you get a good look at his kisser, Urby?"

"No, but you see that fellow standing next to him, the one on his cane side? That's a drummer named Buster Thigpen. A man is paying me big money to reel him in. He's run off with the man's daughter. The man is wealthy…and American."

"What's the man's name? Promise I won't tell a soul."

"Barnet Robinson III," I replied, gambling that I could trust her. Jean filed the name away in her brain. From our first meeting, I had been struck by her amazing memory, and I guessed that she would tell me more down the road.

"Urby, look at the Count, really *look* at him, not at your Buster Thigpen. He's got to be the long lost French father you told me about at Chez Red Tops the first time we met."

I did what I was told and got the shock of my life. I looked in the mirror every morning when I shaved, and the face that I'd see reflected in twenty years was the Count's—like my identical twin but one who'd just aged twice as fast as I had.

"Jesus Christ!" I cried out, then immediately apologized to Jean for swearing. She laughed.

"I've heard a lot worse. But you worry me, Urby. You're a great guy, but you've got ice floes clogging up your veins. Doesn't what I told you mean anything to you? The Count's your old man! That's what I call a BIG surprise. But your only reaction is to say 'Jesus Christ' and then *apologize* to me for taking the Lord's name in vain?"

I felt a burning inside me knowing that there, thirty or so feet away, stood the man who made my mother, a person I never knew, commit suicide from despair.

The Oriflamme was falling back toward the National Assembly. The mounted gendarmes, as if still under the spell of the Count, followed them slowly, making no effort to charge again. The workers had snapped out of their bewitched state, though, and had started to chant l'Internationale again. They rained flaming rivets down on the retreating Oriflamme.

Suddenly, the line of gendarmes opened and scores of Oriflamme reserves came charging through, running directly at us and the workers, swinging their bicycle chains, clubs, and brandishing their brass knuckle-covered fists. Buster was leading a pack of them, jabbing away with, of all things, a spear. From it waved the banner of the Oriflamme. Buster was about twenty yards away and closing, and I started sprinting toward him, my leather-covered sap in my hand. I figured that my best move was to knock Buster unconscious, drag him off, hogtie him, and bring my contract with Barnet Robinson to a quick conclusion.

Jean screamed and I turned to look at her. Blood was streaming down her forehead, and she had fallen against a car, trying to staunch the flow with her silk scarf. I ran back to her, looked toward the rue Saint-Guillaume and saw some space between the workers and the Oriflamme, now wrapped together in hand-to-hand combat.

"Jean, we've got to get you out of here and see to your wound. Can you make it?"

Jean held my hand and nodded yes.

"Let's go then!"

I ran interference for Jean, dragging her behind me, my sap thudding on Oriflamme and workers alike. Finally, we passed the La Petite Chaise restaurant and kept on going until we reached the corner of Boulevard Raspail and the rue de Sèvres. We ducked into the Hôtel Lutetia, opposite the Bon Marché Department Store.

Fabrice was on duty at the swanky Hôtel Lutetia bar. He was a comrade from my Foreign Legion days. The American bar hounds swore that he made the best American cocktails in Paris, although he had told me that his English was limited to recognizing the names of cocktails and booze.

Without waiting for us to order, Fabrice brought us a bottle of calvados and some table napkins and swabbed away at the cut on Jean's forehead. The wound wasn't as bad as it looked, and soon Fabrice had fashioned a stylish bandage that he tied around Jean's head. She looked like a pirate modeling for Chanel.

Fabrice put away the cheap calvados he had used on Jean's cut and filled two brandy snifters with fine Domfront calvados, which is distilled from apples and pears. He knew that I preferred it to the more widely known Pays d'Auge applejack.

We told him how Jean had been wounded in the battle raging in the streets a few blocks away. From his reactions, it was clear that Fabrice's sympathies lay with the Count and his outfit, not with their left-wing opponents.

The calvados soon revived Jean's spirits, and she made faces at herself in the mirror behind the bar.

"That bandage suits you," I laughed. "Makes you look like a pirate."

Jean suddenly turned serious. "A gold-colored eye patch would look better."

"Like the one the Count was wearing?"

"Yes, like the one your dad was wearing. But you don't care about all that. You're Urby the Iceman, right?"

For the first time in my life, I felt the presence of my mother deep down inside me. She was real, at last. My feelings toward the Count could flare into hatred and murder down the road, and I would again become the killing machine that the Foreign Legion had forged. But I did not want to go there. Not yet. Buster was in my crosshairs now.

"Right. I don't feel anything one way or the other. That's just the way I am. An Iceman."

Jean looked at me, a hint of tears in her eyes. "It's the war that's changed you, right? That's killed something inside you?"

It was time to dissemble again.

"It's just me, Jean. The way I play the cards that life deals me. The war was one card. Now the Count is another."

Jean looked at me steadily as if she were seeing something in me for the first time. Then she chuckled and punched my arm. "We've got some talking to do, when we get through this. You've got to run me through that story about you being a foundling again so I can do some checking."

"Checking" meant, I reckoned, rummaging through the circus-stunt memory I discovered that she had when I first met her last week.

"What I want to know is what Buster Thigpen is doing with the Count's people," I said, trying to change the subject.

"Maybe he's passing himself off as someone else, like pretending to be you." One look at my face made her realize she had gone way too far. "Sorry," she said, looking contrite. But she returned to the attack, as I knew she would.

"Another thing, Urby. I ran the stuff I know about the Count through my head, and I know he was in New Orleans back in the nineties, when you were born. He's your old man, for sure." Jean laughed before going on. "And think about it. 'Urby' is a weird first name in English. Sounds more like a take on 'Uribé' to me."

I felt my anger toward the man who made my mother suicide herself rise a few more notches. Jean was staring at me; she had recalled something else.

"I remember where I heard about your client Barnet Robinson III. You know Cole Porter?"

"Yeah. I've played his music. We've swapped French Foreign Legion tall tales at Chez Red Tops."

"Well, old King Cole is a Hoosier, like me, so he can't put up with a lot of guff. We got plastered at Le Grand Duc one night listening to some great jazz band, and we got to naming Americans we wouldn't like to run into in Paris. Robinson III was in Cole's top three. Cole said he had met him when he was planning to invest some money in commodities. They palled around for a while in New York right after the war, but Cole got sick of him pretty quick. He told me that Barnet was a Princeton man through and through, even wore orange and black scarves. For a Yalie like Cole, that's like waving a red flag at a bull." Jean shook her head, chuckling as if she could not believe her own story. "Robinson's so crazy about Princeton that he built a mansion a few miles away, near Hopewell, New Jersey. He and Charles Lindbergh have neighboring estates. In fact, they're big pals." She made a face and continued. "I don't like Lindy at all. He's a rotten egg. But it's lousy that somebody kidnapped and murdered baby Lindbergh even though Lindy coughed up the ransom. With Robinson III's help, I've heard."

I hadn't followed the story of the kidnapping very closely, so I simply said, "Mr. Robinson was wearing orange and black suspenders when I met him."

Jean laughed and clapped her hands. "That phony crap really gets Cole's goat."

The booze was beginning to take hold of me, and I knew that I had to get some sleep soon, so I prodded Jean along. "I still don't see why he hates Barnet Robinson. I took the job because a great friend of mine vouched for him."

"Well, Cole says he's a liar, a traitor, and a swindler. That for Barnet III the sun rises and sets on the Teutonic Empire. His mother's some kind of German princess with two 'vons' in her maiden name. She and

Robinson III were raring to sign on with old Kaiser Bill during the war, until his old man, Barnet Robinson II, threatened to divorce her and disinherit him. I'll tell you all about that later, as soon as the brain grinds into gear." Jean tapped her forehead, took a big swig of calvados, and went on.

"After the war, Cole says III made a mint sneaking banned metals and commodities into Germany by bribing the right people. He pumped a lot of spondulicks into the Nazi party, which boosted Hitler's rise to power. A grateful Adolf extended a personal invitation to Mama von Robinson von Robinson, Robinson III, and his daughter, Daphne, to visit him in Berlin late in the twenties. Robinson III bragged to Cole that Hitler bowed and scraped to them and gushed that they were perfect Aryan types, whiter than white. Any more questions about why Cole detests him, Urby?"

"It's hard to believe that he's so mad about the Boches. He told me they'd killed his wife and her parents in a torpedo attack on the *Lusitania* in 1915."

Jean smiled wickedly. "Hold on, lad. All will be revealed."

I sipped some more of the good Domfront calvados.

"When Robinson II heard that his wife, Robinson III, and his granddaughter were hobnobbing with Hitler and the Nazis, he blew a gasket," Jean continued. "He called them on the carpet and swore again that he'd give her the old heave-ho and leave them penniless if they ever set foot in Germany again or even whispered 'Hitler.' And Robinson II forced him to stop forthwith all business ventures with Germany when Adolf'—she put a two-finger mustache under her nose—'came to power.'"

"Robinson II sounds like a good man."

"He's a great one compared to his son," Jean said. "Robinson III and Ma Robinson are so scared of the old geezer that they've clammed up about Adolf and haven't put a toe into Germany since he blew them off. Here's to Robinson II, says I." Jean lifted her glass in a toast and knocked back some more calvados. Fabrice had been hovering close to us, polishing glasses and checking bottles. I would have sworn that he was listening in on our conversation, except that he had told me that he didn't speak or understand any English, aside from words used for ordering drinks.

Jean said she was going to telephone a friend of hers. I studied Fabrice. He looked toward the wall where the telephone was hanging before she asked, in French, if she could use the telephone. Things were not what they seemed with Fabrice, I realized.

When Jean returned to the bar, she told me that she had called a fellow with a car who worked in the *Chicago Tribune*'s Paris Bureau. I protested that I could have walked her home, after she told me that her apartment was on the rue Jacob, which was in easy walking distance. She waved me off, saying that she was too "tipsy" to stagger as far as that.

Jean smiled at Fabrice and touched her empty snifter. She held her thumb and forefinger a quarter of an inch apart. It was two in the morning, well past closing time. But Fabrice was a friend, and he knew that I would return the favor someday.

"Encore un," Fabrice said with a wink aimed at me. He poured Jean double the calvados she had asked for.

"One for the road," she promised, smiling at him. Jean knocked it back in one smooth motion, smacked her lips loudly, and rose, unsteadily, to her feet. She looked in the mirror, straightened her bandage, and handed Fabrice a handful of franc notes. Jean looked into my eyes with a somber gaze and said, "If I were you, Urby, I would check back with your friend about Barnet Robinson III. From what Cole Porter told me, and Cole does not lie, no 'great friend' would vouch for him."

We heard a horn honking repeatedly.

"That's Freddy," Jean said. She held out her arm for me to steady her on her way through the swinging door and out to the curb. Freddy was waiting for us in a banged-up red Renault, the engine running. He motioned to Jean to hurry up.

"One last tidbit," Jean said. "The old brain has saved the best for last. I've heard a rumor that Daphne's not Robinson III's daughter, but his half-sister. His mother had a late dalliance before the war with no less than Kaiser Bill the Second, got pregnant at thirty-nine, and Kaiser Bill, Barnet III, and his mother arranged for Ma Robinson to have an extended visit in Germany to 'catch up with her relatives,' so that she could give birth there without Robinson II being any the wiser."

"Come on, Jean, that's just craziness. I mean, the Kaiser is as ugly as sin. He looks like a constipated junkyard dog. There's no way that Daphne can be his daughter."

She scoffed, tossing her head back and laughing out loud. "You're really a naïf deep down, Urby. Let me finish the story; it gets crazier. Robinson III's mom delivers Daphne in a posh secret birth clinic in Bavaria, handpicked by the Kaiser. As soon as the baby is born, the Kaiser packs Ma Robinson, baby Daphne, and a few nannies onto the *SS Kaiser Bill II* before the Kaiserin twigged what was going on. They steam off to New York and break the world record time for an Atlantic crossing. Meanwhile, the Kaiser and Ma Robinson have given III's teenaged wife, the only child of her doting parents, a million bucks of hush money to pretend that she's lying in in a private, German-owned and staffed New York clinic on the Upper East Side, awaiting the birth of our Daphne."

"You're making this up," I said.

"Nope. Gospel truth, Urby. Barnet II is off on business, and he doesn't give a damn about III anymore 'cause the kid's gone against his advice and, in his junior year at Princeton, married a social climbing tootsie he deflowered on their first date. So, II cold-shoulders them from then on." Jean was chuckling so hard that she couldn't finish her story.

"Jean, your friend's real nervous."

Freddy was drumming his fingers on the steering wheel, either worried about the riots and dying to get to a safe spot or bored with waiting and wanting to join in the action.

"Let me finish, Urby. After the *SS Kaiser Bill II* docks in New York, baby Daphne is spirited into the clinic and—*hey presto!*—out she pops from between the million-dollar thighs of Robinson III's baby wife, and nobody is the wiser. The Germans staffing the clinic are sworn to secrecy. Neat story, non? The Boches really know how to pull off stuff like that. It all means that III ain't her daddy; he's her half-brother. Her grandmother is her mother, and Robinson II isn't kin to her at all. Anyway, Robinson's child bride and her parents don't get to enjoy their filthy lucre from the Kaiser and Ma Robinson. Ma beguiles the morons into leaving Daphne with her to take a luxury liner to England to celebrate hitting their jackpot—in wartime, no less. On Ma's advice, they take the *Lusitania* in May 1915, and the Boches's U-Boat torpedoes her off the coast of Ireland, on the direct orders of Kaiser Bill. They perish, along with over a thousand passengers. Guess who turns out to be the sole heir of child bride and her parents? Robinson III, that's who. He gives all the dough to Mama, and she splits it with the Kaiser. Got to love the Boches, non?"

Just then we heard an ear-popping explosion and machine gun fire. We both looked toward the National Assembly and saw flames arching up into the sky. There was more scattered small arms fire and ratatats from machine guns and the distant hubbub of voices and wailing sirens. Freddy honked and gunned the engine.

"You better go now, Jean; otherwise, Freddy's cutting out."

Jean smiled and kissed me on the cheek, her eyes gleaming. "Goddamn it! Urby, I love France! We could wake up in the morning with the same old crooks in power, with a king, an emperor, a dictator, or a new French Fourth Republic. Anything can happen in this place! Beats Indiana, hands down. In fact, it beats New York, London, Berlin, you name it."

I poured Jean into Freddy's car, and she waved at me. I saw her talking to him. He kept shaking his head no, but he finally started racing down the Boulevard Raspail, toward the National Assembly. Jean flipped the bird at me, making faces through the rear windshield until she was out of sight. She lived in the opposite direction. She was heading toward her story.

CHAPTER 4

Paris, Wednesday, February 7, 1934

What Jean had told me confirmed my first impression that Robinson was as phony as a three dollar bill. My dislike for him was the clincher. But the man had serious money for sure.

Was Jean's story that Daphne was really Robinson's sister true? And, if it was, did it make any difference? The contract was to track her down and return her to Robinson III, and I needed the money. As for Buster Thigpen, he was now part of a band of uniformed Fascist, monarchist nuts trying to tear down the French Third Republic under the leadership of a loony French Count who, Jean Fletcher had convinced me, was my father. Did that make any difference to me? The answer was no. So far.

In the middle of it all, the most violent combat that I had seen or heard since the war was still raging within earshot, and I might wake up in the morning to a whole new France.

My mind was overloaded and I was drunk. There was only one person in the world who could help me make sense of things at times like these, and he lived on the rue Caulaincourt in Montmartre. It was half past two in the morning, and Stanley Bontemps would be making his rounds of the jazz clubs in Montmartre and the bars and a whorehouse or two in Pigalle. He would head to Mama Jane's Eatery off the Place

Pigalle at exactly 6:00 a.m. for a real down-South breakfast with all the trimmings.

I decided to walk to Mama Jane's real slowly. I needed to let my brain cool down before I could talk sensibly to Stanley. Sporadic police vans were still heading toward the National Assembly and the Place de la Concorde. I wondered how many "forces of order" were left in reserve. I could still see the light from flames in the distance and hear amplified cheers and shouts coming through megaphones. The Eiffel Tower loomed like a giant black skeleton in the darkness.

The stores and cafés and banks were shuttered. The back streets were deserted as I headed toward the Seine, knowing that I had to save some strength for the climb up to Montmartre to meet up with Stanley at Mama Jane's.

When I walked into Mama Jane's, I was back in the Deep South, with the smell of fried chicken, collard greens, pigs' feet, corn bread. This morning the place was packed with jazz musicians hung over from their night and hungry for some Deep South chow to help them face another day.

I was sitting in a booth by myself gnawing on some barbecued chicken wings when the noise stopped and people started whispering, giving reports of Stanley's movements.

The door flew open and there stood Stanley, of medium height, thin as a rail, brown-skinned, and swaying on his feet. He was resplendent in a big white Borsalino hat and an all-white suit with a black shirt and tie under his white woolen overcoat. His black and white two-toned shoes glinted in the dim light, and a beautiful copper-colored woman carried Stanley's saxophone case. Stanley saw me and came over, arms wide open for a French-style hug. The copper beauty looked at the men staring at her with their tongues hanging out, shivered, and vanished. Mama

Jane came to our table, carrying plates piled high with bacon, scrambled eggs, sausages, biscuits, pancakes, corn bread, and hominy grits. She placed them in front of Stanley and beamed. He lifted his shaggy eyebrows, took off his jacket, and rolled up his sleeves.

Stanley wolfed down the piles of food, covering them in gluey cascades of dark Karo syrup and molasses. Mama Jane stacked more plates in front of him and watched approvingly as Stanley splashed syrup over the eats and scoffed them down.

Mama Jane shook her head, grinning from ear to ear. “That ain’t no man,” she said. “That be a wolf!”

“I’m sure gone to wolf down these eats,” he said, adding more syrup to the mix.

When Stanley had finished, I counted up the stacks of empty plates and paid his bill for once, feeling rich with my golden dollars in my pocket. The other musicians in Mama Jane’s took out their instruments and tried to get an impromptu “jam session” going, and Stanley was ready to rip. But I made a sign by raising my eyebrows and, understanding it, he staggered to his feet.

“Sorry I gots to be leaving you good folk, but me and mon petit Urby here got to talk, so, au revoir ’til later.”

Stanley had a penthouse on the fourth floor of a luxury apartment built in the Haussmann style of Napoleon III’s time. It was sometimes hard to remember that Stanley came from St. Vincent’s Colored Waifs’ Home and was the son of slaves. But then Louis “Strawberry” Armstrong, over six years younger than me, had been a colored waif, too, and he was even higher up in the world than Stanley was.

Stanley went to his bar, took out a bottle of rye whiskey, some Bohemian crystal glasses, and a bucket of ice cubes. He set them down on a curved, clear-glass pane on top of what looked like a pair of big, ruby-red crystal lips. We eased ourselves down into white leather couches shaped like saxophones and drank that rye until Stanley had the whole story of what had happened from the time he saw me meet up with Robinson III at the bar at Chez Red Tops.

It was eight o'clock in the morning, and Stanley had swallowed enough food to feed a platoon and smoked enough hemp to float any normal human into the sky to keep the stars company. But as we worked our way through the rye whiskey, Stanley seemed to sober up. He had a telephone call, muttered some words in French, smiled, and then poured himself some more rye. He had puzzled over every detail of what I had told him and finally said, "Mon petit, show me the money this white man give you."

I took the five strange-looking gold-tinged twenty dollar bills out of my pocket and handed them to him. He stood up, walked to a floor lamp, and screwed a jeweler's loupe into his eye to examine the dough.

"UMMMUMMMPH, sure be the prettiest cash I ever did see, Urby. And it ain't be no fake."

"Robinson says it's good as gold. Seems like the government will give you genuine gold, if you hand one of those dollars over to them."

Stanley looked at me and then unscrewed the loupe to contemplate the ceiling mural of himself and Louis Armstrong in diaphanous togas, basking in the sunny radiance of heaven, playing jazz to God. Then he started laughing his big wheezing laugh with a lot of cricket sounds in it.

"Onliest one little problem wit' dis here dough. That Robinson be playin' you for a fool!" he said, angrily. "Louis Armstrong told me America gone off of the gold standing last year. It ain't even legal for y'all to have even one of these here gold certificates now, and you got *five* of them. Old J. Edgar Hoover catch you and he get his G-men to throw yo' ass *under* the jail, especially he find out you colored."

Stanley seemed as angry about Robinson III and his funny money as I was.

"I'm going to go straighten the man out—right now!" I said, enraged. As usual, Stanley cooled down first, using his brain to check out future moves, like a chess player.

"Let's ease up, and think this through, Urby. Old Robinson need you doin' somethin' for him real fast without gettin' his hands dirty. I mean fetchin' his daughter from Buster who be crazy as a coot and dangerous. Robinson don't want you never to say nothin' about it to nobody afterward. And you won't if J. Edgar Hoover got you buried in some Deep South jail 'cause of that gold money." Stanley gargled down more rye, and then his eyes glittered. I knew that he now had a plan.

"Still and all, you play your cards right, you can make a lot more money out of this than that man even thinkin' about payin' you, even with straight dough. Urby, you got to act like everything be copacetic, and don't let on you wise to him." He peeled five green-back twenty dollar bills from a wad in his pocket and told me to take the money and let him put the "gold backs" in his safe until he got advice on what to do with them from a friend in Germany. I would pay him back later after we settled affairs with Robinson III.

"So, I do the job he's hired me to do? Find Buster T. and his woman Daphne Robinson and then we demand a bonus to punish the man for cheating me? Is that what you're talking about, Stanley? Bonus money?" I liked the idea of squeezing more dough out of a cheater.

Stanley grinned slyly. "I be talkin' 'bout we hold onto his daughter 'til he pay you righteous money."

That really knocked me back on my heels. "You're talking kidnapping? Holding her for ransom? I don't..."

He waved his reefer at me impatiently. "I be talkin' 'bout you gettin' yo' just deserves for solvin' a hard case with a lots a angles. We not talkin' kidnappin' here; we talkin' adduction," he said, almost angrily.

I thought about what he meant, and then it all fell into place. "So how do we pull off this fake 'abduction'?"

Stanley started laughing again, as if I was saying the word incorrectly. "We goin' to flush Buster out and get him away from that girl and that Count. Get Buster to bring the girl with him. You know Buster. One thing he gone want to do is show off to the girl what a big shot he be. We gone make them come to us."

I had begun to see where Stanley was going. "You going to ask him to music with you at Chez Red Tops?"

"No, mon petit. I'm goin' to put on a show at La Belle Princesse and ask Buster to be my drummer. You know that Count be runnin' a politics party. That phone call I just got was from a friend of mine in the government tellin' me the Count and his peoples got busted up by the cops real bad last night, so they ain't takin' over no France no time soon. You find out where the Count's politics party be at, and you go and deliver the message that Stanley want Buster to be his drummer at La Belle Princesse on Saturday night. Charity concert, with no 10 percent rule, for thems got killed or hurt in the riot, be they workers or dukes. We rehearses on Friday, and it's there we grabs the gal and hands her over to her daddy against straight dough."

I looked at him skeptically.

"Urby, I know this goin' to work," Stanley insisted. "We gone let Redtop and Baby Langston in on the plan since Baby be workin' at La Belle. If needs be, we gone get him to help us grab Buster and his Daphne while we squeeze the money out of her old man with lagniappe for his cheatin' you the first time. Then we turns his gal over to him." He paused and said, indignant again, as if I had accused him of a crime, "You can't call that no kidnappin' for no ransom money."

I knew that Redtop was going to be let in on the plan because she was Stanley's closest friend in Paris besides me. He didn't want any heat to fall on Chez Red Tops in case anything went wrong with his "charity concert" scheme. But I also knew that he didn't like or trust the owner of La Belle Princesse, Rawlston "Hambone" Gaylord. By choosing his nightclub as the venue for the concert, Stanley could deflect the heat onto Hambone in case everything blew up in our faces.

I reckoned that he would keep Baby Langston in a limited role because he worked for his Uncle Hambone as the barman and general factotum of La Belle Princesse, and Stanley needed an inside man to help him make whatever arrangements he was cooking up to snatch Daphne and Buster. Knowing Stanley, I figured that he trusted Baby Langston enough to do what he told him to do and shut up because Baby's head lived in a world far removed from his Uncle Hambone's. He kept body and soul together by working for his uncle at La Belle Princesse, while he scribbled away in his garret, dreaming of becoming the colored Walt Whitman, as Langston Hughes had proclaimed.

I didn't know a thing about poetry, but I reckoned that if a man wrote it, he must have caught the bug from a woman who was important to him, like his mother. But Stanley had told me that Baby's mother, his Uncle Hambone's baby sister, Magnolia Swilley, was one of the deadliest gangsters in Harlem, male or female. The story on her was that money, power, and sex were what made Magnolia tick, not poetry.

CHAPTER 5

I had read in Léon Blum's Socialists' newspaper *Le Populaire* that the attempted Fascist takeover of the National Assembly had ended in a shambles. After hours of skirmishes lasting until the morning, the riot police had forced the Fascists and monarchists off the Concorde bridge and cleared the Place de la Concorde. That put an end to the *coup d'état*: the Third Republic was alive and kicking until further notice.

As I hurried through the debris littering the rue Royale, I passed some men in morning dress staggering into Maxim's, sporting bloody bandages like they were ribbons on Croix de Guerre medals. I wondered how many men and horses had drowned in the Seine last night. I figured that Count d'Uribé-Lebrun wasn't among the victims.

I turned left in front of the Madeleine church onto Faubourg Saint-Honoré and then made a right onto the rue Boissy d'Anglas. I checked the address that Redtop had found for me in the telephone directory and stopped in front of an elegant building. On a gilded nameplate were engraved the words, "Le Comte Import-Export, Premier étage gauche."

I had arrived at the headquarters of the Oriflamme du Roi. I pulled on a metal contraption on the door, saw the door click open, and I walked into the dimly lit hallway. Immediately, three burly men wearing the storm trooper uniforms and Oriflamme du Roi armbands seized me and marched me up the staircase at double-quick time.

They pushed me into a brightly lit room, and two of them pinned my arms behind my back. They looked at me and their jaws dropped. The third man, who seemed to be their leader, recovered fastest, took one look at me, and then frisked me, his hands lingering on my shoulders, arms, and calves, sizing me up.

He marched me to an oak door, which he hammered on. I heard a handbell ring, and then he ushered me into a large office. The man who was holding my arm and I had seen each other in New Orleans half a lifetime ago, and neither of us had forgotten the time or the place. He was the foreigner who'd been hanging out with the police and the Ku Klux Klan loyalists when they burned the St. Vincent's Colored Waifs' Home to the ground on July 5, 1913.

The Count, looking like my identical twin, except for his age and the gold-colored silk eye patch, sat at an ornate desk on which were planted three gold-colored box files, each one stamped with a crest that I recognized immediately. He was skimming through sheets of paper yellowed with age. He didn't look up. Oil paintings of his ancestors covered the walls.

An elaborate gold writing set, the gleaming silver handbell, and two photographs in gold and silver frames were the only other items on the desk. I recognized the handbell, which bore the same crest as the one on the box files: a crowned two-headed black eagle traversed by three arrows, perched on a golden scroll with the words "Jamais ne serai vaincu" written on it. I had its identical twin in a safe in my office.

I was shaking with anger while the Count's goon and I stood at attention, waiting for the master to acknowledge us. He kept on reading his papers. Finally, the Count said, "Pierre, seat our guest, please, then leave us. Lock the door after you."

I was glad to be able to place the name "Pierre" on the face I'd seen in my dreams and nightmares for more than twenty years. Pierre instantly pulled up a leather armchair. He pushed me down into the chair gently, stood behind me for a second, then clicked his jackboot heels. The next sound that I heard was the turning of the lock. The Count continued working.

I glanced at the photographs. The first one, in the gold frame, was a color portrait of the Count and a beaming Adolf Hitler standing in front of a huge red flag bearing a black swastika on a round white field. The silver-framed black and white photograph was of the Count in a Brigadier General's uniform with a somber-looking Marshal Pétain pinning the Croix de Guerre on his chest.

All of a sudden, the Count looked up. I glanced at the golden eye patch that sheathed his right eye, but it was the cold blue left eye that was drilling into me. He contemplated me in silence for what seemed like minutes and then sighed. Finally, he tendered me a gold cigarette box.

"Virginia tobacco?" he asked.

I nodded and took one of the cigarettes. I noticed that the cigarette box bore the same crest as the one on our handbells.

"Calvados?" he asked out of the blue. That worried me a lot but not as much as his next question. "Domfront calvados, of course?"

I stared at him for a moment and then he smiled.

"That is where the Château d'Uribé-Lebrun has sat for six hundred years. In the Domfront region in Normandy, near Bagnolles-de-l'Orne. You know the region?"

"I know the calvados. It's my favorite. How did you know?"

The Count smiled but did not answer my question. He spoke excellent English, with a New Orleans lilt. He smiled again and pointed to a rosewood bar against the wall to my right.

"Help yourself. You probably know the best one to choose, and bring me the same, if you please," he said.

I helped myself to the best one that I could find among the many excellent bottles of Domfront calvados in his collection. I poured us both generous snifters. With a sudden chill, I realized there could be only one explanation for his knowing my tastes in calvados: he must have me under observation. I thought instantly of Fabrice at the Hôtel Lutetia because I had been there last night and caught him in a lie about his inability to understand English. But the Count could have found out about me from scores of other people.

The Count sniffed at his glass, and a smile creased his face. "Tchin! Tchin!" he said, lifting his glass without clinking it against mine. "This is my favorite, too." Then he inquired, "To what do I owe the pleasure of this visit? Mr.…?"

"Brown. Urby Brown."

The Count repeated my name to himself, his expression becoming distant again.

"A friend of mine, a great musician, has discovered that you have a fine musician of his acquaintance in your employ," I said, carefully.

The Count sipped at his calvados, his face giving nothing away. Then he said, "No doubt you are referring to Mr. Bartholomew Lincoln Thigpen Junior?"

Bartholomew Lincoln Thigpen Junior? I said to myself, chuckling inwardly. I knew that I had some blackmail potential for bringing Buster Thigpen into line if I threatened to tell people his real moniker. I kept my composure and answered, "Yes, he's a fine musician, and Mr. Stanley Bontemps would be very much obliged to you if Mr. Bartholomew Lincoln Thigpen Junior could be his drummer in a charity concert he's organizing this coming Saturday night, 10 February, at nine. A number of other great musicians living in the American expatriate musical community in Paris will be participating."

The Count sipped the calvados and then swiveled in his chair, turning his back to me. Then he suddenly swiveled back to confront me head on, his face reddening. "Charity begins at home, non? So, what charity would Mr. Bontemps want Bartholomew for?"

"Mr. Bontemps loves France and wants to help those who've been harmed in the recent…disturbances, regardless of their political affiliation." It was a mouthful, but I'd been rehearsing those lines for hours. The smile on the Count's face made me think that my hard work was paying off.

"You mean, people like my Oriflamme, two of whom were shot dead by French soldiers on the Place de la Concorde? They are going to be helped by this charity concert?" he asked.

"If not them, their loved ones. That's the message that Mr. Stanley Bontemps wishes that I convey to you."

"My followers get all the money they need from me. We do not need charity from a Jewish-Negro musical conspiracy called jazz to help us." He said this calmly, but his face was flushed.

"But other people need that help, and it would be seen as a measure of your generosity if you let Bus…Bartholomew, a great jazz drummer, display his talents beside one of the greatest jazzmen in the world, Mr. Stanley Bontemps."

"I will agree then, on one condition," he said. "That you play the clarinet during the charity concert."

At my look of complete surprise, he grinned from ear to ear.

"I was once a resident of New Orleans. I liked much about it at that time in my life: the jazz, the beautiful women, especially the women of color."

If he noticed my rage, he concealed it very well.

"I have been told that you were once called the 'Mozart of the Creole Clarinet,'" he said, smiling. "A very apt nickname, from what I've ascertained." He smirked and continued. "New Orleans was alluring, but I returned to France to answer the call of my ancestors to serve in her armies." He pointed to the portraits of men in breastplates and armor and powdered wigs on the walls. Among the serried ranks of military portraits, I noticed a recent oil painting of the Count decked out in a French general's uniform from the Great War, with rows of medals on his chest.

He went on, "I have been confirmed in the rightness of my decision to return to France by my great friend Maréchal Pétain. And since my contacts with Il Duce and..."—he picked up the photo of himself with Hitler—"my dialogues with mon cher Adolphe, I have seen the errors of my youthful ways. All of the sins that I committed in New Orleans are dead and gone." His cold blue eye fixed on me before he added, "Or soon will be."

We stared at each other for a while, and then I placed my empty glass on the table.

"Thank you for your cooperation and your hospitality. Mr. Bontemps would be more than grateful if Bartholomew could be present for a brief rehearsal on Friday, say, at six in the evening. It will acquaint him with the program—"

"I have one further condition," he interrupted, "and then *all* is agreed. I wish to be invited to the charity concert on Saturday, with a few of my men to provide protection in case some unsuitable elements choose to create disturbances. Say, five of my men?"

"I'm sure that Mr. Bontemps will find that arrangement satisfactory," I answered. It would be all the more satisfactory, I thought, since we planned to abscond with Buster and Daphne at the Friday rehearsal, and there would not be a charity concert on Saturday at all, I reckoned.

"Please take good care of Bartholomew; he is very dear to me, and his face always brings back pleasant memories of a very good friend from my young days. He is like a son to me, barring the matter of his racial origins, of course."

"We will take care of him, I assure you."

He looked at me approvingly for the first time.

"You yourself are of a higher order than Bartholomew, one can see that. You are as white-skinned as myself. People have even detected a resemblance between us." His widening smile was goading me deeper into rage. I knew that it was time to leave before I committed mayhem on the man, who seemed to know a whole lot about me, to my surprise.

"You honor me, sir. Thank you, again, for your cooperation—and for the wonderful calvados from your Domfront region."

We stood to shake hands. We were the same height, the same build, even identical in skin color if he spent a little more time in the sun. I wondered if he knew that I had the same handbell as his, stashed away in my office safe. Father Gohegan had passed it to me seconds before he burned to death in the fire at St. Vincent's Colored Waifs' Home in New Orleans over twenty years ago now. A fire that the Count's main goon, Pierre, who had ushered me into his office a few minutes ago, had probably started or helped to start.

"Urby Brown," he said. "An interesting name. You are, of course, aware that 'Brown' translates into French as 'Lebrun'?"

"Yes," I said to my older replica.

"An interesting coincidence, is it not, if one believes in coincidences? I even used the name Brown sometimes in New Orleans, to make it easier for the natives of that city to understand it."

Before I could answer, he picked up the handbell. "Have you ever seen one like this before?"

"No," I lied. He looked quizzical and then smiled.

"Maybe yes, maybe no?" he asked. He rang it twice. "I think yes," he said with finality.

Pierre unlocked the door and came rushing into the office. He led me out and through the front door of the building and onto the rue Boissy d'Anglas. He gave me a wolfish smile and said, in English, "See you again soon, Mr. Urby Brown. Very soon." When he drew his right index finger across his throat to intimidate me, I reached out, grabbed his right hand, and yanked him off balance by pulling him toward me. Then I head-butted him with the crown of my Homburg hat. In fact, it was a metal helmet, covered in felt and shaped to look like a Homburg. It was a birthday present from Stanley. I knew that it was going to hurt Pierre real bad, but it was time to send him a message that he could understand.

"First blood always goes to the best hunter," I whispered in his ear as he lay writhing on the sidewalk, his face covered in blood. He was too stunned and in pain to go for his gun.

Hitting Pierre made me feel that I had finally paid a first installment toward avenging Father Gohegan and the colored waifs. But he was just the organ grinder's monkey, and I was aware that the Count must have ordered him to destroy my world.

CHAPTER 6

As I hurried away from the Count's headquarters, my run-in with Pierre brought back memories of July 5, 1913:

Hannah Korngold waits on the sidewalk outside the St. Vincent's Colored Waifs' Home in New Orleans. The sun beats down on her mercilessly. The word has just come down: the city is closing the Waifs' Home due to budget cuts. In other words, the Klan had decided to close the school, although officially the Klan no longer existed.

Hannah waves to me. Surprised, I walk away from her. She calls out, "Can we talk?"

I notice two white men standing across the street, leaning on a black Ford, pretending not to look my way.

Hannah follows me. I don't break my stride. I keep walking as if I don't know her. All the while, I watch the two men out of the corner of my eye. One of them I recognize as a plainclothes policeman from the NOPD. Louis "Strawberry" Armstrong has pointed him out to me before. The other man—I now know—is Pierre. He sports a gray Borsalino hat and, despite the heat, wears a gray linen suit with matching spats over his black patent leather shoes.

The policeman throws his cigarette butt onto the sidewalk and stamps on it, looking disgusted. I duck through some back streets, trying to shake off Hannah and make sure the two men aren't following me. I step inside a doorway and see the black Ford cruise by at the end of the street. Relieved that I'm alone, I walk on, whistling one of Stanley Bontemps's riffs. Someone taps me on the shoulder, and I turn around to see Hannah blushing angrily.

"I'll ask once more. Can we talk?"

I make sure that no one is watching, take off my "Colored Waifs' Home" shirt. I tuck it under my arm, leaving me in a dingy undershirt.

"Let's walk," I reply. We keep talking during our long ramble.

We walk through the French Quarter under balconies draped with Confederate bunting, past the throngs, to the Mississippi River. We sit down on the grassy bank to watch the riverboats pass by.

"Be nice to be sailing far away," Hannah says with a sigh.

"Real far," I agree.

"Far as New York?"

I don't answer.

"You going there?" Hannah repeats.

"Yes'm."

Hannah looks at me, irritated.

"People say it's the greatest place for a musician."

"Guess they ain't been to N'awlins, Miss Hannah."

"You hate my father for letting you go? Someone burned a cross on our lawn last night."

I feel bad about that but say, "That be what the Klan do in N'awlins. They s'posed to be shut down but they still got the votes and the guns. They done nailed the Waifs' Home shut, too." I pause and say, "Why should I hate your father? He been good to me. He give me a clarinet for my birthday yesterday, which gone get me out this place. Nobody done gifted me nothin' before."

Hannah looks nervous and then asks, "Do you hate me?"

Her question really surprises me. "Why? Ma'am, you somethin' else."

"What else?"

"I'm still workin' on that, ma'am", I say, and I see a soft look in her eyes.

"I got some questions for you," she says. "Like, why don't you ever look me straight in the eye when we talk? How come you keep calling me 'ma'am' and saying 'yes'm' when we talk?"

"You know why. You white, that's why."

"I'm not going to scream for help, you know."

A horn sounds on a riverboat, and jazz blasts from it. I start laughing. "Hear that clarinet? Fool think he be Stanley Bontemps."

"But he be nowhere near as good as ole Stanley. Nooo... ma'ammm!" Hannah says, mimicking me.

I'm surprised at how good a mimic she is. We laugh.

"I'm going to New York, too," she says quietly.

"You done told your folks?"

"They can't stop me. I'm going there to study the violin," she says, defiantly. Then, "Why don't we meet up in New York? My father asked me to give you his cousin Jack Firestone's address. He's a musician's agent working in Tin Pan Alley."

She hands me a piece of paper with a note from her father and her uncle's address.

"You going to look him up?" she asks.

"Yeah, thank your daddy for me. Thank him for everything. He been good to me."

"You didn't answer my other question," she says. "Are we going to meet up in New York? Ever see each other again? Or is this as far as we go?"

A lot of different ideas running through my brain, I shake my head no and stand up to go. Hannah pulls me down on the grass, rolls on top of me, and kisses me hard. I look around, frightened.

"Swear you'll never call me ma'am again, or I'll scream," she says.

I kiss her back, jump up, and bolt to St. Vincent's.

Later, I riff on Scott Joplin's "The Entertainer," playing the clarinet that Hannah's father, Abe, had given me as an eighteenth birthday present the day before. My friend Louis "Strawberry" Armstrong, who is six years younger than me, blows his cornet, also a birthday present from Abe. The other boys gather up their things and file out of the dormitory door. Most are dressed in the rough clothes that they will wear back to the Battlefield in the Back o' Town neighborhood.

Strawberry and I wrap our horns up in newspaper and gather our belongings.

"You sure you want to head to Chicago first?" I ask him.

"Yeah. Got to see some folks there, then I be headin' on to New York for us to duet up again." He was a month shy of twelve, but looked, and acted, years older. He was already a genius on the cornet.

"Don't waste no time gettin' there, Strawberry, 'cause my next stop's Paris, France."

"Say what?" Strawberry says, amazed.

"Father G told me yesterday some white Frenchman name of Brown fathered me be livin' there. My mama was a quadroon whore done suicide herself on his account."

"That's some bad stuff, man."

"I'm gonna rake me up some money in New York and then track Brown down."

We leave the dormitory room and immediately see smoke billowing through the corridor. Flames lick around the door to Father Gohegan's office. We run toward it. Through the burning door I see Father Gohegan on his knees, head bent forward, hands clasped in prayer, holding a silver handbell. He turns to look at me as I start breaking flaming shards from the door frame, trying to get to him. With his last strength Father Gohegan throws the handbell through the door and screams, "Urby, your father gave the handbell to your mother! Go find him, in France!" Then Father Gohegan is engulfed in flames. Clutching the handbell, I feel Strawberry's hands on my back, pushing me out the front door of the building as it collapses in a gush of flames. We lie on the ground, struggling for breath. I see the plainclothes policeman and Pierre. Pierre is holding a can of kerosene, his eyes searching the crowd of colored waifs who watch the blaze impassively.

I pull Strawberry down out of their sight. "I seen them two before, Straw," I say.

"They been watchin' the home for days. That sharp dude done set the fire, I reckon."

I suddenly realized why the men were there. "They be lookin' for me, Strawberry. They seen me with Hannah."

"You best git, Urby. Stay away from them main roads much as you can. See you in New York, man." Strawberry strolls toward the fire to join the other waifs watching their home burn down.

I slip away into the night, moving away from the fire. I carry the silver handbell in a burlap sack along with my clarinet and my few possessions. I look back one more time. Firemen and policemen, joined by men in Klan robes, stand watching the blaze. They smoke cigarettes and cigars, drink from pint bottles, and laugh uproariously, enjoying the spectacle.

Pierre stands beside the plainclothes policeman, who now has the kerosene can in his hand. They run over to the line of Waifs' Home boys retreating fearfully from them. I see Buster Thigpen, now a big-time drummer in Harlem nightclubs, who had returned to New Orleans and St. Vincent's to show off his flashy clothes and car to the colored waifs.

I yell out a warning just as a policeman wrestles Buster to the ground and forces his hand around the handle of the kerosene can. They throw Buster into a police van, which howls away, groups of cars with flashing headlights following it.

CHAPTER 7

Paris, Friday, February 9, 1934

With a name like The Beautiful Princess, you would expect Hambone Gaylord's nightclub just off Place Pigalle to be as elegant as Maxim's and as big as La Coupole, the enormous restaurant-brasserie that had opened with great fanfare in Montparnasse a few years ago. But La Belle was no bigger than four VIP booths in Johnny Sutton's Blue Heaven Club in Harlem.

There was a bar where seven or eight skinny people could drink together if they didn't wave their arms around too much. A dozen or so tables were crammed together near a small stage, and the place always looked like three o'clock in the morning in a murky bar in Harlem.

But some of the best jazz in the world and Hambone's charm had brought celebrities there from all over the globe. First time I went there about seven years ago, Redtop was doing the hostessing. It was before she got her own place. Redtop brought so many famous people into La Belle Princesse that crowds would form outside the club, waiting to catch a glimpse of Charlie Chaplin or Picasso or the Prince of Wales or Mistinguett or Josephine Baker.

I turned up at La Belle at 5:00 p.m. on Friday, as arranged with Stanley, Redtop, Hambone, and his nephew, Baby Langston. Buster was due to arrive in an hour, and he had phoned Stanley at the club a few minutes before to let him know he would be on time and to ask him if, as a favor, he could bring his girlfriend to the rehearsal. Stanley hemmed and hawed, winking at us. Finally, he consented, and the trap was set to close on Buster Thigpen and Daphne.

Stanley's plan was simple: to snatch them and then hide them in a disused stable block that he owned in a remote thicket in the Bois de Boulogne. Meanwhile, he would present a list of demands to Robinson III, mainly that he pay me my fee in straight money with a generous bonus for the "dangerosity" of the job. That was the way we had arranged things between us because none of us wanted to have problems with the French police.

Stanley used his stable block to store, or stash, some of the many items that he dealt in to supplement his considerable income as a musician. No one knew its exact location, except Redtop and me.

Buster and Daphne would be abducted from La Belle Princesse by two of Hambone's associates, whom he called "the Corsican Twins." I would deliver her to Robinson a few hours or, at most, a day later after freeing her from the stables when Robinson III coughed up my fees and bonus as arranged by Stanley. I would pretend that I had tracked her down and saved her from kidnappers, and I would have damage on my face to back up my story. I'd also let Robinson III know that the kidnappers were wise to unpleasant stuff that wouldn't look too good if it got into the newspapers. The unpleasantness I had in mind was the stories that Jean Fletcher had told me about the family Robinson in the Hôtel Lutetia bar after we fled from the rioting last Tuesday night. If Robinson swallowed the bait, he'd fork out the dough gratefully for our returning Daphne safe and sound. If things turned sour, Buster was there to take the fall.

Putting Robinson III and Daphne to one side, Buster Thigpen was still a big problem. He was washed up as a drummer stateside due to his bad reputation as a drug addict and a violent womanizer with a quick temper and a fast blade. Paris was the only place where he had any kind of backing, thanks to the Count. Buster's only hope of avoiding ending up with a bullet in his brain was to stick as tight to the Count as white on rice. If things went well for Buster's Fascist and monarchist buddies, and if they succeeded in bringing the government down on their next try, old Buster would be sitting pretty.

That was where the Corsican Twins came in. Once I turned Daphne over to Robinson, I was thinking of going back to the stables, fetching Buster, and turning him over to the Corsican Twins, unless Stanley had a better plan for dealing with Buster.

I reckoned that the Corsicans could make it clear to him that he had better keep his trap shut about the snatch, stay away from Daphne, and get out of France as soon as possible. I figured that, although the Count might have two hundred uniformed storm troopers to do his bidding, the Corsican Twins could muster even more men from their clan at a moment's notice. I doubted that the Count had enough foot soldiers to face down the cream of the French underworld.

I was taking no chances with the rehearsal. I had brought along my clarinet and its case, but if things went to plan, I wouldn't even play one note. Still, in case I had to defend myself, I had a hidden compartment in the case concealing my Colt M1911 with two spare clips, each carrying seven rounds of .45 caliber bullets and a silencer.

It was already getting dark when I arrived at La Belle Princesse. I went past Baby Langston who was polishing the zinc bar. He nodded toward Hambone Gaylord's office and said, "Everybody's waiting for you."

I knocked on the door, and the burly, black-skinned Hambone and I shook hands. The walls of his tiny office were covered with photographs of celebrity patrons of the club, which they had signed with fond messages. There was a battered table, even smaller than my office desk, next to which Stanley was rocking in a mahogany rocking chair, wearing powder-blue threads from head to toe. Next to him sat the Corsican Twins, two tough-looking youngsters wearing dark pinstriped suits, black Fedora hats, and spats. They looked around calmly as if they could handle any situation without mussing up their duds. Their well-tailored suits had thin bulges in a few places, inside which were thin guns and razor-sharp stilettos. Their swarthy faces were expressionless, and they looked at Hambone Gaylord as if he was their clan leader. Redtop was watching the Corsicans with a worried look. I had never seen her so nervous before.

"Soon's Buster and his goldilocks come in, the Corsican boys gone to come running in the front door all tough, waving they pieces," Stanley said. "They gone attack Baby Langston at the cash registry and grab all the takings. Then these here Alfieris gone sap Baby on his head, and they do the same to you, Urby. They gone menace me with they pieces and tie gunny sacks over Buster and Daphne. A getaway car be waitin' for them in the back alley." Stanley was getting more excited by the plan, his voice rising as he warmed to it. "The driver, a Corsican like these here boys, gone take Daphne and Buster to the meetin' place and then hand them over to friends of ours who gone take them to the hidin' place."

Stanley's eyes twinkled. I realized that he wasn't giving Hambone and the Corsicans very many details.

"Then we start playin' the game with this Robinson man of yours," Stanley continued, looking at me, "and you best believe he gone keep the police out of it, 'specially with all the stuff Urby has on him." Stanley did not let on to Hambone or the Corsicans what I had on Robinson III. If they knew too much, they might pull off a real kidnapping and hold the girl to ransom themselves.

I liked the plan, but I had learned in the war that even the best plans had a way of going haywire in the heat of battle. But I felt pretty confident that with the Colt in my clarinet case and the Corsican Twins in on the action, I stood a pretty good chance of getting myself, and Daphne, out of this mess in one piece. One thing intrigued me, though: Robinson III had told me that when she had sent him an SOS asking him to help her escape from Buster, he had told her that he was engaging me to track them down. I wondered if she would remember my name and realize that Buster was being set up so that I could rescue her.

Redtop said her good-byes all around. She was probably heading back to Chez Red Tops for her Hispano-Suiza. She would come back for Baby Langston after the snatch, drive to a place where they would rendezvous with the Corsican Twins and their driver, and then ferry Daphne, Buster, and a blindfolded Baby to the hideaway.

A few minutes after Redtop left, Baby Langston gave a warning whistle that meant that Buster and Daphne were entering La Belle Princesse. Stanley leapt to his feet, fast as a cat, grabbed his powder-blue Borsalino and his soprano saxophone and, together with Hambone and me, went forth to meet them. The Corsican Twins took their cue to slip out the back door and prepare for the snatch.

When Buster and Daphne saw the welcoming committee, Buster started grinning from ear to ear and sashaying around, showing off to his girlfriend.

Buster Thigpen had not changed much over the years. He was still a fine-looking man, but the drugs and booze had turned out the lights in his yellow-green eyes. Still, he moved warily and menacingly, like a big cat in the jungle, and his eyes never stopped tracking. He looked like a hard man to take by surprise.

He and Stanley flung their arms around each other.

"Mr. Bontemps, I be honored that you wants Buster on the drums for this here charity concert tomorrow night. It gone to be like the good times in Harlem. Remember that golden gig we played with the Duke on piano, Bubber Miley on the trumpet, and Charlie Dixon on the banjo at Johnny Sutton's Blue Heaven Club?"

Buster was really laying it on thick for Daphne, but she was studying Stanley's face, and she wasn't buying any of Buster's jive. It didn't help that Stanley's eye tic flared up while Buster kept recalling "the golden gig" back in Harlem.

According to Stanley, Buster was so drugged up that he couldn't find the drumhead with his sticks. This happened in front of a packed house at the Blue Heaven Club with Louis Armstrong, Eubie Blake, and Noble Sissle in the audience. Johnny Sutton got so angry that he stopped the quintet in the middle of Blake and Sissle's "I'm Just Wild About Harry," hauled Buster off the bandstand, dragged him across the floor amid tables of cheering patrons, and tossed him outside into a December snowstorm.

Daphne watched everything with the same intensity as her father (or brother?) Barnet Robinson III. Up close, she was breathtakingly beautiful with white-blonde hair that fell to the small of her back. The wave of hair covering her right eye only made her violet-blue left eye look more startling. She wore a long, white silk dress cinched at the waist by a blue leather belt that set off her curves real nicely. Daphne was so beautiful that I tried not to look at her. Each time I did, something fluttered in my chest, and I lost my concentration on what was going to happen in a few minutes. Suddenly, I wanted to protect this woman with every fiber in my being. I wanted to be alone with her somewhere with warm sand, palm trees and an azure blue-violet sky, the color of her eye, reflected in the sea.

Daphne turned to me and locked her gaze into mine as if she could read my mind and liked what she saw there, too. There was a faint hint of surprise in her expression. When she finally spoke, her voice was low and husky, a voice more knowing than I expected from a twenty-year-old coed who came from a rich, upper-class background and was the daughter of Kaiser Bill to boot, if Jean's "sources" were right.

"This be Hambone Gaylord, and this man be his nephew, Baby Langston," Buster said, introducing Daphne all around.

Of course, he saved me for last. "This be Urby Brown," Buster said, yanking a thumb at me by way of introduction.

She flashed her beautiful smile at me, but if my name meant anything special to her as Robinson III's bloodhound, she was not giving anything away.

"Urby Brown. I like your first name. It's unusual," she purred.

I liked it only when *she* said it.

"Buster told me that you met as schoolboys in New Orleans," she went on.

"Yes," I answered, going along with Buster's lie about us meeting as "schoolboys." I felt heat on my neck just looking at her. "Buster and I go a long ways back. So does Stanley. But the main thing is we're still musicianers," I concluded, lamely.

Daphne laughed and clapped her hands in delight.

"'Musicianers.' That's such a quaint word, when Buster's old friends from New Orleans use it. It sounds nicer than 'musicians.' It conjures up high priests of jazz with a language and ritual all your own. As if you hold secrets of the temple that only the initiated may know. Like Wagner."

I was enjoying listening to Daphne almost as much as looking at her, except for her comparing our music to Wagner's. Some high-falutin French music critic said something similar at Chez Red Tops a few years ago, and Ernest Hemingway socked him in the jaw so hard that the man had to be taken to the Hôtel Dieu hospital to be revived.

Daphne kept her eye locked on mine. I wished I could see her other eye peeking under the wavy white-blonde hair, so that I could know what she was thinking. I looked at the poet, Baby Langston, standing behind the bar. His eyes were glued onto Daphne, and he was taking in her every word. I was sure that Baby was already working out a poem that would transform Daphne into a goddess out of Greek mythology.

I was beginning to get cold feet about Stanley's plan because I didn't want to see the Corsican Twins throw a sack over Daphne's beautiful face and body, and I didn't like the thought of her fear while Stanley kept her and Buster in hiding until he negotiated terms for my fees and "lagniappe" with Robinson III. Daphne must have sensed that something was wrong, and she put her velvet-gloved hand on my sleeve.

"Is something wrong, Mr. Brown? You've gone red in the face like you have a fever." She actually took her right glove off and put her soft hand on my forehead. So soft and perfumed was her hand that I had to restrain myself from kissing it then and there. Buster took it all in with an ugly sneer twisting his face before he said, "Don't you worry none about Urby, baby. He be tough as they come, almost as tough as me. Ain't that right, Urby, my man?"

He was really skating on thin ice now because the last time we fought at St. Vincent's, I beat him up so badly that he had to limp into Father Gohegan's office to find sanctuary.

"I think Mr. Brown has a fever, Buster. Maybe he should be in bed under warm blankets with pots of tea and lemon and dry toast in easy reach. I could take him to my—"

Just at that moment, there was a commotion at the door, and we all looked at each other. Only Buster seemed truly surprised. Daphne was not fazed at all; she looked amused by the goings-on.

An instant later, pandemonium reigned in La Belle Princesse. One of the two masked men had slugged Baby Langston and was rifling through the cash register, while the other pointed a sawed-off shotgun at us.

"Que personne ne bouge!" he shouted.

"Les mains en l'air!" We all raised our hands. Buster was wide-eyed with terror, but Daphne was as cool as if armed robberies were a matter of routine. Playing the role assigned to me, I leapt at the gunman, and he brought his sap down on my head so hard that I slumped to the floor and saw a lot of my blood on my hand when I removed it from my temple. Soon I was only semiconscious, but then I felt Daphne's hand on my cheek, and her honeysuckle scent filled my nose.

"You didn't have to do that," she hissed at the Corsican. "He was only trying to protect me…like a gentleman."

"Shut yo' mouth, woman," Buster quailed. "Elsewise they turn on you. These here men just wants to take the money in that cash registry and be gone like a cool breeze."

The first Corsican had filled a bag with all the money in the cash register, and then he turned to Buster and Daphne. "Vous parlez trop," he said to them. The second Corsican tied their hands behind their backs so tightly that Buster let out a yelp. Daphne went a little red in the face. The Corsicans threw big burlap sacks over Daphne and Buster that almost fell to her ankles.

"Avancez," a twin barked out as they pushed them toward the alley door with the barrels of their shotguns aimed at their backs. Buster was shaking and moaning like a man going off to the guillotine, but Daphne didn't make a sound.

The four of them slipped out the back door. We heard the distinctive roar of a Citroën "traction avant" revving up and then the squeal of tires as the Corsicans raced off with Buster and Daphne to rendezvous with Redtop and Baby Langston.

The moment the car roared off, Stanley slapped palms with Hambone Gaylord, and they both made that cricket laugh in their throats. Baby Langston was wiping at the scratch on his forehead with a handkerchief, but when he saw the cut on my temple he poured gin over it and swabbed the blood away.

"Those boys sure play rough," Baby Langston said in his soft voice. "I sure wouldn't want to be around when they do it for real."

My head was throbbing. I was wondering why the Corsican had sapped me so hard. But, mainly, I was worried about Daphne. She seemed cool enough, but I didn't want to think of what the twins might do to her if they got hot eyeing her on the way to the rendezvous with Redtop and Baby Langston. They probably wouldn't be able to master their urges for too long.

"Are your Corsicans on the level, Hambone?" I asked.

"They my men," he replied coldly. "I done dragged they Daddy off the barbed wire at Verdun. The whole Alfieri clan at my beck and call."

Stanley gave me a big wink and wagged a finger at me. "You sho' taken to that Daphne and she to you, mon petit. Ooooeeee, I can still feel the heat. Don't worry, your doll gone be free in twenty-four hour, Mr. Robinson play ball."

"What about Buster?" I asked.

"Well, you told me he was tight with the Count. Let's see that little Hitler sweat when he try to get that no-count Buster back from them Corsicans. But you let me handle it. We gots to be careful that it don't bite back on us. I gone phone the police right now 'bout the robbery and snatchin' of goldilocks and Buster. You keep a rubbin' on that cut so's the blood keep gushin' outta it."

My blood, I thought bitterly. I hadn't lost a drop of it during four years in the Great War, and now I was bleeding in a faked abduction over a question of money.

"The mo' blood and bruises them Frenchy po-lice sees, the mo' they likely swallow our story," Stanley said. "We got to rough Baby up some more in case they come back to question y'all again about the robbery and the snatch."

Stanley looked like those photos of King Vidor directing *Hallelujah!*. He sat Baby Langston down at one of the tables and slapped him across the face until Baby was sobbing in pain with tears flooding his cheeks. I could see that Hambone was straining to keep from jumping Stanley. Then Stanley threw me to the floor so that my back was angled against the bar, and he rubbed one of the white cloth napkins across the cut on my forehead so hard that it soaked up the bleeding instead of making it worse. When I dabbed at the cut with my handkerchief, it had already dried up.

Stanley flung a few more chairs and tables around and threw bottles of wine at the bar toward both sides of the cash register. Shards of glass ricocheted around La Belle Princesse, and Hambone was looking seriously irritated. Stanley smiled at him slyly and said, "Hey, Bone. Gots to make it real nasty in here so them police don't look around too much. They don't like to get real down and nasty and mess up they pretty uniforms and shoes like the cops back home."

Hambone scowled even more as he took in the mess, and he looked frightened when he saw the state of his nephew Baby Langston. Stanley threw more fat on the fire.

"Hambone, mon grand, when the police arrives you gots to be lookin' mo' upset about losin' all that money and havin' yo' club all trashed up. But don't worry. The girl's father goin' to pay Urby some big money to get his daughter back, and you goin' to get a nice slice of it, pay for some new furniture for yo' club. Sho' needs it."

That really did it. Hambone raised himself to his full six feet three inches and shook his ham-like fists at the slight Stanley.

"You wants me to look *mo'* upset?" Hambone said. "*Mo' upset!* Sheeeitt, Stanley, I be mo' upset, you be missin' half yo' mouf. This caper best be worth my while."

Stanley sweetened Hambone up by forking over a large wad of franc notes as an "advance" on the proceeds. After eyeing the wad and making fast mental calculations, Hambone suddenly became so enthusiastic about playing the role of a robbery victim that Stanley had to keep him from busting up all of his own chairs.

I heard the roaring of a car engine, and then Redtop burst into the room. She checked out the devastated nightclub and shook her head nervously.

"The firestorm's about to blaze," she said. She crossed herself and looked as if she were about to cry. I was surprised because Redtop was one tough woman. She went over to the miserable Baby Langston and yanked him to his feet. "Let's git, Baby. We got to meet up with them Corsican boys and fetch Beauty and the Beast off to Stanley's hideaway."

The chief inspector of police apologized to Hambone for the "inconvenience" that the robbery had caused. Hambone declined his offer of help to tidy up La Belle Princesse for tomorrow night's charity concert. Hambone didn't want policemen lingering around the premises because he probably felt that they might uncover something that could get him deported.

The police examined my wounds, careful not to get blood on themselves. When the chief inspector learned that, like himself, I had known the carnage of the Battle of the Somme, he carried my clarinet case out to his car and drove me to the Hôtel Dieu hospital himself, the siren wailing at full blast.

Fortunately, he didn't open the clarinet case and find the weaponry in its hidden compartment. That would have got me kicked out of France quicker than you can say Jack Robinson, war hero or not.

I was released from Hôtel Dieu six hours later, at just past one thirty in the morning. A team of doctors had spent most of that time debating whether I needed stitches on my temple and, at long last, concluded that I didn't. Finally, I asked them to put liquid court plaster on the cut. Then I combed my hair over it, said my good-byes, and headed for Chez Red Tops. I was anxious to find out how Daphne was doing.

CHAPTER 8

Paris, Early Saturday morning, February 10, 1934

Chez Red Tops was unusually empty for two o'clock on a Saturday morning. The Paris taxi drivers were nine days into their strike, and it was getting hard to move around in the city, day or night. People were still lying low after the riots, avoiding the Fascist gangs licking their wounds in bars and restaurants on the Right Bank and assaulting anybody who looked foreign or like a workingman. They were limbering up for another attack on the National Assembly if the order came down.

The colored American owners of businesses in Harlem-in- Montmartre were ready for them, guns and knives and baseball bats on hand, in case the Fascists aped their Klan brothers in the South by attacking their businesses.

Redtop was all alone, standing behind the bar looking blue and down. I had never seen Chez Red Tops so empty, and I had never seen her so low. She sipped at the straight gin in her glass, smoking a gold-filtered Russian cigarette with a trembling hand.

When I asked her about the "hostages," she said, "Buster's ice queen be really somethin'. Don't nothin' faze her. Them Corsicans say the girl be quiet as a morgue, but Buster be whinin' like a baby so much they etherize him and ice queen a little bit before turnin' them over to me and Baby Langston to take to Stanley's hideout. Urby, you ought to have seen them when we opened their sacks to check them out. Buster be out cold and lookin' scared to death, and the ice queen be like Sleepin' Beauty with no fear in her. Me and Baby ain't said a word the whole time, so there ain't no way Buster or the ice queen can tell who we is. I left Baby with them to hold the fort when they wake up until Stanley make his move."

"How come Buster's acting like that? He's all front, but I've never seen him act so cowardly."

Redtop's gold tooth shone. "I think he scared to death that Daphne Daddy goin' to cut a deal for her and leave him to them Corsicans, and he know what they capable of doin'. Between you, me, and the lamp-post, Buster ain't worth flea farts and ain't worth savin'."

I had discovered a frightened Redtop at La Belle Princesse earlier, but I saw a panicked one now. She pulled at her curly red hair, bit at her claw-like, lavender-painted fingernails.

"This deal gettin' too big, Urby," she went on. "Smells to me like cops and politickers and other big white fish goin' to get swimmin' around in this thing. That got to be a worry for my bidness and our folk here in Montmartre." She paused and squeezed my arm, the first time that she had ever touched me.

"Urby, they throw me out of France, and I ain't got no place to go. There ain't no way I'm goin' back to America and all of that Jim Crow lynchin' and everybody black and white be hatin' on me 'cause I makes love to women instead of men. No way I'm goin' back." Redtop reached under the bar and held up a sawed-off shotgun. "I'm goin' to swallow this baby's barrel and pull the trigger if the Frenchies deports me."

"What you got there?" I asked Redtop, stroking her shotgun. I was trying to get the old smile back on her face and to cover up my shock at what she had said about suiciding herself. "Looks like when your baby grows up, she's going to be a Browning A-5."

"Sure is," she said, smiling. "And I knows how to use her. Them French Nazis better not try to bust in here. You packin'?"

I reached inside my overcoat and made a fast draw from the custom-made speed holster strapped to my chest. Then I twirled the Colt around, doing Tom Mix gun tricks. Redtop whistled and then tapped me hard on my Homburg helmet for good luck, a little too hard judging from her pained look as she sucked at her knuckles. I screwed the silencer onto the Colt and put it back into the holster.

"You sure is ready, Urby," she commented, admiringly. "When Baby Langston phone me just 'fore you come in, everything be copacetic, 'cept Buster awake now and he lettin' rip. He shoutin' about tellin' the Count them Corsicans stuck up Hambone's place and snatch up him and ice queen, unless somebody cut him loose from his gunny sack. The girl ain't open her pretty little mouth one time."

"You tell Stanley about the way Buster's acting?" I asked.

"Stanley says he got a plan for Buster. Meantime, Baby Langston keepin' a close eye on them through a spy hole in the stable wall. Baby finally had to hogtie Buster. Man goin' to end up scarin' hisself to death. Thank the good Lord, he don't know me and Baby in on it. He think it be the Corsicans."

"Can I look at them through that spy hole?" I asked.

Redtop gave me a knowing grin and said, "Sure, you can take a peek at her. I got itchy feet too, Urby. I'll drive you there myself."

"Has Stanley talked money to Barnet Robinson yet?" I asked.

"Stanley told me he decided to get a white friend of his to phone him at the Ritz where he be stayin'. Around lunch time. The friend goin' to lay it all out to Robinson so that he pay what he owe you big time when you brings the girl in."

"What's Stanley's plan for Buster?" I asked.

"He goin' to ax Baby to put on one of them French accents he can do and warn Buster that the Corsicans gone cut him into little pieces and feed him to the sharks, he open his mouth about the snatch. Also, he gone promise Buster if he hush up his mouth, he be back to his Count in no time flat."

Stanley's plan sounded good to me, but I knew we couldn't trust Buster to go along with it quietly. He was bound to do something crazy.

"You think the girl will talk?"

"Naw. You goin' to bust into them stables and save her soon as Stanley white friend settle your bidness with her daddy. You be her hero then. I think she like you, too."

Redtop closed her empty nightclub, leaving the Senegalese bouncer to stand guard. She seemed to have calmed down and was acting like her old self: tough as nails and warm as the sun.

We hopped into Redtop's Hispano-Suiza. She had slung her baby shotgun out of sight under her coat. She revved up the engine, and we sped off to Stanley's Bois de Boulogne hideout using back alleys and side streets. I peered behind us. It didn't look like we were being followed. But I had an uneasy feeling that something was out there. Redtop knew Paris as well as any taxi driver, and we hurtled along so fast that anybody tailing us would have to show his hand.

I saw a glint of light on a car well behind us. "Redtop, I think somebody's tailing us." Just then, it turned down a side street and disappeared.

"Call me jumpy," Redtop said, "but we best slip around another way, so ain't nobody follow us without us knowin' it."

She stopped the Hispano, turned off the engine and the lights, and we waited for five minutes to see if the other car reappeared. While we were waiting, Redtop opened her coat, unslung her shotgun, and put it in my lap. No car appeared, so Redtop started up the engine, and we moved along a road in the Bois de Boulogne with the lights off.

Suddenly, Redtop veered off the road and we skidded across the grass, the frost crunching under the tires. We stepped out of the car and looked around. Even with our coats on, it was chilly, and the bare, rimy tree branches looked sinister swaying in the wind in the dim moonlight. We struggled through a mass of tangled bushes that tore at our clothes. Redtop led the way, swinging her mini-Browning like a scythe. By reflex action, I unlocked the safety on my Colt.

We could make out the outlines of the stables when they were about ten yards away. The sounds from Paris were faint, and the woods were silent. Suddenly, I heard a cry like a hoot owl, right in front of me. I heard Redtop chuckling. She had made the hoot owl sound and thrown her voice. She put her finger to her lips and we waited. We heard a hoot owl replying.

"That be Baby Langston," she said. "Let's go." Redtop slung her shotgun, but I kept my Colt's safety off. She hooted more loudly as we reached the stables and then she walked inside and I headed toward the spy hole.

Something hard hammered against my metal Homburg. As I fell, I drew my Colt, ready to hit the ground shooting. I must have blacked out for an instant. When I came to, I heard Redtop cursing and screaming inside the stable, and I peered through the hole in its wall. In the light from a kerosene lamp, I saw that Buster had broken loose, and Baby Langston lay unconscious on the ground next to the tire iron that must have bounced off my Homburg. Buster was holding Redtop's Browning to her head. Luckily, he didn't know that I was conscious.

Buster looked like he needed some drugs real fast. Killing me, Baby Langston, and Redtop must have seemed to him to be the fastest ticket to drug heaven now that he held the upper hand. When Buster cocked the shotgun, ready to blow off Redtop's head, images of him from the time that I first saw him at St. Vincent's flashed through my mind. I wished there was a way to stop him from shooting Redtop without killing him, but I drew a bead on Buster's ear hole through the opening in the wall and pulled the trigger.

The bullet made a *phttttt* sound passing through the silencer and then punched its way through Buster's ear. The force of it made his head jerk sideways, and blood spattered from the wound as Buster toppled over, dead before he hit the ground. I heard Daphne cry out, but by the time I had charged into the stable, she must have fainted and now lay immobile in the burlap sack.

"Thanks, Urby," Redtop whispered. "I ain't about to forget you done save my life." Baby Langston moaned and started rubbing his head vigorously where Buster had slugged him.

"Let's get Buster out of here now, Redtop," I said quietly. "We'll deep-six him and leave Baby to keep an eye on things until I can take her to her father."

Redtop nodded, still in a daze. We wet down horse towels and bandages and cleaned up every speck of blood we saw and then I tied cloths around Buster's head to staunch the bleeding and put him back inside the burlap sack. I checked the stable walls and floor for traces of a bullet hole or fragments and didn't see any. Redtop and I dragged Buster to her car and stuffed him into the trunk. I put some ropes and a blacksmith's anvil into the sack with him and then tied it up tightly. My blood-covered hands were trembling violently.

I knew that the best way to make Buster disappear for good was to cast him into the waters of the Seine at Argenteuil, where the river reaches its widest and deepest point. I had always had a hunch that Buster was heading for a bad place, but I never thought that I would be the one who put him there. I had killed before, too many times, but I had never killed someone I knew.

We opened the other burlap sack to check on Daphne, who was still unconscious. Baby Langston was on his feet, and he nodded to us that he was all right. He looked scared when we told him that Buster was dead and stuffed inside the trunk of Redtop's Hispano for burial. I told Baby that Redtop and I had cleaned Buster's blood up as best we could but asked him to go over the place again to make sure there were no traces of blood or struggle anywhere. Baby fell to it with mop and pail. By the time we were ready to leave, he was scrubbing the floor as if he were back at La Belle Princesse, making the place spick and span for showtime.

We looked over at Daphne's inert form again. She had not moved a muscle. We took Baby outside and whispered to him that if she came to and wanted some water, he should first put on the Balaclava hood and gloves he had been supplied with so that she could not recognize his face or his color. He was not to utter a word to her. The success of Stanley's fake abduction depended on Daphne's being sure that the Corsican Twins and their accomplices alone had snatched her and Buster.

Redtop told Baby not to say a word about Buster's death to his uncle or anyone else, and he swore not to. We knew that Baby would keep his mouth shut about it, if he swore he would. The only danger was that he might write a poem about Buster's death someday, turning him into some kind of tragic hero.

When I came to Daphne's rescue in a few hours, nothing that she could say to her father or the police could implicate Stanley or me or any of the others, because the only people she had seen or heard speaking during captivity were the Corsicans.

If everything had gone according to plan, I would, at some time in the afternoon, have had my revenge on Robinson III for passing me funny money to track down Daphne and Buster. Stanley would have negotiated a big payout from our fake abduction of his daughter. The Corsicans would have warned Buster to keep his trap shut about the snatch before he had a chance to start shooting his mouth off to the Count about what had happened at the rehearsal at La Belle Princesse.

But with Buster dead, the problems were beginning to pile up. When Buster didn't appear, the Count was going to fix his suspicions on me. I had roughed up the Count's main storm trooper, Pierre, real badly when I left his headquarters. Still, that hadn't stopped the Count from letting Buster show up for the rehearsal because *I* had convinced him that Buster was the musician Stanley wanted for the gig. I saw only one way out of keeping the Count from going after me: to make him think that Buster was ransoming Daphne to feed the hungry monkey on his back. When Buster's scheme had failed, he had evaporated into thin air. Still,

I felt guilty about killing Buster. If I hadn't been so angry at Robinson III, he'd still be alive.

Yet, Buster had to take the fall, now that he was dead. The problem was getting the Count to believe us because he had said that Buster was like a son to him, and that meant he must have seen something useful in him somewhere.

I was hoping that the Corsicans were as tight with Hambone Gaylord as he said they were and could help us to face down the Count and his men if we couldn't make Buster take the fall. And would Daphne go along with it? She had seen Buster's fear and known that he wasn't playacting. Daphne could make the whole thing unravel if she wanted to.

On the drive to Argenteuil, I kept thinking about Buster. He would have killed Redtop and me and Baby without a second thought because he needed another high from his drugs. In the end, that was all he was, a need that could never be filled. But I had known Buster when there was a glimmer of hope that he might turn out to be better. Now, I had taken from him the only thing that had kept that hope alive—his life.

Lights swirled past the car window as Redtop raced toward Argenteuil along deserted roads. My eyes kept closing, and then I fell asleep and remembered how Buster was a long time ago:

> *The police car stops outside St. Vincent's, and the Irish policeman unlocks my door and leads me straight to Father Gohegan's office. He knocks on the door and stands at attention, making me do the same.*
>
> *"Come in!" Father Gohegan shouts. When we walk in, he is standing behind his desk, all smiles at the policeman. I stare at the worn oak floor not raising my eyes.*
>
> *"Good morning, Father. We've found him for you," he says.*
>
> *"Usual place?" Father Gohegan asks.*
>
> *"Yes, Father. Sitting on the same bench, looking at the same riverboats. Been sitting there all night, he said."*

"At least we always know where to find him. How's the family, Patrick?"

"Everybody's fine. We miss you at mass, though. The diocese is wasting you here, Father, if you don't mind me saying so."

"I'm doing the Lord's work, Patrick. But it sure is hard to fathom what He has in mind sometimes." They both chuckle. Father Gohegan makes the sign of the cross, and the policeman crosses himself and leaves the office, with a wave at the door.

I keep my head down, staring at the floor. Father Gohegan goes to the door and shouts, "Buster!"

I hear the sound of bare feet slapping on the floor of the corridor, and then Buster comes into the office, a smile of anticipation on his face. Father Gohegan takes a small leather whip out of the top drawer of his desk. Buster grabs it eagerly, flicking it on his palm.

"Five, Buster, and mind that you strike only his left hand."

Buster sneers at this command and marches me into the small adjoining room, where punishments are meted out.

"Hold her out, boy," Buster says.

I hold out my left hand and watch Buster brace himself on his legs as if ready to take a swing at batting practice. Then he brings the whip down hard three times. He wants to keep going, but Father Gohegan has had second thoughts, and he rushes into the room and pulls the whip away from Buster.

Buster looks surprised. "Father, if you too easy on him, he just gone run away again."

"Three is enough for now," Father says, irritated that Buster is challenging his authority. Then, with a dismissive gesture, he says to us, "Go, both of you. Urby, you run away again, and I'm going to take Buster's advice."

Buster shoves me along the corridor into the small passageway leading toward our dormitory. I'm catching up to him in height and muscle, having put on a spurt of growth over the last few months.

I feel that the time has come to put an end to Buster's bullying, once and for all, while he is disarmed inside the home.

"Why you hit me so hard?" I ask, feeling my rage turn to flame.

"Hard?" Buster says. "Me, I got worst when I run away. I caught ten. On this here right hand. Father G hisself whupped me, and you got to believe that hurt. But 'cause you the Clarinet Man, he ease you up, like you a little girl."

"You better ease up the next time, boy."

He is so amazed at me talking back to him that he falls silent for an instant. Then he sticks his face into mine, his yellow-green eyes full of menace. "Me ease you up? Sheeit! Next time, you dead, whitey. What you gone do then, sick your mama on me?"

I look away and bow my head as if giving up, but then I quickly spin around and head-butt him on his breastbone so hard that Buster is propelled backward as if blasted by a cannonball. His head bounces on the floor. He tries to stand but sprawls face down, unconscious, arms outstretched.

"Don't never mouth me again, you bastard! I'm gone kill you, you mess with me, you hear? I'm gone kill you, you bastard!" Then I slam my foot down hard on Buster's right leg. I keep on kicking him in the leg until Strawberry hears the ruckus and comes racing out of the dormitory to drag me away.

My talk of killing Buster was just a frightened street-fighter's dreams, shouted out loud to scare a dangerous opponent, that was all. Except that they'd become a nightmare for Buster early this morning, and he was dead for good and forever, not just badly hurt. I tried to sleep despite the roar of the Hispano-Suiza's engine, but I was sure that I'd never know dreamless sleep again. Like him or not, I knew Buster too well to kill him.

PART II

CHAPTER 9

Paris, Early Saturday Morning, February 10, 1934

Baby Langston saw flashes of light like fireflies. His head hadn't stopped hurting since Buster Thigpen had broken free and walloped him with the tire iron. He'd felt all right when Urby and Redtop had left the stables. They'd asked him to clean up all traces of Buster's blood, and he'd done it eagerly to clear his aching head. The girl lay still in the gunny sack. He was beginning to worry that she might be dead.

Baby Langston put on his Balaclava hood and gloves and opened the girl's sack. In the dim light from the kerosene lamp, she looked paler than when he had first seen her at La Belle Princesse. Baby pulled the sack off, removed his hood and gloves and put his ear against her heart. He heard it beating, but contact with her breast made his head ache badly again.

He wondered why the girl had gotten mixed up with that "no-count Buster," as his Uncle Hambone called him. She had everything that Buster didn't. She was beautiful, rich, and well-educated. But what attracted Baby Langston to her most, from the moment he heard her speak at La Belle Princesse, was her breathy voice and her precise use of language. As a poet, Baby Langston appreciated people who spoke English elegantly.

Even in the dim light in the stables, beauty glowed from her flawless face. Her long, white-blonde hair, which spread across the burlap, gleamed like platinum. Baby Langston's head throbbed even worse as he tried to recall the lines written by his favorite poet, Keats, in his ballad "La Belle Dame Sans Merci":

I met a lady in the meads,
Full beautiful—a faery's child,
Her hair was long, her foot was light,
And her eyes were wild.

To make sure that she was still breathing, Baby Langston put his head against Daphne's breast again. Though it was soft and inviting, he pulled his head away as if scalded. Baby Langston had been born in Nashville, Tennessee. He had heard so many stories about colored men being lynched for only making eye contact with a white woman that touching Daphne seemed fraught with danger. He wanted her to be comfortable, though, so he loosened the rope that the Corsicans had tied around her wrists. It had left welts on her skin. Suddenly, he felt an urge to free her. More words from "La Belle Dame Sans Merci" seeped from his memory:

She took me to her elfin grot,
And there she wept, and sigh'd fill sore,
And there I shut her wild wild eyes
With kisses four…

He tried to remember the rest of the poem. Exhaustion gripped him, but he had to stay awake until Stanley Bontemps or Urby Brown told him what to do next. He hoped he would get the word early in the morning because he didn't feel that he could stand much more pain.

Staggering over to the watering trough, Baby turned on the faucet and let the cold water splash over his head. He heard a sudden swish of cloth and turned his sore head slowly. He stared into the girl's wild eyes and saw her upraised arms. Was she an angel spreading her wings to fly away to heaven? Those were Baby Langston's last living thoughts as Daphne connected solidly to his head with the tire iron, putting all of her considerable strength into the blow.

Daphne had been conscious from the moment the "burglars" had abducted Buster and her from La Belle Princesse, except when they had put them under ether because of Buster's whinings. She had bided her time when she came to because she knew the power that her beauty held over men. Because of it, they would make mistakes, and she had to be ready to seize her chance.

When Urby Brown had shot Buster, she felt as if a powerful charge of electricity passed through her. She was excited because she knew that Buster had served her purposes and would only stand in her way from now on. Urby, the man her father had hired to track them down—she remembered his strange first name from her father's telegram—would be her man now because he had felled Buster. She wanted to make love to him as soon as possible to bind him to her.

Buster had needed little convincing to go along with her scheme to stage a false kidnapping of herself and to arrange for her father to pay a large ransom for her return. Central to its success was luring her father to Paris by cabling him that she needed to be rescued from the colored jazz musician named Buster Thigpen. She had asked her father to stay at the Ritz Hotel because she needed an easy address for forwarding ransom demands. She had puzzled over how to deal with the private eye her father had hired to track her and Buster down, but now that Urby had killed Buster, more possibilities had opened up for her scheme to succeed.

She had thought at first that the men who had taken them from La Belle Princesse were Buster's friends and that he had come up with a clever ploy to make their kidnapping look genuine. But, once again, she had let her sexual attraction to Buster blind her to his stupidity. He could never have come up with a neat idea like hiring fake kidnappers to make things more plausible to her father. She realized when the Frenchmen tied her wrists so tightly that they were real kidnappers who could derail her scheme. They must have been working for the owner of La Belle Princesse, she thought, the man Buster introduced to her as Hambone Gaylord. Why else would that nephew of his, the man they called Baby Langston, be standing watch over her when she came to from the Corsicans'ether?

Urby Brown must have somehow gotten wind of where the kidnappers were hiding them and had come to free her. Buster would be alive now if he hadn't panicked and tried to shoot the woman Urby called Redtop. Urby had killed Buster to save her.

She had to get away in case the two French kidnappers reappeared, but she was paralyzed with fear whenever she looked at the huge man, Baby Langston, dead on the ground, blood still oozing from his mangled head.

She wondered what her father would think if he knew that she had now become a killer to achieve her goal of serving the Fatherland. He was a weak man who could have been strong had he, as she had, heeded the call of his mother's aristocratic Prussian blood, "Die Stimme des Blutes," the voice of the blood. Her grandmother had told her that "the voice" was calling all true Germans to return to the Fatherland now to help the new Reichskanzler Adolf Hitler restore Germany to its rightful place as the first among nations. Daphne had her own vision of how to help him.

During laborious sessions, Daphne had dictated and spelled out the ransom note to Buster, which he had transliterated in the scrawl of the near-illiterate that he was. She was demanding a ransom of one hundred thousand dollars, a drop in the bucket for her father and only twice the amount that the kidnappers had demanded for the return of the baby son of their New Jersey neighbor, Charles Lindbergh. Daphne looked down on "America's hero," whom she considered to be an uncouth, lanky grease monkey with pilot's wings. His only saving grace, in her eyes, was that he was an Aryan type who seemed to be an admirer of Germany.

One hundred thousand dollars might be pocket money for her father to obtain her "freedom" from her fictitious kidnappers, but Daphne considered that it would suffice, for now, to make her independent to travel to the Fatherland. Her father would not dare to follow her himself into Germany if he realized he had been duped.

She would be free to fulfill her vision: to marry Adolf Hitler and help him to make Germany the most powerful nation on earth and him the most powerful man. But as his beloved Aryan bride and the mother of his children and of the renewed Aryan race, she herself would have ultimate power.

She had met Adolf Hitler with her father and grandmother in Berlin when she was sixteen. He had been very complimentary about their Aryan qualities, but he had singled her out for praise because of her beauty. After asking her father's permission, he had his chauffeur drive the two of them to Berlin's Tiergarten, or Garden of the Wild Beasts.

They had stopped near a leafy glade and walked in silence in the dappled light. He had briefly held her hand, and they stopped and looked deeply into each other's eyes. He was over twenty years older than she was, but electricity passed between them; she was sure of it. He stammered that she was beautiful and then turned abruptly on his heels and marched back to his limousine with her trailing in his wake.

Since that moment, her greatest desire had been to be left alone with him, and she dreamt of arousing him to shouting out his desire for her in his stentorian voice. Buster had taught her every art of arousing men to heights of sexual frenzy. She had served her apprenticeship with Buster and had been his whore, accepting humiliation and his unnatural desires; now, she was confident that she could conquer any man.

If everything went according to plan, her father would be receiving the ransom note in a few hours. One of Buster's most trusted friends in the Count's Oriflamme du Roi group would use a contact at the Ritz Hotel to slide it under her father's door.

Daphne had used up a lot of her own money keeping Buster drugged up enough to go through with her scheme. She had promised Buster one half of the ransom but had no intention of keeping her part of the bargain. By killing him, Urby Brown had spared her the trouble of ridding herself of Buster. But with Buster dead, she had to find a new ally to help her collect the ransom and protect her from the Frenchmen who were now trying to kidnap her. Hambone's people, she thought to herself. Could she turn Urby into that ally? She was sure that she could because she sensed that he had fallen under her spell.

Daphne looked at Baby Langston's body again. Nobody would believe that she could have killed a large black man so brutally. She smiled to herself; her beauty turned all men into fools. No, the killing of this black man bore all the hallmarks of Buster Thigpen's brutality. And Buster was, judging from what Urby had said to the woman Redtop, on his way to burial in a watery grave. She would make sure that blame for the killing of Baby Langston fell on Buster.

She suddenly heard the sound of breaking branches and footsteps approaching. Was it the French kidnappers? Coolly, she dipped her hands in the blood gushing from Baby Langston's head and swabbed it over her dress, face, and hair. Then she tied the ropes back around her arms and wrists and sprawled out on the burlap sack, pretending to be unconscious. There was a knock on the door, and then it was pushed open warily. Daphne heard the sound of two men speaking rapid French. Daphne recognized the voice of Count d'Uribé-Lebrun, and for a moment she was frightened, not knowing how he had found out where she was.

The Count was growing increasingly worried that Bartholomew Thigpen had not yet returned from the charity concert rehearsal at La Belle Princesse nightclub. Then Pierre had received a phone call from a contact who told him that Corsican friends of his, driving a black Traction Avant, were dropping off two "packages of interest" at the intersection of the Boulevard Malesherbes and the Place Wagram at 10:00 p.m. The packages would be picked up by a métisse woman and a black man driving in a Hispano-Suiza automobile. Pierre tried to find out more, but his contact would only tell him what he safely could.

Pierre reported the information to the Count right away. He was very interested because Bartholomew had not yet returned from the rehearsal, and the Count was sure he would take his beautiful blonde girlfriend Daphne with him. Bartholomew might be involved with the "packages" in question. The Count's instincts told him that some plot was being hatched, probably by Bartholomew, to obtain money or something that could be turned into money to feed his drug addiction.

Perhaps this time he had come up with some "louche" scheme to make himself financially independent. This thought displeased the Count, who wanted to keep Bartholomew on a short leash so that he could be used for the major operation that the Count was plotting against the Socialo-communists: the assassination of the Jew and Socialist leader Léon Blum.

Egged on by curiosity, the Count decided that this matter of the "packages of interest" was too delicate to be delegated to his hotheaded acolyte Pierre. No, he would accompany Pierre and find out what, if anything, Bartholomew was plotting.

Pierre and the Count had driven to the rendezvous point indicated by Pierre's contact in an inconspicuous black Renault. They had arrived early and waited near the statue of the painter Alphonse de Neuville, their engine idling. They had a perfect view of the Corsican youths manhandling two large sacks into the trunk of the Hispano, helped by a large black man. The person driving the Hispano, who appeared, in the low light, to be a woman, got from behind the steering wheel briefly to peer into the sacks. The Corsicans had driven away, and they had followed the Hispano as far as the outskirts of Neuilly. Approaching a traffic light, the Hispano sped through the red light, and the Count and Pierre were forced to stop to avoid colliding with a truck. By the time the light changed and they moved forward, the Hispano had disappeared. Irritated, the Count said, "Mon petit Pierre, you let yourself be outmaneuvered by them."

Pierre, abashed, stuttered an apology.

The Count decided that the "packages" were headed for the Bois de Boulogne. Where they had stopped was a good place for observing if there were any further collaborators in the affair. There was a lone open café nearby, and the Count asked Pierre to buy some sandwiches and wine to sustain them while they waited.

The Count's instincts told him that some others would join the woman driving the Hispano and her black helper. Those joining them would be the masterminds, probably Bartholomew and Jean, his closest friend in the Oriflamme. He decided to wait, until dawn if necessary, to see if his hunch proved right.

Some four hours later, the Hispano-Suiza passed by again. This time, the Count recognized the driver as the famous métisse cabaret owner Redtop. He was surprised to see Urby Brown in the passenger seat. The Count nudged Pierre to follow them. This matter was more interesting than he had anticipated.

"Make no mistakes this time, mon petit," he said to Pierre.

They shadowed the car until the Count was sure that they had been spotted. He ordered Pierre to take a side street, which the Count knew would allow them to drop behind the Hispano and follow it at a distance. They saw the car stop and the woman and Urby get out of it and enter a remote thicket in the Bois de Boulogne. Pierre started to get out of the car to follow them, but the Count stopped him.

"Let's wait, mon petit. We will see what happens." The Count was rewarded when the woman came running back alone, drove the Hispano across the frost-covered grass, and then returned five minutes later with Urby still in the passenger seat. The Hispano sped off toward Paris.

The Count signaled to Pierre to follow the Hispano's tire tracks into the wood.

Pierre was the first to spot a dim light glowing in a thicket. They stopped the car, got out, and crept forward, Pierre carrying his Beretta and the Count his trusted Berthier. About ten yards ahead of them, they saw the outlines of a stable and tracks of footsteps in the frost. The Count asked Pierre to reconnoiter the stable. Soon he came running back, wild-eyed.

"Mon général," he said. "The black man who was in the Hispano earlier appears to be dead. He seems to have killed the mistress of Monsieur Bartholomé."

The Count and Pierre crept cautiously into the stables and, immediately, the Count saw that the black man was definitely dead. But a quick glance at Mademoiselle Daphné made him suspect a "mise en scène," that she was feigning an injury. He motioned to Pierre to fill up a bucket of water. He watched the girl as the water filled the bucket. The faint expression of consternation on her face convinced the Count that he was right.

He signaled for Pierre to douse her with water. She leapt to her feet, soaked and sputtering the water out of her nose and mouth. The Count laughed at her expression of surprise and then anger that her subterfuge had been discovered.

"You have some explaining to do, young lady," the Count said to her in his soft New Orleans drawl.

When she had regained her composure, Daphne stared at the Count, thinking at first that her eyes were playing tricks on her. He looked exactly like Urby Brown, the man who she sensed could help her gain independence from her father and achieve her dream of ravishing Adolf Hitler. She had had a fleeting instinct of the resemblance when she had been introduced to Urby hours before. There must be some connection between them, she thought. She felt her confidence swell at the prospect of using both of them to serve her ends.

CHAPTER 10

"Dispose of that cadaver, Pierre. We leave no bodies behind," the Count ordered, jabbing toward Baby Langston with his cane. Pierre obeyed instantly, hefting the large corpse onto his powerful welterweight's frame and then manhandling it into the trunk of the Count's car.

The Count waved his cane at the stables and made a match-striking gesture to Pierre whose eyes gleamed with pleasure.

Pierre took a ten-liter jerrican of gasoline out of the trunk and poured its contents over those strategic points, which Pierre, whose greatest pleasures came from arson, knew would accelerate the burning of the stables.

The Count and the girl watched him dart around, pouring gasoline against the wooden walls of the stables. He then put the empty jerrican on the ground next to the girl and went inside. Pierre returned with a piece of newspaper, which he screwed into a torch. He passed a hand over it like a magician and said, "One match is all that I need." He lit it and touched it to the wall. There was a sudden *whoosh* as the stables went up in flames. Pierre smiled as the blaze spread. He heard clapping and turned to see the Count applauding his prowess.

"Like magic, Pierre. To Paris now," the Count said, all the while studying the girl. He planned to question her in detail about Buster's whereabouts as soon as they reached his headquarters. He also wanted to find out what Urby Brown and the woman, Redtop, were doing at the stables and why they had not taken her with them. As for the corpse they had found with the girl, the Count trusted Pierre's magic to make it disappear.

The Count watched Daphne, who was staring at him from the other side of the desk in his office. The Count had had his maid draw a bath for her in the gilded bathtub in his late Countess Hélène's chambers, which had been unused since her death.

Daphne was rehearsing, in her mind, answers to his inevitable questions. She had to make an ally of him.

He sighed after a while, lifted his gaze, and said, "I hope that you have found everything that you need."

"Everything was so beautiful that it was like being in paradise. Your wife's boudoir?"

"My late wife's," the Count answered. "She died of the Spanish influenza, a week after the armistice." Precisely on November 19, 1918, he remembered, a week and a day after the armistice ending the Great War had been declared. His chief, Philippe Pétain, had been promoted to the rank of Marshal of France that day and the Count to the rank of Brigadier General. The Count was in Paris having his brigadier's star pinned on when a somber Marshal Pétain informed him that his Countess had died from Spanish influenza a few hours before.

"I'm so sorry," the girl was saying to him now. "She must have been a woman of exquisite taste. And she was beautiful. I saw the photograph of the two of you on her dressing table."

"Yes, she was all of those things." He waved his hand dismissively. "But that is the past. What interests me is the present and what has happened to our mutual friend Bartholomew Thigpen."

Daphne looked blank.

"He bears the vulgar nickname Buster," the Count said, smiling.

Daphne's face darkened. "I thought that he cared for me, but he was only after my father's money. He and a black man called Baby Langston arranged to have some Corsicans kidnap me at a nightclub called La Belle Princesse where the black man works for his uncle who owns the place. We had gone there for Buster to rehearse for a charity concert for the families of the dead and injured in the riots last Tuesday." Daphne felt real tears running down her cheeks, and the Count handed her a handkerchief with an air of total indifference.

"Please go on," he said.

"The Corsicans pretended to be burglars and slugged Mr. Urby Brown when he tried to stop them from robbing the cash register. They put Buster and me in burlap sacks as if they were planning to kidnap both of us. They blindfolded me and put some ether or something over my face, and the next thing I knew I woke up with my hands bound behind my back." Daphne broke down, but her tears subsided when she noticed that the Count looked bored rather than sympathetic.

"Please make an effort to go on, my dear," he said, drily.

"When I woke up, the Corsicans were gone, but Mr.Langston and Buster were there. Buster untied my hands and forced me to help him write a ransom note to my father. He wanted one hundred thousand dollars in banknotes and gold for my safe return." She paused. "One hundred thousand dollars! Then he told Mr.Langston to deliver the note to my father at the Ritz Hotel. Buster tied me up again and put me inside that bag to wait until Mr. Langston returned. He promised to untie me when there were two of them to keep an eye on me. Then he raped me, again and again, with my hands tied behind my back! We've made love lots of times; he didn't have to do that." Her face had flushed as if she was still outraged by it all.

The Count made no attempt at sympathy. He pressed on, "Do you think that the owner of La Belle Princesse was complicit in the kidnapping? Or the famous musician Stanley Bontemps? Or Urby Brown?

After all, Mr. Brown came here to ask my permission for Bartholomew to take part in the charity concert."

Daphne paused as if thinking it over. Then she said, "I'm sure that neither Mr. Brown nor Mr. Bontemps had anything to do with it. I don't know about Mr. Langston's uncle. He certainly didn't try to stop Buster and Mr. Langston the way Mr. Brown did. And Mr. Bontemps seemed shocked by it all."

"How did the big black man Langston end up dead?" the Count asked, studying her reaction.

"When Mr.Langston returned from the Ritz and saw what Buster had done to me, he got angry and said he wanted no part of the kidnapping. While he was untying me, they had a violent quarrel, fought like wild animals, and Buster finally got the upper hand and killed Mr. Langston with a tire iron. Buster got frightened when he realized what he'd done, and he just ran off after begging me not to tell anyone what had happened. To say that Mr. Langston had kidnapped me and that a white man had found us, killed Mr. Langston, untied me, and run away. If I know Buster, he's lying low until he can collect the ransom from my father, and then he'll disappear. He always talked about hitting the jackpot someday and going off to Spain or Italy to live like a grandee. I didn't think he planned to hit the jackpot by kidnapping me and holding me to ransom!"

"How did the ransom note reach your father? If this black man Langston delivered it, it would have raised eyebrows at the Ritz."

"Buster told Mr. Langston to ask a French West-Indian cleaning woman he knew to slip the note under my father's door."

The Count studied Daphne's reaction to his next question very carefully. "I think that I saw Mr. Urby Brown and a red-haired métisse woman called Redtop leaving the stable in a car before we found you."

Without hesitating, Daphne said, "I was groggy, but I remember thanking them for tracking me down so fast. They untied my ropes, and then I told them to go to the police right away and get them onto Buster's trail fast, before he left the country. Then I must have fainted."

Daphne put her head in her hands and wept, all the while keeping an eye on the Count's reactions.

Finally, he sighed and said, "I owe you an apology on behalf of Bartholomew, my dear. I know that he has bad sides to him, but he has been most helpful to me, and we have grown quite close. I would never have allowed him to take part in the charity concert if I had known that he was planning to kidnap you."

He seemed to Daphne to be truly sorry; his head had slumped forward, as if to hide his emotions from her. In fact, the Count was thinking to himself that he had heard many stories in his long life, and that he had a fine-tuned sense of the difference between a lie and the truth. This time, though, he was uncertain.

Bartholomew had a violent streak of savagery in him, he knew. He had a penchant for fast women and drugs and gambling, which meant that he needed a constant supply of money. The Count had been happy to supply the money to Bartholomew, up to a point, because of a curious attachment that he felt toward him. He had decided to instill some discipline into Bartholomew and make him work for the money he gave him by forcing him to take a more active part in the attacks of the Oriflamme on the workers and the Socialo-communists.

The Count felt that Bartholomew had distinguished himself in the attack on the National Assembly last Tuesday, although the enemy had won the battle. In fact, he was so impressed by Bartholomew that the Count now planned to mount a counterattack next week, on Ash Wednesday, by having Bartholomew assassinate the Socialist leader Léon Blum. Bartholomew's sudden disappearance had jeopardized the Count's plans.

The Count kept sizing up the girl as she seemed to wait nervously to hear his next words.

The Count recalled his surprise when Bartholomew had first turned up with the girl before him who, though American, had breeding. She obviously came from a wealthy background. She was beautiful and of a pure Aryan type. His instincts told him that beyond her seeming fragility, she possessed a steely will. The Count suspected that Bartholomew was a means of sexual initiation for her, but he had also felt from the outset that there was more than sex involved. She was playing Bartholomew like a musical instrument, just as he was.

If, as he sensed, she was behind the kidnapping scheme, he might claim a share of the one hundred thousand dollar ransom. The money would be very useful at this time; many people who would have been generous to his movement were in difficulty due to the Depression and to the catastrophic bursting of the financial bubbles blown by the Jewish swindler, Alexandre Stavisky. For his Oriflamme movement, outside financial support was as essential for toppling the French Third Republic as it had been to Hitler's Nazis for conquering Germany.

"Would you like me to contact your father to let him know that you are safe?" the Count asked finally, having decided that her reply would be decisive in determining his course of action.

"Of course," she answered, without conviction. "But I know that he'll book us a passage on the next liner for America, so that I can get back to my studies and graduate with my class at Smith College in June. Unless I have it out with Buster first, I'll spend the rest of my life wondering if every man who makes love to me is just doing it for my father's money."

Her answer convinced him that she was involved in her own kidnapping and that the idea of the ransom was hers. Bartholomew was not ambitious or imaginative enough to elaborate, by himself, a kidnapping scheme to extract one hundred thousand dollars from a white man of wealth and power.

"You put me in a very delicate position, my dear," the Count said, gently. "You are a young woman of breeding, and I feel that it is my duty as a gentleman to report to your father that you are safe and sound. It will then be up to the French police to undertake the necessary—"

"But Buster said that you were like a father to him!" she interrupted him, angrily. "If the French police get their hands on him, I'm sure my father will arrange for him to spend the rest of his life in a French prison. Or even worse, he'll get him extradited to America to spend the rest of his life in an American prison. He wouldn't last very long. I don't know if you have any idea about the racial situation in America…"

"I know the situation," the Count replied, before continuing, "and Bartholomew *is* like a son to me. I would like no harm to come to him in France or America."

Daphne thought to herself that she was now ready to spring her trap on the Count. She knew that Buster was dead and that, as she had overheard, Urby and the woman, Redtop, had taken him away to "deep six" him. Daphne had killed the black man they called Baby Langston, so she was the sole witness here to Buster's death.

"I think that you should look for Buster," Daphne finally said. "Buster has told me a lot about your political movement. I agree with your ideas. I'm in no hurry to go back to America. Under President Roosevelt, socialism is gaining ground every day. At least, that's what my father says."

"I have a question, my dear, and please don't take offense."

"Shoot," Daphne said, sensing what the question would be.

"Assuming that the one hundred thousand dollar ransom came into your hands, and not Bartholomew's, what would you do with it?"

Daphne pretended to mull things over and then fixed the Count's blue eye with her violet-blue eye, beauty and innocence radiating from her face and her soft red mouth.

"I would give half of the money to a movement like yours and spend the rest getting myself set up in Germany. I have relatives there. Germany is the coming country, and I would like to meet Herr Hitler, the coming man," she said.

As if in reply, the Count picked up the gold-framed color photograph of himself and Reichskanzler Hitler from his desk and handed it solemnly to Daphne. She took the photograph, held it lovingly, and then smiled winsomely at him.

"You know him? If I went to Germany, would you give me a written introduction?"

The Count put on his best smile. "Of course. But there is the matter of the ransom. And Bartholomew. And your father."

"You and I could arrange for the ransom to be paid over. While you continue to search for Buster, of course."

The Count pretended to be taken aback by her proposal. "But, surely, my dear, your father would expect your immediate safe return as a counterpart to paying the ransom."

"I have read that there are such things as multiple kidnappings in France. Where a ransom is paid and the person doesn't turn up, being kidnapped by another party for a new ransom." Then she added, seemingly as an afterthought, "Buster asked for my father to pay a hundred thousand dollars in untraceable banknotes in small denominations and in gold, fifty-fifty."

"So you..."—he hesitated and corrected himself—"we would collect the ransom, you would turn half of it over to me, and you would use the other half to visit relatives in Germany and use my introductions to make contact with my dear Adolf, while I and my associates search for Bartholomew? Is that a fair résumé of your proposed course of action?" He arched his fingers under his chin while he awaited her answer.

"Yes. I think that you have the means to find Buster quickly. As to yours truly, I'd like to go to Germany and meet Herr Hitler as soon as possible," she said with conviction.

The Count was impressed by the sheer audacity of the young woman, by the boldness of her vision, and the diamond-like hardness at the core of her being.

"An interesting proposition, young lady. Intrepid, even. But, as a gentleman, though not, unfortunately, a father, I feel that you should know that a beautiful young woman like yourself—may I be bold enough to say, the very portrait of Aryan beauty—might easily fall prey to overexcited German men. Even men from Herr Hitler's disciplined ranks. You would be safer with a male…companion to watch over you. I would strongly advise it."

"I couldn't agree more. I know just the person for the job. I didn't mention to you that Mr. Urby Brown is a private investigator. My father hired him to track me and Buster down. If I go to Germany and my father got word that Buster and I were there, he would surely ask Mr. Brown to run us to ground, wouldn't he? I'm sure that Mr. Brown would do everything possible to protect me until he can bring me back." She paused before continuing, "Except I don't intend to come back right away, so he'll have to protect me until I decide to leave Germany." She said it in such a way as to convey to the Count that she would be irresistible to Urby Brown.

"Urby Brown?" the Count asked, seeming to search his memory for the name. "Oh yes, I *have* dealt with him in another affair."

"He bears an amazing resemblance to you, you know," Daphne said. "Who knows? He may become a pal of Herr Hitler's, like you have," Daphne said, picking up the gold-framed photograph.

The Count suddenly realized that the girl had come up with the perfect solution to many of his problems. His son's exposure to the workings of the Nazi party and to Herr Hitler would surely convince him that Adolf and his ideas and Germany were irresistible. Germany would be a training ground for him. Afterward, he would return to France and invest himself in the Oriflamme cause and, one day, become the rightful heir to his name and his movement.

The beautiful, clever, and ruthless girl sitting in front of him was obviously sexually drawn to his son, and she appeared certain that he reciprocated. Their eventual marriage would produce legitimate heirs to the d'Uribé-Lebrun bloodlines.

In the meantime, the Count would set Pierre and his colleagues the task of finding Bartholomew Thigpen so that he could be assigned the mission of assassinating Léon Blum.

As for the girl, his complicity in helping her to carry out her plans gave him power over her. He would know how to make her and "Urby Brown" do his bidding, when the time came. All of these thoughts pleased him, and he smiled warmly at the dangerous young beauty sitting opposite him.

"Young lady, I think that your ideas are sound. We shall proceed as you desire."

"Great. I think that when Mr. Brown returns to the stable and discovers that it's burned to the ground and that I'm gone, he'll need to find me, thinking that afterward he'll return me to my father at the Ritz Hotel. I'll have to disappear again when my father gets Buster's ransom note. That's when you step in, whisk me off to Germany, collect the ransom, and get my father to set Mr. Brown on my trail. You can wire me my share of the booty while I'm in Germany." Daphne smiled, eager to get on with her plans.

The Count marveled at the girl's sangfroid. She was acting as if she were heading off to the French Riviera or to the casinos of Monte Carlo for a holiday.

"All is agreed, my dear," the Count said finally.

She clapped her hands, leapt to her feet, and came around the desk to envelop him in her soft, beautiful body. He smelled the faint hint of incense of Hélène's favorite perfume, Poiret's Nuit de Chine. The girl had dabbed it on her earlobe and her graceful neck; the scent of it on her body made all of his senses come alive again. He desired the young Daphne as much as he had ever desired Josephine, but the pain in his groin brought back the memory of the loss of his manhood at Verdun.

"I will prepare the necessary introductions to my dear Adolf Hitler for you. You will leave for Berlin in a few days. Pierre and his assistants will give you all of the details of your arrangements for the coming days. Don't worry, my dear, everything will go well. You may stay here meanwhile."

Daphne felt that she had played the Count expertly and that she had taken a giant step toward achieving her goal of getting to grips with the Führer.

When Daphne left his office to retire to Countess Hélène's bedroom, the Count sprang to his feet and rushed to open a safe concealed behind the seventeenth-century portrait of Count Maximilien d'Uribé-Lebrun, Marshal of France under Louis XIII. The Count rummaged around in the safe for a minute, extracting the three gold-colored box files bearing his family crest and numbered from one to three in Roman numerals. The Count had written the name "Le Comte Charles-Emmanuel d'Uribé-Lebrun" on each file in his precise French copperplate script.

File I contained written reports about "Urby Lebrun," which he had jotted down after conversations with Pierre on his return from dsicreet visits to New Orleans over the years to check on Urby, the Irish priest, and the Jews Urby frequented, namely one Hannah Korngold and her family of lowly rag-and-bone merchants. There were also masses of information about Urby and his frequentations from the time of his arrival in France twenty years ago up to the present. This material had been provided by the Count's network, which included functionaries in the police and the Paris Prefecture, waiters at restaurants and barmen, including Fabrice Lourmel at the Hôtel Lutetia.

File II held information on Urby's military service in the French Foreign Legion and the American-volunteer Lafayette Flying Corps of the French Army, with evaluations of his performance and accounts of the deeds of heroism, for which Urby had received his military decorations. It held a copy of the Count's letter to Capitaine Lacroix, ordering Urby's transfer from the French Foreign Legion to the Lafayette Flying Corps. The Count deemed that service in the air army posed less of a risk to Urby than fighting in the trenches with the Legion. Lacroix had also intervened, on the Count's orders, to avoid Urby's expulsion from France after the incident with the American soldiers before the Victory Parade in 1919.

The file also contained newspaper clippings about Urby's career as a musician and the rise and fall of his Montmartre nightclub, "Urby's Masked Ball," which closed following the departure of Hannah Korngold to America. The Count smiled, remembering the temptations that he had arranged to place in Urby's way until he succumbed to cocaine, as he had in Harlem.

As the Count had anticipated, the Jewess had left his addicted son to return to America. Fortunately, the Count reflected, his son had overcome his addictions, once again showing the strength of character imbued in him by his d'Uribé-Lebrun lineage.

The Count smiled wryly to himself, remembering that he had also played a further role in the closing of Urby's nightclub and crippling the growth of American black jazz in Paris. Acting behind the scenes, he had successfully manipulated the French musicians' union into agitating for the enforcement of an old law imposing a 10 percent limit on the number of non-French musicians employed in a jazz band or orchestra in Paris.

His son was now reduced to running a private investigation agency, which the Count conspired to keep on the edge of bankruptcy. However, he had ordered his agents in the Prefecture of Police not to close it down because its precarious existence enabled him to keep tabs on Urby's doings. At the same time, the continual menace of a deportation order hanging over his son's head kept him in line, although there was no danger of his being deported. The Count intended to keep his son in France at all costs because he intended to make him his successor.

The Count mused upon his son's destiny: Urby had been living under the illusion that he was a free man from the moment he had "escaped" New Orleans after Pierre had put the torch to the Colored Waifs' Home and destroyed the Irish priest. But, that had been the Count's opening gambit in a match whose endgame was his son's arrival on French soil.

File III was entirely devoted to the correspondence with which the Irish priest from New Orleans had deluged him. It was in this file that the Count searched for the priest's first letter, which he had reread countless times over the years.

The letter, yellowed with age, was dated July 10, 1895. In it, Father Gohegan wrote that the Count's quadroon lover, Josephine Dubois, had confessed to him that the Count had fathered her son, making the boy an octoroon, of one-eighth African blood, by the race laws prevailing in the South. She had pleaded with Father Gohegan to let the boy be raised as white. When he refused, she had fallen at his feet and begged him to send the baby son to his father in France. The Count had told her, she said, that they weren't so harsh about race there.

A week later, the priest had written to announce that Josephine Dubois had hanged herself. The priest felt guilt over her death. Afterward, the priest had sent the Count letter after letter, imploring him to send money so that he could finance the boy's travel to France to join him, as his mother had wished.

Some twenty years had passed since his son had arrived in France after the Count's various machinations. He had kept track of his movements and, unknown to Urby, had intervened a number of times to shape the direction of his life. But the Count had resolved never to meet with him face to face, unless the vicissitudes of his own life left the Count no other option.

The February 6 debacle with the failure of the Fascist and monarchist coup d'état against the French government made him realize that the moment had come for him to reclaim his son and chain him to his destiny as heir to the lineage of the d'Uribé-Lebrun. He had been considering how to do that when his son had appeared in his office of his own accord, requesting permission for Bartholomew to play in tonight's charity concert.

Urby Lebrun, to whom the Count had assigned the name Charles-Emmanuel d'Uribé-Lebrun, in keeping with the traditions of his family, was the only child that he could ever have because his grave wounds from shrapnel to the groin at the Battle of Verdun had precluded him from ever having another heir to his own d'Uribé-Lebrun bloodlines.

Now sixty years old, the Count felt that his hours on earth were dwindling and that he must now prepare his son for his predestined role.

CHAPTER 11

Paris, Saturday morning, February 10, 1934

Disposing of Buster had taken its toll on me and Redtop, physically and emotionally. We had finally found a secluded stretch of shore just outside Argenteuil near a jetty with a rowboat moored to it. I had had to drag the sack with Buster and the anvil inside out of the car and manhandle it into the rowboat. I had boarded the boat and rowed out into the Seine as far from the shore as I felt I could swim back to if the rowboat swamped. The hardest part was casting the body overboard. It had taken me an hour to inch the body over the side. I had to struggle to keep the boat from capsizing and plunging me into the icy water with Buster.

When I was near my breaking point, I gave one last heave and Buster was gone. I had drifted out so far that it took me another hour to row back to the jetty and catch the rope that Redtop threw me to moor the rowboat.

Dawn was breaking by the time we finished. My clothes were soaking wet, so I took them off and wrapped myself in some blankets that Redtop kept in the trunk of the Hispano-Suiza. I shivered all the way back to Paris, although Redtop had turned the heat up to full blast.

When I woke up, we were back in Paris. I looked at my watch: it was nearly 7:00 a.m. The streets were emptier than usual for a Saturday morning, so I was able to slip out of Redtop's car, wearing the blankets and carrying my clothes. Redtop was so frightened that she had gone mute. I told her that I needed to catch a few hours of sleep and asked her to tell Stanley that I would meet him at his place at ten.

I dragged myself up the flight of stairs to my office. I fumbled the keys out of my waterlogged pants pocket and looked in on my office on the first floor. Things looked the same, but nothing would be the same again I said to myself, remembering the sight of Buster's head jerking from my bullet to his ear. I climbed another floor to my apartment, locked the door behind me, walked quickly to my bedroom, and threw myself into my unmade bed. I started to set the clock but I must have passed out…

I wonder if I'm dreaming that I can hear a loud knocking, like a club smashing against a door. Suddenly, I'm surrounded by poor white toughs in the white neighborhood beyond the Battlefield. They walk around me, as if I'm invisible, although it's broad daylight. Crowds flow past me, drawing me along in their wake. Shouts of "lynch the nigger!" grow louder. An old white man with a bright red beard smiles at me and grips me by the shoulders, staring into my eyes.

"How old are you son?" he asks.

"Near fifteen," I answer.

"You ever seen a lynchin'?"

"No, sir."

The man gives out a loud whoop of joy and pushes me to the front of the mob. "You a virgin, boy. Time to lose your cherry!"

PART II

An old black man, blood gushing from his nose, lies on the ground, books strewn around him. He has been thrown out of a police van by a group of policemen and men dressed in Klan robes. They throw more books out of the van, rip them up, and add them to a bonfire started by the mob. A cheer and rebel yells rise from the crowd. A stern-looking woman, standing beside her pretty blonde daughter, pokes me in the chest as I turn my head away. The daughter, who is a few years younger than me, rubs a hand over my ribs. She has long, white-blonde hair, which covers one of her eyes. The one that I can see is violet-blue. Her mother looks at the two of us and smiles.

"That darky a teacherman," she says. "The police heard him teaching 'bout Yankees freeing the darkies. They always gonna be slaves, whatever them Jew Communists say."

Around me, children chant "lynch the nigger!" in high-pitched voices, as though they were singing in a children's church choir. Her daughter joins in, but I remain silent. The woman eyes me suspiciously and says, "You deaf and dumb? Join in, boy!"

"No, ma'am, I can't say them words," I answer.

"You a nigger lover, son? You sure had me fooled. Thought you was one of us." She cups her hands around her mouth, ready to call the mob onto me.

"Lynch the nigger! Lynch the nigger!" I shout, singing along with the others. The woman beams, hugs me.

"Give him a kiss, Delphine," she says to her daughter.

The men in Klan robes hoist the old black man to the roof of the police van, and one of them makes a noose, which he slips over the black man's head. They tie the other end to an overhanging branch. A policeman shoots his service pistol at the sky, and the van accelerates away.

The black man dangles in the air. Applause and rebel yells boom out. I stare at the black man's jerking feet. I feel Delphine's hand on my arm and turn toward her. She flicks her wavy blonde hair away from her face and her other dark green, reptilian eye. She grabs my head and kisses me hard on the lips, her tongue darting inside my mouth. She tightens her arms around me and grinds her pelvis into me, moaning. As the crowd passes the police van, they give it a friendly knock. The knocking gets louder and louder, drowning out Delphine's moans...

The knocking got louder, and I heard a voice shouting downstairs "Mr. Brown, Mr. Uhby Brown. It's uhgent!" I looked at the clock. It was 9:00 a.m. I ran to the door and shouted, "I'm coming. Give me a minute to get dressed."

I quickly threw on a sweater and some slacks and socks and shoes. I bolted down the steps and found Barnet Robinson III pacing back and forth in front of my office door. He was red-faced with anger, disheveled, trembling, and shaking a sheet of paper around in his hand like a madman.

"You better take a look at this, Mr. Brown. It's a damned ransom note!" My look of surprise was real. A ransom note was not part of Stanley's plan. One glance told me that Buster had written the note. I knew because I taught him how to write. It was the punishment Father Gohegan gave me for beating up Buster at St. Vincent's those many years ago. For all my efforts, all I could get out of Buster was a messy scrawl. I stared at the words; they weren't Buster's. There was no way on earth that Buster could come up with this:

> Dear Mr. Robinson,
>
> I am holding your daughter hostage for a ransom of one hundred thousand US dollars. I have no intention of harming her if you are good enough to cooperate with my demands. Any attempt on your part to bring the police into this matter or to alert the press will result

in fatal damage to your daughter. I will communicate the time and the place where you are to leave the ransom money in a few hours, to enable you to make the necessary arrangements. Half the money should be in small denominations, not exceeding twenty US dollars, and the bills should be used and contain no markings, consecutive serial numbers, or any other means of identifying them. The other half should be in untraceable gold bullion. I have experts at my disposal who will check that the ransom is sound before I release your daughter. I hope that this affair reaches a felicitous conclusion.

Thank you in advance for your understanding. I remain your obedient servant, Bartholomew Lincoln Thigpen Junior, alias Buster Thigpen.

Robinson III observed me intently, awaiting my judgment.

"It's definitely his handwriting, but somebody else came up with the words."

"You're sure?"

"One hundred percent. I've seen his writing before. The man's nearly illiterate. Somebody's masterminding this."

I also knew that Buster would not be taking part in any kidnapping because I had cast him into the Seine a few hours ago. Buster, and whoever he was in cahoots with, must have set their scheme in motion just after I had seen the Count on Wednesday about Buster taking part in the rehearsal and the charity concert. Barnet Robinson III was standing there, twisting his hands together, giving himself an Indian burn.

"It's just like what happened to Chahlie Lindbug's baby. I got the money together for Chahlie Jr.'s ransom. The demand is the same, small dollah denominations, except we slipped in some gold certificates. Maybe a worldwide kidnapping organization's at work."

At the mention of the gold dollar certificates, I got angry, remembering what Stanley had said, but Robinson III was not watching my reaction. I said, "I'll go photostat this ransom note in the back of my office."

Barnet Robinson III hesitated, as if wondering whether he should let me deal with the matter or go to the police.

"Don't think about going to the police," I said. "Buster is a desperate man, and he'll carry out his threats," I lied. "Let me handle the kidnapping investigation, and I suggest that you think about how to come up with the money, in case it comes to that."

He had waved his hand dismissively when I said "money," as if that was the least of his worries. "Ah you sure that you can get my Daphne back safe and sound? Chahlie Jr.'s kidnappers said not to go to the police, and we paid the ransom and they killed him anyway."

"I can guarantee that you'll get her back safe and sound. Trust me. But you mustn't tell a soul about the kidnapping and the ransom note. Give me a day to investigate this. I'll report back to you at noon tomorrow. Do you know the Coupole in Montparnasse?"

"Isn't that the hangout of a lot of those…intellectuals?"

"Yes, but we'll be less conspicuous there than at the Select or the Dôme because they're always crowded on Sundays with people looking for actors and music hall celebrities. If…"

"If what, Mr. Brown?"

"Maybe you could wear more…wintry clothes to the Coupole."

He smiled for the first time.

"I'll reserve a table for one o'clock. In my name."

"I understand. Incognito. No gaudy Princeton stuff," he said. He threw me his intense look again.

"No offense meant, Mr. Robinson," I said.

He gave me a really warm smile, the first one since we'd met.

"You know, Mr. Brown, the more I get to know you, the more I think Mr. O'Toole was right to suggest you for this job. I think you'll bring my Daphne back to me safe and sound."

"Thanks," I said. Unfortunately, I was far from sharing his confidence. When Robinson III finally left the office I made two photostats of the ransom note, put the original and a copy in my safe, and took one with me to meet up with Stanley to plan our next move. Our faked abduction scheme was dead in the water.

Stanley had never learned to read or write words or music. He had me read the ransom note out loud and then, resplendent in his chartreuse silk dressing gown, he leaned back in his armchair, scratching his chin. He sat like that in silence for a long time, and then he signaled for me to get some rye from his liquor cabinet and to bring two of his Bohemian crystal glasses.

It was ten in the morning, but Stanley was well into his day in terms of eating and drinking. Stanley lit up a Cuban panatela cigar and eased himself back into his futuristic armchair.

"You say this be Buster handwritin', but Buster be floatin' with the fishes, no?" I nodded and he went on. "I done believe all along that Buster want to make some money off'n his rich goldilocks and her daddy to feed his nose and whatnot. His usual style be to pimp his women for dough, but goldilocks he cain't pimp 'cause she too high-toned. So, Buster gone to study how to pocket her daddy money. Be what I be thinkin' all along."

He flicked the ash from his cigar into a gaudy pink crystal ashtray. He went on, as if talking to himself.

"That be why I wants to pull off our snatch first and get her daddy to pay you your money before Buster pull off somethin' like this." Stanley picked up the ransom note and said angrily, "But this here note mean Buster be playin' *us*. He weren't never studyin' to turn up for no charity concert tonight." Stanley started laughing with his whole body, slapping a thigh and dancing around. He managed to wheeze out, "Old Buster had him some style, after all." Stanley cricket-laughed and then went on.

"But there ain't no way Buster be usin' words like thems in that note, what come from another planet to Buster. So who put them words in Buster's mouth, Urby? Onliest colored men I know can make such words be Langston Hughes, Baby Langston, and you. And, it ain't be you nor Langston Hughes." Stanley lit up a panatela.

"You think Baby Langston was in on it with Buster?" I asked.

Stanley took a long swig of rye and studied the light playing through its amber color. "Might be your Count in there somewhere, too, holdin' the whip hand over Buster. But I be thinkin' that Baby be the last one left with goldilocks. Urby, I want you to go out to the stables and have a look-see. Baby Langston still be there with her, that let him out. They be gone, that open up a whole new can of worms. Like Hambone Gaylord and them Corsicans be in on it. Or your daddy, the Count."

I'd been keeping my connection to the Count secret from Stanley, but he always ended up finding things out. He passed me the keys to one of his cars and told me to go to Pine Thicket Drive and then foot it from there, making sure no one was tailing me. When I left Stanley's, we agreed to meet back at his apartment as soon as I scouted out the stables.

Stanley had lent me his blue Citroën C4G Berline, which was the least conspicuous of his fleet of cars. The traffic was light but it was cold outside, and snow flurries were brushing against the windshield. I turned on the wipers and the heat. I kept myself awake by humming Armstrong's trumpet riffs. Then Stanley's soprano sax riffs. The music was coming back.

I reached Bosquet des Pins Street and parked the car behind a coal truck. Despite my fatigue, I'd been keeping my eyes peeled to make sure that I hadn't been followed. As I walked toward the cutoff into the Bois de Boulogne, the first sign of trouble was the blaring of the sirens of the fire engines speeding past. They were stopped up ahead, surrounded by rubberneckers. I kept hearing the words "Etables incendiés," stables burned down. People in this wealthy part of the sixteenth district of

Paris were blaming the fires on the Communists, the Socialists, and the anarchists, although it was their own kind, the Fascists and the monarchists, who had been putting parts of Paris to the torch and trying to bring down the government.

"They're even attacking horses now!" someone shouted indignantly, the Longchamps racetrack being nearby. I could sense the panic in the well-heeled people questioning the firemen. I kept thinking that these rich folks were the natural allies of the Count and his Fascist and royalist supporters. They had a deep blood memory of the French Revolution and the Paris Commune Workers' Revolt of 1871. The events of last Tuesday had them feeling the blade of the guillotine, still in use for public executions, whispering on their necks. They could picture snipers perched in every leafy horse chestnut tree, aiming their guns at them. They were prepared to do anything to save their lives and their wealth, even if it meant going to war with their fellow Frenchmen. I reckoned that they would readily jump into bed with Hitler and Mussolini and the Count himself to halt the spread of the Red Menace in France.

I saw smoke and flames pouring from Stanley's stables which were clearly visible now that the dense thicket concealing them had burned to a crisp. My heart started pounding as I thought of Daphne, and I sprinted toward the smoldering remains of the hideout. Scores of firemen were directing their hoses at it, and more firemen and policemen were arriving in waves, their sirens blaring. I spotted a young fireman with an elaborate mustache who was looking angrily at the rich gawkers commenting on the scene. Figuring that I was a working-class man like himself, he answered truthfully my fearful question about possible victims. "There are no victims," he said. "Just razed, dilapidated stable blocks. There were some pieces of old furniture and some framed paintings that went up in flames. Perhaps they had some value. But, frankly, comrade, my lieutenant thinks that it's the work of professional arsonists working for property developers who will now try to buy up the land and"—nodding with disgust toward the elegant buildings nearby constructed by Baron Haussmann in the late nineteenth century—"construct more buildings for those wealthy parasites."

"Thank you for your frankness, comrade," I said, relieved. I didn't know where Daphne was, but at least she hadn't burned to death in Stanley's stables. I was going to find her, but first, I needed to check out the scene for clues to what had happened. The young fireman smiled when I whispered to him, "The party was publishing tracts in those stables, to help the cause. We suspected that the Fascists were wise to us, so, fortunately, we removed our printing presses to a safe place. Between us, I think the Fascist militias have set the blaze. Is there any way that I can get a little closer to inspect the site?"

The fireman nodded for me to follow him. He picked a spare respirator off his fire engine and passed it to me.

"The police," he said to any firemen who challenged me.

Whoever had set the blaze had done a thorough job of it. I paced the length of the smoking stable block and saw places where the fire seemed to have burned more intensely than in others. There was no trace of Daphne or of Baby Langston. No burned corpses. Maybe Baby *had* been in cahoots, as Stanley thought. But as I walked in the burnt-out thicket near the stables, I saw a half-burned safety match and some charred bits of newspaper.

The fireman was right; this was the work of professionals. My memory of the fire at St. Vincent's all those years back made me think of Pierre, which, in turn, made me see the Count's hand behind Buster's ransom demand. I wondered whether he had been involved in this business all along. Maybe he had masterminded Buster's kidnap attempt and dictated the ransom note, possibly for funds to get his Oriflamme movement back on its feet again after its lost battle of last Tuesday.

That would mean that the Count had found out Stanley's hideout for holding Daphne and Buster. Maybe my instincts about Redtop and me being followed had been right, and we had led him to them. Or had Baby Langston tipped them off? And, if he had, were Hambone and the

Corsicans involved? They weren't the Count's natural allies, so it had to be a question of hard, cold cash.

And where did Daphne fit into the puzzle? She was obviously the prize, since Robinson III would only fork out a hundred thousand dollars if she were returned to him without a scratch.

I thanked the "comrade fireman" when I returned the respirator to him. He looked around and, surreptitiously, gave me the clenched-fist anti-Fascist salute. I gave it back to him and then headed to Stanley's Citroën C4G and climbed in, just as more police cars and fire engines arrived.

I had to report to Stanley about what was going on, but I needed more rest first. I drove to my apartment building, managing to stay awake just long enough to park the car, slouch up the stairs to my apartment again, and throw myself into bed. There were no nightmares this time, just flat-out sleep.

CHAPTER 12

Paris, Saturday afternoon, February 10, 1934

I arrived at Stanley's four hours later at around half past three in the afternoon. The events of last night and the early morning seemed a long way away. Stanley was still sitting in his futuristic tiger skin armchair, as if he hadn't moved since I left him.

The only difference was that the ashtray was overflowing with panatela cigar butts, and Stanley was well on his way into finishing another quart of rye. It didn't seem to have any effect on him, though.

He motioned for me to pour myself some rye and sit down. He had gone quiet the way he did whenever something important was on his mind.

"They gone," he said. It was a statement of fact, as if he had been at the scene himself.

"Yeah," I said. "No sign of the girl or of Baby Langston. Your stables have burned to the ground."

Stanley lit up another panatela and smiled.

"I done sold them six month ago and collect cash money. Sure hope the new owner got him some fire insurance." He passed me the bottle of rye; I poured myself a good shot of it.

He said, "I figure they be gone. I reckon Hambone and them Corsicans done snatch the girl, and they goin' for the hundred grand ransom." He was so calm that I thought he would fall asleep.

"Stanley, I promised the girl's daddy that I would have news for him tomorrow about the kidnapping and the ransom," I said, exasperated.

Stanley wheezed some laughter. "You goin' to have news, Urby. We just won't know what news until after the gig tonight."

"We're going to go through with the charity concert at La Belle Princesse?"

"Sure. We goin' to play out our hand to the last card. I already got Lonny Jones to be drummer, 'stead of Buster. Lonny near kissed my hands when I told him he was gone to be playin' besides me...and you."

"I haven't played in a long time," I said.

Stanley sighed and looked me straight in the eye. "Urby, you was the best Creole clarinet when you was a boy in knee pants, and you still the best. I know you ain't played since Hannah done left, but, boy, you got to get back on that bone. You got mo' music inside yo' pinky than most musicianers has in they whole body."

I thought about Stanley's words, and I knew that he was right. Hannah's leaving me had dried up my music, but since I'd first set eyes on Daphne, I felt the hunger for the music coming back. The time had come for me to do more than just hum Louis Armstrong's and Stanley's riffs, which I was doing more and more when I was alone. Stanley and I looked at each other, and I nodded. He flashed a smile at me, knowing what I'd say.

"I'll be ready, Stanley," I said.

"Urby. You gone be fine. I wants you to bring yo' clarinet and yo' Colt, 'cause I reckon we goin' to have a showdown with the Hambone and his Corsicans. They be tryin' to steal that ransom money for they own self. They crazy axin' for a hundred grand to give the man his own daughter back. That just ain't righteous."

The odds didn't look good to me. I'd have my Colt, and Stanley would have his own Colt within easy reach. Hambone Gaylord had never had any of his patrons at La Belle Princesse frisked, but he might try to pull something different if he and Baby Langston and the Corsicans were behind the double cross. And he knew that the Count and his Oriflamme storm troopers, as well as the workers, would be crowded together in the small space of his nightclub.

There was likely to be bedlam and brawling and that meant cops. The Count was coming with five of his goons, including his main man Pierre. They would see that Buster was missing, and they would suspect that Stanley and I had something to do with that because of the way Buster had played us. The Oriflamme would all be packing some kind of weapon, and Pierre, especially, was fixing to wring my neck unless I told the Count why Buster hadn't turned up for the concert.

Stanley was looking at me serenely. He wagged a finger.

"Don't you be studyin' the Count and his bully boys. I got peoples comin' who be packin' guns, shivs, brass knuckles, saps, you name it. I got peoples comin' so ugly, they make the baddest Harlem gangsters look like French ladies at a tea party with old Marie-Antoinette, holdin' they teacups with they pinky stickin' out. Hambone and his Frenchy eye-talians try nothin' with us, and his club gone to be blown to glory."

"We've got to be careful with the Corsicans and the Count, Stanley. They're Frenchmen on their own ground."

"I got me some Corsicans, too, Urby, and they don't like Bone's Corsicans. They settle it French to French. We got some French workers comin' for the charity concert, too, and they bound to keep the Count and his bully boys in line. What we got to do is get our hands on the Hambone and Baby Langston and squeeze out some answers about where goldilocks be at. We gone know by the end of this evening, and we gone take back that girl. I reckon we still good to ask her daddy for ten grand for yo' troubles when you return her, not no hundred grand for no ransom." He blew a perfect smoke ring, stabbed his panatela through it, and went on.

"Ten grand in good old-fashion greenbacks. Dropped off where the police afraid to go, like the Versailles forest. Then you turns the girl over to him honest-like, 'cause you ain't a cheat like him. And you learns him not to fool colored folk with goldback money get us jailed up by J. Edgar and his G-men."

"The ransom note asks for one hundred grand. If the press and police get wind of it, like they did with the fifty grand ransom for baby Lindbergh that Jean Fletcher told me about, we'd be in for a heap of trouble, Stanley. If the cops pinned a kidnapping on us, even for ten grand, they'd ship our behinds back to Jim Crow land to stand trial. I say we find her, get the fee I signed on for with Robinson at the outset, and drop the rest."

"Believe me, Urby, we bring home the bacon for ten grand, Robinson be so happy he be dancin' the cancan with us at the Moulin Rouge and servin' us champagne in gold goblets. 'Cause we not talkin' no hundred grand, Urby; we talkin' ten. Any man know in his soul that be righteous. But we gone hold off for now, you so worried."

I was relieved, but a lot could still go wrong.

The more I thought about Daphne, the more I felt the music burning in me like lava, and my fingers had taken on a life of their own, as if already playing the keys on my clarinet. I was nervous about how things would go, but I was excited about playing the clarinet again. I had six long hours to wait until the charity concert began.

I went over the program with Stanley. It would be a repeat of the last gig we had ever played together at Johnny Sutton's Blue Heaven Club when Buster Thigpen was, for one night, the best drummer on the planet.

The only worry I had about finding my music again was that it was all because of Daphne. I didn't know anything about her except that she was the most beautiful woman that I'd ever set eyes on, but I'd loved a lot of beautiful women in my heyday. None of them turned out to be good for me, except Hannah Korngold, and a bad Daphne could send me back into the pit, without a Hannah around to rescue me.

CHAPTER 13

Paris, Saturday evening, February 10, 1934

Mardi Gras would fall on Tuesday, February 13, in three days, so Hambone Gaylord had a New Orleans Mardi Gras Masked Ball as the theme of the charity concert, just as it had been the theme of my and Hannah's nightclub. He told the audience crammed into La Belle Princesse that he had chosen the masked ball theme to honor the three "great" New Orleans Creole musicians in the quartet (Lonny Jones, the drummer, was from Mobile, Alabama): Stanley Bontemps on the soprano saxophone, myself on the clarinet, and Buddy Baudoin on the cornet.

As customers filed in, they were handed New Orleans Mardi Gras carnival masks. Hambone had piled folding chairs into every nook and cranny of his club. Celebrities milled around the bar. Workers in their blue overalls and cloth caps puzzled over their carnival masks, and the women with them gawked at the celebrities. One overly made-up prostitute spotted the movie star Charles Boyer at the bar and unabashedly opened the top of her dress and asked him to autograph her slip, which he did with a laugh and a big kiss on her cheek. The workers' section cheered. Boyer motioned for them to don their masks and mimed how to put them on. The workers copied him, and Boyer ordered bottles of wine and doled them out. He made an elaborate bow and toasted them as applause rang out from the workers.

A half dozen "celebrity tables" had been placed next to the stage, and the chanteuse Mistinguett was laughing uproariously as she and the actress Yvonne Printemps pulled at the masks of Maurice Chevalier and the boxer Georges Carpentier. The writers James Joyce and Samuel Beckett, not wearing masks, were speaking earnestly with empty glasses littering their table.

The hubbub in La Belle Princesse rose even higher when Jean Cocteau came in with Pablo Picasso. Someone had told them about the Mardi Gras theme, and Picasso had made masks for the occasion which some of Stanley's friends were staring at with very quizzical expressions on their faces.

Stanley and Redtop had called out the reserves for the charity concert. I recognized some of the leading figures in the Harlem-in-Montmartre scene, not the owners of bars and restaurants and nightclubs, but their most highly trusted enforcers. They sat together in La Belle Princesse where they could watch everything that was going on. It was obvious that they were packing serious hardware; as they laughed and drank, they clanked against each other, the sound of the guns, metal pipes, and shivs that they were carrying making a metallic din as they grew more and more boisterous.

In another section of the nightclub stood Hambone's backup, a group of Corsicans whose looks were improved when they put on their masks. They were dressed impeccably, nearly identically, wearing black Borsalino hats and gray and white pinstripe suits with matching vests and black and white two-toned shoes. They were all packing weapons, which were slim-lined handguns and stiletto knives that did not rumple their suits.

I felt nervous, not so much at what might happen but at playing the clarinet again after two years. But I knew that it would go well. The music was boiling inside me again, and I felt the same excitement I had twenty years ago playing a gig in Harlem. In my mind, I was dedicating my music to Hannah Korngold, but I was kidding myself; deep down I knew that if I made my clarinet sing tonight, Daphne was my muse.

Suddenly, La Belle Princesse fell silent as the Count, followed by Pierre and four other Oriflamme, came in. The workers nudged each other, and a few of them had to be restrained from attacking them. The Count and his men refused to put on the proffered masks and hunkered down at one of the celebrity tables that Hambone had reserved for them on Stanley's orders. After a brief pause, the noise level rose, and then there was silence again as a professorial-looking man wearing a thick mustache and glasses entered the club. He was immediately greeted by applause and cheers from the workers who leapt to their feet and flashed him clenched-fist salutes. The man saluted back to louder cheers from the workers. They started chanting, "Léon Blum, Léon Blum, Léon Blum." He smiled and waved and put on a carnival mask and sat down among the workers. I looked over at the Count and his followers. As if by reflex action, their hands went to the parts of their bodies where they were carrying their weapons. The workers started singing the Internationale with Léon Blum joining in.

I felt a nudge in my ribs and turned around. It was Jean Fletcher.

"Hi, kiddo," she said. "Good luck tonight. I hope you've got your metal Homburg somewhere. With Léon Blum and your daddy in the same room, things could get ugly."

At that moment, Lonny Jones played a drumroll, and Hambone Gaylord bounded onto the small stage. The feeble lights around it went up, and Hambone cupped his hands like a megaphone to shout, "Welcome to La Belle Princesse in Nouvelle Orleans, Paris."

There was loud applause from everyone. Hambone continued,

"Hambone thanks y'all. We all come in peace tonight, in aid of the victims of the…troubles of last Tuesday night. The proceeds from our concert will all go to the victims and they family."

"That's right, brother," Hambone's backup men intoned. "That sure be a fine thing for ole Hambone to do, ummmmummmphh."

Hambone continued, “Ain’t none of these musicians gone take home nary a penny. No sirree. All the money we gone collect, gone go to the victims. Now, we gone pass the collection plate around at the end of the service…the concert…and I ax y’all to be gen’rous. I don’t wanna hear no metal in them plates. I wants to hear silent money. French francs and dollars be welcome but, please, give us paper money and not them itty-bitty pieces of metal.

“Now we got some fine New Orleans lagniappe lined up for y’all tonight,” Hambone continued. “We got a battle of the bones, ’twixt the old-timers and the new-timers. First up: New Orleans and Paris own Stanley Bontemps, king of the Creole soprano sax.” There were cheers and the stomping of feet as Stanley stood up in his white silk tuxedo and white shoes to acknowledge the applause.

“Next up, we got Buddy…Baudoin, the baronet of the cornet.” Buddy played a few flashy riffs stolen straight off Louis Armstrong.

Mistinguett leapt to her feet, waving her fur boa around, and everyone cheered, more for Mistinguett than for the great Buddy Baudoin.

“Then we got my man making his return engagement tonight after two years where he ain’t done touch his clarinet not once. I’m talkin’ ’bout the man they done called the Mozart of the Creole clarinet, Mr. Urrrrrrbyyyy Brownnnnnnn.” There was wild clapping, and Jean Fletcher and Redtop leapt to their feet. To my astonishment, the Count stood up to applaud.

Hambone rushed through the rest of his spiel. “Last but not least, we got Lonny Jones on the drums. This here boy can really make them drumskins sing.” Hambone’s backup muscle boys all leapt to their feet, whistling and making a lot of noise. Hambone shushed the audience with a finger to his lips. He hummed some kind of lullaby. “Folks, forget you in Paris and dream you is far away in New Orleans for Mardi Gras, so ‘laissez les bons temps rouler.’”

Stanley donned his mask, gave the downbeat, and the quartet broke out into a frantic “Tiger Rag.” The audience burst into applause. Suddenly, a small masked man jumped onto the stage and twirled his horn. From his first riffs, I recognized the inimitable clarinet style of Sidney Bechet, even before he took off his mask. The audience stood up and applauded, some crying out, "Bechet, Bechet." Sidney and I started a clarinet duel, "cutting and bucking" against each other like cornet players. I improvised fantastic runs and riffs, and Bechet responded. The other musicians stopped playing to listen, open-mouthed. It was like the old days; I was deep down into the music, listening to it roaring from my brain to my lips and fingers, but I could hear the comments around the stage crystal clear. One man, really surprised, said, "Sidney playin' real good." He hesitated. "But Urby carvin' him up!"

I heard Jean crying, "Play it, Urby. Play it!"

Sidney Bechet looked at me with a sweet smile on his face as he ducked under my riff and let me carry the music for a while; he was figuring out my next notes, waiting to ambush me with better ones as soon as I let him in.

The bucking went on through chorus after chorus. I lost count how many. Finally, Sidney started playing more softly and slowly, but I kept blowing harder, shaping my phrases like I was painting with light and fire. Then I heard just the sound of my own horn and its images and touches reeling through my senses; I saw again the look of concern on Hannah's face, felt Daphne's soft hand on my forehead. I smelled the perfume on her hand. My music curved and swept and moved alone through the air.

Sidney Bechet was sitting down now, watching me with a sweet smile on his face and his head bouncing in time to the rhythm. Sidney stood up, shrugged his shoulders, and mimed throwing his clarinet to the floor in surrender. The audience had gone quiet, listening to every note. Stanley, Buddy Baudoin, and I played the final bars with the skillful drumming of Lonny Jones so fine that he sounded like Baby Dodds—or Buster when he was clean and happy. We finished "Tiger Rag" in a cacophony of sound, all golden and rich. Stanley hugged me, and there was wild applause at the finale. Sidney got up again and waved his hands around, urging the audience on to clap and cheer me even harder. I saw the Count smiling, pretending to be proud of me. Jean vaulted onto the stage and planted a sloppy kiss on my forehead.

"You were great," she said. "You were really great."

Hambone was making his way to the stage to announce the next number when a scuffle broke out between Hambone's Corsicans and the workers surrounding Léon Blum. Word had got to the Corsicans that a major prize was in their midst, and the Alfieri clan had decided to try to kidnap Blum then and there.

The workers pulled out their saps and brass knuckles and bicycle chains and were facing down the Corsicans, the incredibly calm Léon Blum standing, arms folded, among the workers. Then the Oriflamme rushed the workers to join forces with the Corsicans, and Buddy Baudoin blew the call to charge on his cornet. Redtop raced out the door with James Joyce and Samuel Beckett hot on her heels.

Suddenly, Stanley's backups, dressed up in Mardi Gras carnival Indian masks, rushed across the nightclub to join the fray, attacking the Corsicans and the Oriflamme with sawed-off baseball bats, straight-edge razors, and their huge ham-sized fists. Lonny Jones had tackled Hambone on the stage, and he was holding a straight-edge razor against his jugular vein.

The Count was watching the fight dispassionately, seeing his Oriflamme goons being driven back by the enraged band of Stanley's friends. Then he just smiled, tugged at Pierre's sleeve, and walked majestically through the heaving, thrusting bodies, clearing a path with his ivory cane. He turned as he passed me, smiled, and patted me on the shoulder. Then he kept on walking as Pierre joined him with an angry snarl directed at me. They walked straight out the main door and onto rue Ordener.

Stanley took out his Colt, raised it to fire a shot into the ceiling, and then lowered it. He did not want the police to come to break up the fray.

Stanley nodded at Buddy who blew another series of loud blasts on his cornet that imitated the sound of a fire engine. That stopped the fighting, and everyone looked toward the stage, where Stanley stood, waving his Colt.

"Clear on out," he shouted. "Y'all clear on out. We don't want no cops in here." I could see Léon Blum conferring with the workers, who then escorted him through the door, forming a bodyguard around him. The Corsicans followed, brushing the dirt off their suits. One of the three remaining Oriflamme had been knocked out by a blow from a baseball bat and had to be dragged out by his colleagues.

Stanley went over to his group, slapped backs, and handed out wads of franc notes to the enforcers of his nightclub owner friends, and they went off into the night to party on elsewhere.

The last patrons left in the club were the celebrities who had watched everything with enjoyment. They were toasting Stanley with champagne as Hambone squirmed on all fours on the stage in the vise-like grip of Lonny Jones.

Stanley went over to the celebrities, all smiles, whipped out some photographs of himself from an inside pocket of his all-white tuxedo, and autographed the photos for them. He promised Picasso that he would pose for him, and then they all left the club, the great Mistinguett giving me the "bise" on both cheeks, Jean Cocteau and Picasso shaking my hand. Picasso's dark eyes burned into mine, and I wondered if I would end up in one of his strange-looking paintings.

For the celebrities, it had been an exciting spectacle, a settling of accounts in the Harlem-in-Montmartre underworld with a dash of jazz and high politics thrown in. I was sure that they would return to the nightclub with more of their coterie after word spread about the Mardi Gras brawl in La Belle Princesse.

We had done big publicity for La Belle Princesse, but Hambone was in a tight spot right now, pinned to the stage with Lonny's blade against his neck. Jean was the last to leave. I had searched the club for stragglers and flushed her out of her hiding place near the toilets. She always, she had said, wanted to be in at the kill. But this time, there might be a real one.

"Time to go, Jean," I said. She smiled at me and gave me a peck on the cheek. She was as sober as I'd ever seen her.

"You were nothing short of genius out there tonight, Urby," she said. "Promise me you'll tell me no later than Monday what befalls our dear Hambone. Looks like he's in a tight spot."

My promise given, I walked Jean to the door, and she stepped out into the night as Stanley's chauffeur glided up. She got in, waved goodbye, and headed off to the Left Bank.

Buddy Baudoin picked up his illegal wages and cut out, leaving four people in the club: Stanley, me, Lonny Jones, and Hambone Gaylord.

After everyone had gone, I locked the main door. I went behind the bar, took down a bottle of calvados, and filled a tumbler with it. Stanley nodded to me, and I got down the rye and poured him a glass of it straight, no chaser.

Lonny was still holding the gigantic Hambone down with one arm as if he had wrestled a steer to the ground. At a nod from Stanley, Lonny pressed his straight-edge razor across Hambone's throat and drew blood. Hambone's eyes moved wildly in his head as he visualized blood spouting out of his neck.

Stanley motioned for Lonny to put his razor away, and Lonny pulled up a chair for Hambone. Lonny stood behind him with his razor at the ready in case Hambone tried to do a runner.

"How much money you collect tonight, Bone?" Stanley asked.

"Nothin'," Hambone whined. "We was goin' to start passin' the collection plates around after yo' next number. Then the thunder come a rollin' down."

"Unh-unh," Stanley said. "I ain't be talkin' about no collection plates. I be talkin' 'bout yo' man Baby Langston. Seem to me and Urby that Baby and Buster be workin' that ransom on goldilocks' old man with the help of yo' eye-talian brothers. So I ax you again, how much you be collectin' from it?"

"Say what, Stanley? Say what?" Hambone sprang to his feet as if Stanley's words had stung him to the core. "I ain't got nothin' to do with it, Stanley. I don't go around messin' with no kidnappin' no rich white women. Sheeit, the Frenchie police catch me doin' monkeyshines like that, they ship me back to the States and bust up my bidness. And, Stanley, the Alfieris ain't no eye-talians, they be Corsican Frenchies like that man Napoleon."

Stanley smiled at that and drank some rye.

"I know that, Bone. Them Corsicans can give you cover from the French police. They do all the dirty work and collect the ransom and can't nobody pin it on you, Baby, and Buster."

I had told Stanley what had happened to Buster, so he had decided to play his hand with a bluff, not telling Hambone about Buster's ransom note or his death.

"I be tellin' you God's truth now, Stanley," Hambone said. "You right about them Corsicans wantin' us to get a bigger piece of the pie, and we was goin' to blackmail some cash out of you when you got Urby money from blondie daddy. But Baby ain't got nothin' to do with it. Fact is, I be worryin' about my nephew all day. It ain't like him not to let me know if he ain't comin' in. No way Baby be kidnappin' nobody. The man a poet, Stanley. You ever seen him wearin' shoes ain't scuffed up and with holes in the soles? Anything happen to him, my sister Magnolia Swilley gone kill me. Baby her onliest child."

Stanley thought long and hard about what Hambone had said, and then he spoke. "Hambone, I'm inclinin' to believe Baby ain't in on it, but that still don't let you and the Corsicans off. You better call in them Alfieris and get some answers to me by tomorrow night. You don't tell me the fullest truth"—Stanley looked around—"and yo' nightclub goin' to have him an accident. Like a four-alarm fire. And that be the last club you ever run, Hambone. No musicianer gone never play for you again. You understand what I'm sayin'?"

Hambone nodded, fear written all over his face.

Stanley gestured to Lonny who stood up, went over to the cash register, rang up a charge, and peered at the money in its drawer. Lonny growled at Hambone, "Stanley and Urby and me deserves to collect for that charity after we done tore up the 'Tiger Rag.' Looks to me like you got some serious money in this cash register, somethin' like two thousand francs."

"We goin' to take one thousand nine hundred fifty and let you slide for the rest," Stanley said. Hambone started to protest but shut up when he looked at Stanley's hard expression.

He said, "Sound fair to me, Stanley. Wasn't yo' fault that ruckus started."

Stanley had put away the money and held out his palm. "How much *you* givin' to our charity, personal-like, Bone?"

Hambone immediately put his hand into his hip pocket, pulled out a big wad of franc notes, and gave them to Stanley. "That be all I can get my hands on tonight, man."

Stanley riffled the wad. "There must be 'bout the same as in your cash registry." Everyone in Montmartre knew that Hambone always traveled with a lot of cash on his person. Stanley stood up.

"This here be enough. We thanks you, Bone. Now we gots to be moseyin' along. 'Member, you got to fill me in on the whole story from A to Z by tomorrow night. I be expectin' you 'round seven o'clock at my place."

"I'll find out what I can. If you see Baby, tell him to get his behind over here, tout de suite."

"Sure thing," Stanley said.

We left the club and Stanley passed some cash to Lonny and said, "Catch you later." Lonny disappeared quickly. It was still early, and with so much money on him, he would be doing some hard partying tonight and the next few days.

Stanley and I left La Belle Princesse and walked through the bustle of a Saturday night in Montmartre. There were a lot of people at the Place Pigalle, and the cafés and bars were thronging with customers. Their week's work was done, and tomorrow, Sunday, was their day off. Tonight was the first time that people could let off steam since Tuesday night's riots.

There were organizers at street corners from the Conféderation Générale du Travail Unitaire (CGTU), the powerful Communist-linked trade union. Fist-waving men and women formed in groups around the Place Pigalle, raging for action to prevent another attempt at a Fascist coup d'état against the government. Red banners with the words "General Strike called for Next Monday!" filled the Place Pigalle.

Stanley followed the frenzied action, bemused. It was so different from a normal Saturday night when the prostitutes plied their trade, the pickpockets scythed through the crowds of tourists, and the French and American rich folk combed the area, slumming.

"These people sure gettin' serious," Stanley said. "They riotin' in cold weather, and they be talk of another civil war here in France, like the one they have sixty or so year ago. Don't these people never get tired of revolutions and riots and such? Shoot, Urby, we only have one revolution and one civil war in America, but these Frenchies seems to need somethin' like that every fifty year or so."

Some of the workers recognized Stanley and came up to him. One of them called out for "our black American brother to join us in our fight against Fascism and racism." Stanley, who could speak Creole French and understood everything they were saying, waved at them good-naturedly.

"We are brothers in arms," he said to them in French and gave them the clenched-fist salute, winking at me behind his other hand.

We walked through the cheers to Stanley's limousine, which had returned from dropping Jean off somewhere. His chauffeur, who had been cheering and whooping it up with the CGT people, snapped to attention when Stanley and I appeared and opened the door for us. The clapping and cheering rose to crescendo as we headed to Stanley's.

CHAPTER 14

Paris, Sunday, February 11, 1934

I arrived at the Coupole restaurant-café a half hour early to scout out the place. I needed a drink before I met up with Robinson III for lunch because I still hadn't figured out how to play my hand. And I had to force myself to act civil to him.

The rage of the workers that Stanley and I had witnessed at Place Pigalle on the Right Bank last night was small beer compared to what was gearing up on the Left Bank. Bands of angry workers roamed Boulevard Montparnasse outside the Coupole, bundled up in heavy coats with their flat-cloth caps yanked down to their ears. They were men spoiling for a fight with the Fascist-monarchist leagues bent on derailing the General Strike planned for tomorrow. Police patrolled the streets in pairs, making their presence known to the workers but avoiding clashes that might ignite an explosion.

The old-time sounds of the Coupole's Sunday tea and waltz orchestra filled the vast space, which usually echoed with the hot rhythms of its biguine band made up of French West Indians not subject to the 10 percent limit on foreign musicians that had practically killed off black American jazz in Paris.

The Coupole was a small town where you could run into people and end up drinking and eating with them for hours. My favorite waiter,

Honoré, pointed out my reserved table, which was a "good" one in the center of the action. I waved some franc notes at him, told him I needed to be in a more discreet location, and he took me to a grubby corner table in the back near the door to the kitchens, where no one was likely to notice Robinson III and me.

"Parfait," I said, and he vacuumed up the francs like a Hoover. I told him that I would be back at the table at 1:00 p.m. sharp when my guest arrived. I asked Honoré to serve our table himself because I was being invited to lunch by a very rich American, and I wanted him to profit from the man's *largesse*. He thanked me profusely and said that he would fix everything with the reservations waiter.

We arranged that I would head to the bar for a few quick ones, stay on the lookout for my guest, and follow him in through La Coupole's main entrance. I don't know what he thought I was up to, but Parisian waiters were used to monkey business from customers, and he took it in stride.

I watched Robinson III enter at five minutes to one. At a high sign from the reservations waiter, Honoré came dashing across the room to escort him to our table. Robinson III was wearing a light gray double-breasted suit, a Burberry trench coat, and an expensive-looking hat. I watched the hatcheck girl take his things, and he strode like a Viking colossus among the tables, guided by Honoré. When he reached our table, I saw him exchange words with Honoré. I figured he was asking him if there was some mistake. He made a move to pass Honoré some money, but the waiter waved him off and sat him down.

Honoré flicked a quick look my way, and I gave him a thumbs-up sign. He went away and brought Robinson III a glass of champagne "on the house" and his bowing and scraping, and the champagne put the semblance of a smile on Robinson III's face.

I finished my drink, sauntered outside, and then re-entered to make a beeline for our table. Robinson III was looking around, his ruddy complexion redder than usual. He looked worried, and his hand shook as he sipped the champagne. I had no idea how to break it to him that I had nothing further to report, except that his daughter was still at large.

Robinson III got to his feet when he saw me coming, a broad smile on his face. That threw me off balance because I expected him to start pounding on the table, demanding immediate results or else.

"Good day, Mr. Brown," he said heartily, extending his hand. While we were shaking hands, Honoré appeared with my glass of champagne. I felt like throwing it into Robinson's cheating mug.

"Sorry about the table," I said to Robinson through the din, "but it's discreet."

"Good thinking," he said. "It's fine."

We started scanning through the menu, and I said, "I guess you want to get right down to business."

"This one's on me. Eat what you want. Any suggestions?"

"The steak with pepper sauce and dauphine potatoes is really good. Rare will do it for me."

"I'll have the same." Honoré hovered over us, pouring out more champagne while we ordered, asking us how we wanted our steaks cooked. He had a great memory and never wrote anything down. Robinson gave me free rein with the wine list, so I ordered a bottle of 1917 Château Léoville Barton St. Julien, one of the priciest. I figured it would even the score a little for those gold certificates he had foisted on me.

Robinson III was smiling at me so friendly-like that I was beginning to feel uncomfortable. I didn't have any news that would keep that sunny smile on his face. We finished our champagne as Honoré brought our food. Robinson III asked me to taste the wine.

"Très bien," I said to Honoré, and he poured out the blood- red Bordeaux respectfully, not spilling a drop.

"I want to toast you, Mr. Brown." He clinked his glass against mine before I could stop him.

"I don't think…"

He reached into his pocket and handed me a note. It had been drafted on Hôtel Crillon letterhead by the star of the penmanship class, who wrote,

Daddy,

Buster Thigpen and a black fellow called Baby Langston have me prisoner. They say a private eye named Urby Brown's hot on their trail, and they're really panicking. Buster's a big pal of Count d'Uribé-Lebrun's and has asked the Count to act as a go-between. If you pay the ransom—one hundred thousand dollars!—Buster swears he will release me unharmed. Please pay it fast, 'cause Buster and this Baby Langston are scared of Mr. Brown and want to scram from France soonest. I *really* don't want to go with them.

Your loving Daphne, XOXO.

"Where…?" I wondered exactly when Daphne wrote her note.

"A cleaning woman found it in the ladies' room at the Hôtel Crillon and took it to the manager. Luckily, the fellow understands English and, aftah he read it, he had it taken to Count Lebrun. Lebrun had one of his men bring it to me two hours ago. How did you get onto Thigpen's trail so fast?" Robinson asked.

I didn't understand the timing; I was getting worried.

"I've got eyes and ears everywhere in this city," I said.

Robinson patted me on the shoulder chummily and said, "I knew I had the best man for the job! Thanks to Mr. O'Toole."

"You got the first ransom note from Buster yesterday morning and this note about twenty-four hours later, right?" I asked.

"That's right, and this one was written by Daphne herself. She's alive. I was beginning to feel she had been murdered…like Chahlie Jr."

"I don't understand why the Count's gotten involved in this," I said.

Robinson III looked irritated. "I don't give a damn who helps me get Daphne back. And the Count told me he knows you, right?" I nodded yes and he went on, "The important thing is that she's alive. And the kidnappers ah panicking because of you!" he said.

"Did the Count's man say anything else?"

"He wanted Daphne's photograph and gave me the Count's telephone number; that's all," he said.

"Her photograph?" I asked, puzzled.

"Yes. The Count arranged for a search to be made in the Crillon. No one identified Daphne from the photograph, and no negroes have been spotted inside the hotel for ages, thank goodness." He paused, red in the face. "Sorry I said that." I waved it away, and he went on, "But the note's definitely from her. I don't know how Daphne got it into the ladies' room, and I don't care. The important thing is that she's alive and the kidnappers ah frightened of you."

"Have you met the Count?" I asked.

"No. But I phoned him immediately. He said to tell you that he's had word from Thigpen—he calls him 'Bartholomew' of all things—about the place to leave the money. He'll make the arrangements with you in his office, when we finish lunch. You have full authority to act for me. He says that if things follow his plan, I should have my Daphne back by tomorrow!" He looked sheepish and then went on, "I've raised the ransom and given it to the Count's agent."

"You've what?" I was floored.

"Given it to the Count's agent. Just the way that Thigpen asked for it, in untraceable banknotes and gold bullion."

His ability to get his hands on so much dough and gold so fast astounded me almost as much as his casualness at doling it out to strangers.

"You're telling me that you turned over a hundred grand to this 'agent,' just like that?"

He wasn't happy to have me questioning his judgment.

"Mr. Brown, all you have to do is make sure that the Count gets the ransom into that monster Thigpen's hands. You don't have to bring Thigpen to me. I just want to get Daphne out of his…grip…as soon as possible. I want my Daphne back before our lives ah ruined for good. Is that so tough to comprehend?"

I didn't like the sudden turn of events, with the Count and me acting as go-betweens for Robinson III to turn over one hundred grand's worth of bullion and banknotes to a corpse lying on the floor of the Seine.

"All right," I said. "I'll deal with the Count. It's true that he's got close ties to Buster Thigpen."

"Yeah, he told me that he feels deeply responsible for what Thigpen's done, and that's why he wants to put things right. I know that I should've told you beforehand, Mr. Brown, but the Count gave me his oath as a gentleman that he'll get Daphne back. He'll hand her over to you, and then he promises to get back every penny of the ransom money from Thigpen and Langston." He looked imploringly at me. "Will you help me? Please. You're the only soul that I can trust in this affair."

Remembering Tex O'Toole, I said, "I'll get in touch with him as soon as we've finished lunch. We have to move fast on this one."

I wanted to make sure that Daphne got out of this business unharmed, whoever was behind the ransom deal. My feelings for her made me ready to risk big if it meant that she'd be back with Robinson tomorrow.

"I feel our luck has changed, Mr. Brown," he said.

What he didn't know was that Buster was out of it. Baby Langston was missing, but I had doubts that the gentle poet was in on it.

Ruling out Buster and Baby left two possibilities: either Hambone and the Corsicans were behind the caper—despite Hambone's denials last night with Lonny Jones's razor against his throat—or the Count was playing some sinister role as the puppet master, pulling all the strings.

"Thanks for the lunch, Mr. Robinson," I said, as we finished the last drops of the great red Bordeaux, from the vintage of the year after the Battle of Verdun. "But I think I'd better look in on the Count right away."

He beamed. "*That's* the spirit! I like men who put business before play." Then, turning somber, he said, "Please bring her back to me, Mr. Brown. You have my complete confidence. Do whatever you've got to do to get her back."

I stood up and we shook hands. He reached into his pocket and brought out a wad of dollar bills. He handed me greenbacks this time, not gold certificates. If he had, I would have decked him then and there.

"You haven't put the bite on me for extra money to cover your expenses, and I appreciate that. But I want you to have enough to wrap up the negotiations with the kidnappers, just in case. I'm giving you five hundred now and a substantial bonus when Daphne's back. Dollahs still OK with you?"

I pocketed the money but couldn't resist asking, "Have you run out of those gold certificates? These aren't as nice."

He smiled, one financial wizard to another. "I need them for another operation," he said. We shook hands.

As we parted, I said, "By the way, it's not my place to ask it, but would you mind being extra generous to the waiter? He's one of my… agents."

"Done, Mr. Brown."

CHAPTER 15

The Oriflamme trooper at the door of the Count's headquarters greeted me warmly this time, like a comrade-in-arms. He ushered me into the Count's antechamber, bowing and scraping before me as if I were some foreign potentate. Even Pierre was attempting a smile, though his twitching right hand belied what he really wanted to do, which was to shoot me.

He was about to knock on the Count's door when the man himself opened it, hugged me, and kissed me on the cheeks four times, twice on each. In France, you did four with close family or old friends. Judas kisses, I thought to myself.

The photographs on his desk had been pushed closer to my chair than before. The Count placed a photograph of Daphne in front of me, together with a copy of the ransom note from Buster that Robinson had already shown me and what looked like a summary of the ransom arrangements, typed out neatly. The ransom was to be left in a locker at the Gare du Nord. Beside my chair was a plain brown leather satchel. I picked it up; it weighed a ton.

"Miss Robinson's ransom in banknotes and gold bullion?"

"Yes," he replied. Pierre went to the rosewood bar, filled two snifters with Domfront calvados, and placed them before the Count and me. Pierre stood at attention, staring at a point a few feet above my head.

"Pierre will track Bartholomew down, aided by some of my crack troops." He rang the handbell twice, and Pierre cut a smart about-face and marched out of the office. After the door clicked shut, the Count continued, "Pursuant to Bartholomew's instructions"—he pointed to Buster's scrawlings—"I should like you to deposit the bag in a locker in the central locker service at the Gare du Nord, and bring me its key." He sipped at the calvados and said, "I can divulge to you that, at twelve thirty tomorrow afternoon, Miss Robinson will be sitting at a table in a private room in the La Pérouse Restaurant, awaiting you for lunch. I have paid in advance for the two of you to celebrate with champagne and caviar before you return her to her father."

"How will Buster...Bartholomew collect the ransom?"

The Count sipped his calvados and then bore his hard blue eye into mine. "All is arranged." The Count's face reddened in anger.

"So, this has all been Bartholomew's doing?" I asked in a cynical tone. "Mr. Count, I've known your protégé for a long time and, excuse me for saying it, but he doesn't have the brains to write a ransom note or to 'arrange' anything." I picked up Buster's nearly illegible ransom note and continued, "I worked my backside off teaching him to write, and this is probably the best penmanship job he's ever done. Somebody else must have come up with those 'arrangements' of his."

"He's more than just a protégé to me," the Count shouted. "And he is not as stupid as you think! He has distinguished himself in my employ."

The violence of the Count's reaction made me suspect that he had manipulated Buster into fronting the ransom scheme from the outset. Now he was using me as a ransom delivery boy for some murky purpose. I wondered again if the ransom would end up in the Oriflamme coffers.

I didn't really care anymore about who was behind the kidnapping or who ended up with the ransom, so long as I could bring Daphne back alive and unharmed. I would have fulfilled my contract with Robinson III and paid Tex O'Toole back for his friendship and for helping me out so much during and after the war. I stood up, looked the Count squarely in his eye, and said, "Can you guarantee that if I put the money in the locker and bring back the key, the girl will be at La Pérouse tomorrow? That I can take her to her father afterward? I don't know what's going on, but I'll do what you ask if you swear…"

He drilled his eye into my face as if boring into my soul.

"I did not believe all of those letters from the New Orleans priest"—he pretended to search for the name—"Father Gohegan, yes?" I nodded. "Until you came to my office last Wednesday and I saw you face to face."

That enraged me, and I yelled, "You're lying! Your man, Pierre, burned down the Waifs' Home. You ordered him to kill Father Gohegan. Why?"

"You will come to understand in due course," he said.

"Why?" I repeated, screaming at him again. His cold blue eye rested on me, then looked beyond me, as if at the distant past.

"The priest knew too much of our history. Yours and mine."

I was the boy at the Waifs' Home again, with Louis "Strawberry" Armstrong beside me, watching Father Gohegan burn to death after throwing me the handbell with the Count's crest on it and begging me, with his last breath, to find the monster before me.

"That's no reason to burn a man to death! To drive us out of the only home we'd ever known," I screamed.

"But yes! Our history is ours to write. Because we are the d'Uribé-Lebrun. You know, when you were born, we were masters of the richest sugar plantations in Louisiana."

I was horrified that he had said "we," and my face showed it.

He laughed. "Yes, my dear Brown, 'we.' You are my son. The last of my d'Uribé-Lebrun lineage."

"You used my mother like a whore, a slave."

The Count held up his hands, trying to calm me down. "She was in no way a slave, I can assure you. On the contrary. I helped her in many ways, even after her death."

I lunged for him then, and he coolly whipped out a gold-colored pistol and motioned for me to sit down, which I did. He placed the gun in front of him, as if daring me to go for it.

"I left New Orleans because I discovered that I loved France more than I could love any person. Your mother is the only woman I have ever loved with all of my heart."

"Don't talk that nonsense to me. You ran back to France because my mother wasn't white enough for you. Look. I'll do what you want if you promise that the girl will be at La Pérouse tomorrow. Then it's over. I don't want you or your men to come anywhere near me again. 'Cause if you or they do, you're going to get hurt, real bad." I took out my Colt and put it on the table in front of me. "You want war, you'll get it. I've got a lot of friends that would love to take you and your Nazis on. Just one question, though, what are you after? You want to be a new Napoleon? Dictator of France? King, Emperor? What do you want, man?"

The Count picked up his pistol, stood up, and walked past the gallery of ancestors peering down from the walls. He twirled around and said, solemnly, "I want to recognize you. With your real name, which is Charles-Emmanuel d'Uribé-Lebrun. I want that, nothing more."

I holstered my gun, put my Homburg back on, and hefted the brown leather satchel, so that I could swing it over my shoulder.

"Father Gohegan named me Urby Brown, and that's final."

"Urby Brown," he said, disdainfully. "That's not your real name, nor is America your real country." He glared at me, snarling and defiant. "We are the last of the d'Uribé-Lebrun. Only you will live on after me to carry us forward."

"Forward?" I asked, pointing at the portraits on the walls and then picking up the gold-framed photograph of the Count and Adolf Hitler. "Forward to them, to him?"

"When Maréchal Pétain takes power, he will restore our family, and France, to their rightful place. He will grant you French nationality immediately. Hitler is only one stepping stone to our future."

I made my way toward the door. "Mister, I'm stepping out of that future right now."

"You have no choice. It's a matter of blood."

"You want my 'tainted' blood in your future?"

"Those who know that have been or will be liquidated."

"Pierre knows, my friends know. You gonna rub them all out?"

"Naturally," the Count replied, indifferently.

The man was a dangerous lunatic. I had to leave now or do him serious harm.

"I'll get the locker key back to you in an hour. I won't be bringing it back, though. I hope never to set foot here again. The man with the key will be a big fellow named Jones. Think of him as an hors-d'oeuvre to a feast of pain for you if Daphne isn't at La Pérouse restaurant tomorrow at twelve thirty in the afternoon sharp."

Lonny Jones delivered the locker key to the Count two hours later, he told me. Five of the biggest Oriflamme men escorted him to the Count's office as Lonny chewed away at his toothpick, eyeballing them one by one. When the office door cracked opened, Lonny said he just threw the key inside, spun on his heels, and sashayed along the hallway, hawking loudly and spitting on the fine Persian carpet on his way out the front door. Lonny said, "Don't worry none, brother Urby. Them snail-chompers wants trouble, my 'peoples' slice them up like bacon."

CHAPTER 16

Paris, Monday, February 12, 1934

The La Pérouse restaurant was in a townhouse on the Left Bank of the Seine, bordering the river on the Quai des Grands Augustins.

La Pérouse was known as a place for trysts. If you had a private room for two, with a dining table and a large couch in it, you could order the champagne for you and your belle from the waiter, and he would come to take your next order only if you summoned him by pressing a bell inside the door.

So you were left alone to enjoy what the French have enjoyed as long as they have been French: food and sex, probably in that order. There were hidden staircases in La Pérouse that let you exit without being seen. Those who wished to be seen could use the main staircase and strut in, or out, through the front door.

I arrived at La Pérouse at twenty minutes past twelve, having walked there. The General Strike was effective so far, and the post, telephone, and telegraph services were down, and public transportation was unreliable. The Paris taxi drivers were still holding out and heading toward the second week of their strike.

Through the windows of the La Pérouse bar, I could see lunchtime crowds walking by on the sidewalks, sheltering from the cold rain under umbrellas. An occasional horse-drawn vehicule would pass in the road, which gave rise to outraged honking by drivers speeding around it in their Citroën and Panhard automobiles. Striking workers, with banners protesting the government's violent crackdown on them after the riots of February 6, marched along the Quai des Grands Augustins in groups, ready to brawl with any right-wing agents provocateurs or vituperative small business owners critical of the union-led General Strike.

I decided not to check my Homburg, my umbrella, and my Harris tweed overcoat. It was better to hold onto my things if I had to make a hasty getaway with Daphne down a hidden staircase.

I gave the name Urby Brown for the reservation, as the Count had instructed me to. I was escorted to one of the private dining rooms for two on the second floor, passing dark brown leather-covered walls with photographs and paintings of past celebrity patrons. The waiter opened the door and seated me on a Récamier couch, covered in dark red velvet. A bottle of champagne awaited us next to a mound of caviar chilling in a crystal caviar server with crushed ice underneath it. The table was set simply, with small caviar plates, dark red damask napkins, and ivory caviar spoons on a matching red tablecloth.

The waiter poured out two champagne glasses of Veuve Clicquot Ponsardin Brut and turned on the Victrola next to the couch. I recognized the music as being from a Wagner opera, which only raised my sense of anticipation to near breaking point. I figured that Daphne must be on her way or had arrived.

I could smell a teasing scent of perfume in the room, like a whisper. I went to look out the window onto the rue des Grands Augustins. At that moment, the heavy, dark red velvet curtain opened, and Daphne stood before me naked, her long white-blonde hair flowing over her breasts and down to her waist. I saw both of her eyes for the first time; they were violet-blue.

Without saying a word, Daphne undressed me, all the while covering my body with her hair as if to protect my modesty. The strains of Wagner rose in a crescendo, and then, to my surprise, Daphne pushed me down onto the couch, mounted me, and started swaying and moving to the rapid rhythms of the Wagner music, spurring me on with her sharp ankles.

"Wait for me, Urby!" she cried out in her breathy voice.

We lay in each other's arms afterward, toasting ourselves with the champagne. Looking at her beautiful body next to mine, feeling the warmth from her soft skin with its faint blonde down, I felt the need rising again.

We made love again in a silence broken only by cries of pleasure.

"Amazing," she said. "Has it ever been as good for you?"

"No," I lied.

"Promise me that you'll stay with me. Always."

She stood up slowly and walked to the table with our glasses of champagne, her back to me. She was perfection in every part of her body. She poured out more champagne as I watched her back and buttocks, entranced. She brought the glasses back, her face still glowing from our lovemaking. We toasted each other again, looking deep into each other's eyes.

"I'm glad that you're back safe," I said. "I'd have moved heaven and earth to find you." Then I grew sad, remembering that I had to turn her over to Robinson III in an hour or so. She had read my thoughts.

"I know that I have to go back to my father and then back to America. Will you come with me?"

"I wish I could, Daphne, but I don't plan to go back to America again. I couldn't live there like a free man."

"We can do anything together, Urby. I have money. You don't have to live out your life as a…" I knew what she was going to say and stopped her.

"I am who I am. I've already tried being what I'm not, and it doesn't work. I'm a lot older than you, too, Daphne. Eighteen years is a lot. It might not seem important to you now, but in a few years, I won't be able to keep up with you." Tears started streaming down her cheeks, and she wiped them away with the backs of her hands.

"Let's finish our champagne and have some caviar. Then I'll get dressed and we'll go. You're right. But it's lovely being with you. I'll never forget you."

"I know you've gone through a lot. But could you tell me exactly what happened when the burglars took you and Buster from La Belle Princesse?" I was trying to find out how much she knew about what had happened to Buster.

"I'm not sure. Those burglars put a cloth over my face, filled with ether I guess, and the next thing I knew…"

Her words were beginning to echo in my ears. I said, "Ether?" And my words came out so slurred that I couldn't understand myself. "Eeetherrr?" I repeated. The room started swaying and then whirling around. I thought I saw a waiter come into the room to remove the champagne and caviar. Daphne seemed to be dressing in slow-motion, buttoning up a dark gray blouse, which she pulled out of a suitcase behind the curtains. Her body was curving in and out like an image in a fun-house mirror. I saw her look toward me as she brushed her hair, quickly, and then she pressed on the button at the door, and the waiter came into the room again.

Good, I thought. Daphne will go to her father at the Ritz. Then my job will be done. It'll be over. I tried to stay awake, but the room kept spinning around. I heard approaching footsteps and then some words that I didn't understand in a language that sounded like German. Then my lights went out.

A few minutes later, the door to the private room opened. Two Oriflamme troopers led by Pierre dragged the unconscious Urby down a hidden staircase. They bundled him into a red and black Citroën waiting on the rue des Grands Augustins. Pierre took a hypodermic needle out of a leather case and injected pentothal into Urby's veins to keep him sleeping.

The Count had ordered Pierre to give Urby an injection every three hours. At three in the morning, he would drive to the Place Vendôme and dump him on the sidewalk outside the Ritz Hotel with a note pinned to Urby's coat saying that he should be taken to Barnet Robinson's room immediately.

PART III

CHAPTER 17

Paris, Monday, February 12, 1934

Ten minutes after Pierre and the Oriflamme troopers drove off with Urby, the Count met Daphne, as arranged, at the same exit through which Pierre and his men had dragged Urby. The Count was holding open the door of a black Mercedes-Benz Mannheim with diplomatic plates from the German Embassy in France. The car was already loaded with Daphne's matching Louis Vuitton luggage. Three people were sitting inside the car, two huge German men and a fat middle-aged German woman.

The Count had arranged with his friend Rudolph Hess that the two Germans, both of whom were working for Hess undercover in the Paris Embassy, would drive Daphne to Berlin in the company of the middle-aged German nurse, Elsa Herbst. Elsa, a spinster, was the head of the household of Adolf Hitler's right-hand man, Hermann Goering.

After checking that Daphne was comfortably seated beside Fraülein Herbst in the backseat, the Count bowed over Daphne's hand, said his good-byes, and then tapped the car's roof sharply with his cane. The engine roared into life, and the Mercedes joined the flow of traffic on the Quai des Grands Augustins.

Once they had arrived in Berlin, the German diplomats and Fraülein Herbst were to install Daphne in the most luxurious suite in the Hotel

Adlon on Unter den Linden Boulevard. From there, she would send a second note to her father, pretending that her situation was becoming increasingly dire and pleading with him either to accede to Buster's new demands or to send Mr. Brown to rescue her. The note had already been prepared and would be sent from Berlin by telegraph before Daphne arrived.

The Count had told Daphne that Rudolph Hess had already arranged for her to join Chancellor Hitler for a gala dinner on Wednesday evening in the Chancellery. The prospect of meeting him again made the long trip to Berlin with the three dour Germans bearable for her. They were strange in the way that they addressed her as "Ihre Hoheit," or "Your Highness," a form that the Germans used for addressing sovereigns or royalty.

She wondered if Chancellor Hitler had said something to Rudolph Hess about her. Despite having a cold, calculating mind and having experienced the reality of sexual humiliation with Buster, Daphne still harbored the romantic notion that Chancellor Hitler would see in her the sixteen-year-old maiden he had walked with in the Tiergarten and would, when he was crowned Kaiser of the new German Reich, choose her as Kaiserin.

The nurse, who with stiff formality introduced herself to Daphne as "Fraülein Elsa Herbst, head of household of the Widowed Prime Minister of Prussia Hermann Goering," could not take her eyes off Daphne. She stared adoringly at her, her Meissen blue eyes seeming to glow in her porcine face. Daphne thought that she resembled her master.

As the car drew closer to Berlin, the three Germans became ever more sycophantic. They probably knew, she thought, that, in a matter of days, she would see their Führer.

Daphne knew that older men were very attracted to her. Buster became her lover when he was more than twice her age, and Urby was almost as old as Buster. Chancellor Hitler would turn forty-five in two months, on April 20th. He would not be able to resist her and, as he grew older, she would grow stronger until she, the mother of their progeny, was firmly in control.

Hours later, lying in the plush four-poster bed in her suite at the Hotel Adlon, Daphne remembered her last sight of Urby, asleep in their private dining room at La Pérouse Restaurant. After submitting to the degradation that Buster delighted in inflicting on her, making love to Urby had stirred her deeply and reaffirmed her belief in her sexual power over men. She regretted that she had to administer the knockout drops to Urby, as instructed by the Count, but she believed that the plan to convince her father to have Urby track her down in Berlin would succeed. She hoped that they would be lovers again in a short time and that making love to Urby would help her to prepare herself for her greatest ambition: subjugating Chancellor Hitler's heart.

Some five hundred miles away, in Paris, Hambone Gaylord had a big problem on his hands. His nephew, Darius "Baby Langston" Swilley, had been missing since the phony abduction of Buster Thigpen and the rich blonde girl from La Belle Princesse.

Now, Stanley was accusing Hambone and the Alfieris, and even Baby Langston, of being in cahoots to kidnap the girl for real and hold her for ransom.

What really angered Hambone was that Stanley was right about his plans for making money off the girl, although he had not been able to put them into motion. Once Stanley and Urby had outlined their fake kidnapping scheme and mentioned how rich the girl's father was, Hambone had figured that having the blonde girl to hand was like "finding a bird's nest on the ground." He reckoned that big money could be made if he played good cards.

So Hambone and the Alfieris had worked out a real old-fashioned kidnapping scheme. The plan was simple, Hambone told himself. Why had it all gone wrong? If his nephew, Baby Langston, had come in on Saturday like he was supposed to, Hambone and the Alfieri brothers would have leaned on him to tell them exactly where Redtop had stashed Buster and the girl, and then they were going to kidnap her themselves. They planned to work a ransom deal of their own on Daphne's father and then blackmail Stanley to keep his mouth shut by threatening to tell the father that Stanley and Urby were behind the girl's kidnapping.

The problem was that his nephew hadn't turned up for the third morning in a row and, because of that, a new and greater fear was gripping Hambone on this Monday afternoon. Stanley's threats were scary, but they were nothing compared to his fear of what his baby sister, Magnolia Swilley, would do to him if she found out that her only child, Darius "Baby Langston" Swilley, had disappeared on Hambone's watch.

Hambone knew that he was a cold killer. His talent for killing had made him a hero to the French and Americans during the Great War. It enabled him to climb to the top of the ladder in the postwar Harlem-in-Montmartre underworld, backed by the Corsicans. The story was that Magnolia, the most feared gangster in Harlem, New York, had never killed anyone herself. But she was so beautiful and powerful that anyone who crossed her got killed in exchange for her sexual favors. And they got killed real nasty.

She had let Darius travel to Paris to pursue his poetry career because Hambone had promised to take him under his wing. Hambone could not refuse her because she owned La Belle Princesse lock, stock, and barrel.

Hambone had had the Alfieris scouring Paris, looking for Baby Langston and using all of their connections to track him down since Saturday afternoon. But so far, they had come up empty-handed. It was very late in the afternoon on Monday now, and there was no further word from them of Baby's whereabouts.

La Belle Princesse closed on Mondays, so Hambone was alone with his fear of Magnolia. He felt like getting drunk and forgetting what a mess he was in. He remembered that there were two bottles of Tennessee mountain moonshine, which he still had tucked away in the cellar. He drank the moonshine sparingly, like the rarest French champagne, because he had only smuggled in five bottles of it when he arrived back in France from his last trip to America many years ago at the height of Prohibition. Whenever he drank that White Lightning, it brought back memories of home and his childhood with his sister, Magnolia, before they grew up and went their separate ways.

Hambone opened the trapdoor down to the cellar and turned on the light. When he reached the bottom of the steps and stood in the cellar, he bumped into the crates of champagne, whiskey, and other items stored there, looking for the hole in the moldy walls where he kept his stash of moonshine. He moved a few cases of champagne aside and then bent down to avoid hitting his head on a low arch. Moving on quickly, he stumbled over something. Hambone felt for his pistol and realized, panicked, that he had left it upstairs behind the bar.

When the thing he stumbled into didn't move, he bent down in the dim light and discovered a body lying face down on the earthen floor. It was a big body wearing big shoes, their soles full of holes. An enormous fear slammed into his heart, and he choked, afraid that he was going to have a heart attack then and there. He wanted to run away and pretend that there was no body there, but he turned it over. His nephew lay dead with his head smashed in. There was no blood; the body had bled out someplace else. He felt terrible for Baby for a heartbeat, and then his fear of Magnolia gripped him again.

Hambone decided instantly to get rid of the body. As long as there was no body, he could make up a story for Magnolia about Darius having left Paris to go traveling. She would be furious that Baby had not left a forwarding address, but as long as she thought that Darius was alive, he, Hambone, had a slim chance of living long enough to find a way to destroy Magnolia with the help of the Alfieri clan.

He looked around the cellar for something to wrap the body in so that he could tote it upstairs. He would drive his car to the street behind La Belle Princesse, using the same back entrance that the Alfieris had taken to make off with Buster and Daphne the night of Stanley and Urby's fake kidnap deal.

Hambone found some old, torn packing materials and some rope and trussed Darius up like an enormous parcel, after searching through his pockets to make sure that there was no identity on him. It was hard work hauling him up the stairs, but Hambone was a big man himself, and Darius felt lighter with the blood drained out of him.

Night had fallen, and the alley was dark. The street lamp was out of order. Hambone was able to bring his car around to the back and load Baby, together with a pitchfork and a shovel, into his trunk without being seen. He reckoned that the best way to dispose of him was to bury him in some deserted spot in the country where he could put down a marker and say Christian words over the remains.

He planned to tell Stanley that Baby Langston had contacted him from a hiding place and asked him to let Stanley know that he had helped Buster to escape with the blonde girl because Satan had tempted him by dangling big dough before his eyes. Baby had seen the error of his ways and wanted Stanley to know that Buster had gone off with the girl and was hiding out with her somewhere in Paris until he collected ransom money for her. Stanley would have his doubts about Hambone's story, but there was no way he could disprove it, Hambone thought. Unless he found Buster and the girl first and they told him a different story.

Hambone drove on through the night. He felt sorry for his nephew, but he calmed down at the thought that, if Stanley swallowed his story, he would unwittingly help Hambone to send Magnolia up a blind alley until he and the Alfieris found a way to destroy her.

CHAPTER 18

Paris, Tuesday–Wednesday, February 13–14, 1934

Auguste, the night concierge-receptionist of the Ritz Hotel, sat at the front desk, alone with the splendors of the Ritz's lobby, which was empty at three in the morning.

He heard the squeal of tires and the repeated honking of a horn on the Place Vendôme just outside the hotel's florid doors. He thought to himself that it must be Socialist and Communist troublemakers who were increasingly targeting luxury hotels with acts of vandalism and sabotage. The unions had called for an extension of yesterday's mainly unsuccessful General Strike, and the hooligans outside had probably decided to start early after building up their courage with cheap red wine and rum.

Auguste left his front desk to wake up the top-hatted doorman who slumbered on a Louis XV chair in a corner space off the main lobby. The doorman leapt to his feet, stretched himself to his considerable height, and smoothed down his long black jacket and top hat, waiting for orders.

"I heard noises outside," Auguste said. "Be careful, though, it may be some of those red vermin."

"I will deal with them, boss, fear not," the doorman said. He came back a few minutes later, dragging a man by holding him under his armpits. The unconscious man was not a good sort, Auguste thought. He wore a felt-covered metal Homburg hat that was pushed down over his head and held on by a chin strap, a species of haberdashery that Auguste had never seen before. From what he could see of the man's clothes under his rough tweed overcoat, they had no doubt been custom made but not with a fine fabric. They marked him out as being from a middling social milieu: not a worker.

After Auguste spotted a tag on the man's lapel reading "Take me to Barnet Robinson right away. I am Urby Brown," he had the doorman take him into a well-appointed room off the lobby to await further instructions. He decided that it was unwise to buzz Mr. Robinson at this hour; instead, he took the elevator to Mr. Robinson's suite. Auguste tapped on the door, and Mr. Robinson opened it right away, as if he were expecting someone. Fully dressed, he looked as if he hadn't slept.

"Yeah?" he asked.

Auguste answered, "A man has just been brought in, unconscious, from the Place Vendôme. A note pinned to him states that he is Urby Brown…"

"Great!" he said excitedly. "Bring him up right away. I've been waiting for him all day."

A sharp whiff of ammonia cleared my head, and I saw Robinson III and two other men standing over me.

"Can you understand me? What's your name?" Robinson asked.

"Napoleon Bonaparte," I answered.

Robinson grinned and said to the two men, "You fellows can go now." He held out some dollar bills. One of the men snatched them and they left.

Robinson looked worried. "When you didn't bring Daphne, I phoned Count d'Uribé-Lebrun. He said things didn't pan out like he planned."

I was really surprised by that, and he must have read it on my face. I said, "I met her at La Pérouse Restaurant, all right."

"He paid Thigpen the ransom, right?"

"That's what the Count told me he was planning to do. I put the money in a locker at the Gare du Nord, had the key left off with the Count, and met up with Daphne at twelve thirty on Monday afternoon."

Robinson looked surprised. "That was yesterday. It's three thirty Tuesday morning now."

It was my turn to be surprised. "Daphne was at the restaurant. We toasted with champagne to celebrate her release, and that's the last thing I remember," I said.

Robinson III looked as if he knew that already, but asked, "How was she?"

"Fine. Shaken up, but happy to be free of Buster Thigpen."

"Thigpen must have arranged to slip you a Mickey Finn…"

"That's impossible," I said without thinking.

"Why impossible?" he asked, suddenly suspicious.

"Look, Mr. Robinson, I've known Buster for a long time. He just doesn't have the…brains to cook up anything like that."

"Maybe the man Baby Langston Daphne mentioned in her note is behind it. The Count doesn't think so, though."

I was confused. I couldn't imagine how the Count knew about Baby. "Baby Langston doesn't strike me as the kidnapping type."

"Daphne said he was involved though."

I thought about it for a while. If Baby Langston was in on the scheme, Stanley was right that Hambone and his Corsicans might be pulling the strings. A Corsican might have posed as a waiter and slipped me the Mickey Finn at La Pérouse. All that I could remember was making love to Daphne. I had to find her because I was beginning to think that I was in love with her.

"It's possible," I finally answered. "His Uncle Rawlston Gaylord runs the La Belle Princesse nightclub in Montmartre and has close ties to the

Corsican mafia. They might have gotten wind of Buster's ransom demand and decided to take the deal over and keep the ransom for themselves."

"The Count's really cut up that Thigpen is still on the run aftah I paid the ransom."

The telephone rang like a sudden scream in the night. Robinson picked up the receiver.

"Yes?" he answered, staring at me. He motioned for me to come closer and listen in with the second earpiece. It was the Count.

"You gave a colleague of mine a photograph of your daughter after they found her note at the Hôtel Crillon," the Count said. "I passed a copy of the photograph to a friend at the Quai d'Orsay who had it circulated to various embassies. She has been spotted in Berlin with a man believed to be of a Mediterranean type. The man may be my protégé Bartholomew Thigpen, alas."

"Daphne's crazy about the place," Robinson said. "But it's a bad spot for your man right now. Seems that Hitler's people attack non-Aryan types on the streets." The Count was lying about Buster; I wanted to know why.

"My contact knows where she's staying. I would go to Berlin myself, but I can't get away because the leftists would use my travel to Germany to brand me as a lackey of Chancellor Hitler. Can you go?"

I studied Robinson III's reactions, wondering if what Jean Fletcher had told me about Robinson II's embargo on his setting foot into Germany was true. He went deathly pale before answering lamely, "Not right now. I have some problems…with the present authorities."

"May I make a suggestion?" I heard the Count ask, suspecting what his suggestion might be.

"Shoot," Robinson said simply.

"I understand that you have a private investigator named Urby Brown in your employ. Perhaps you could send him to Berlin to track down your daughter and settle affairs with my treacherous colleague once and for all. I have friends who can be of assistance to him. I will personally pay for his fees."

Robinson III looked at me imploringly again, and I nodded my approval. He patted me on the back.

"Mr. Brown is listening, right beside me. He agrees to go. How soon can you arrange everything?"

"I strongly recommend that he leave for Berlin on Thursday so that he may still benefit from the element of surprise. I'll prepare the necessary letters of introduction, make funds…"

"Thank you for offering, Count, but Daphne's my responsibility. I will take care of all of Mr. Brown's expenses."

"As you wish," the Count said.

"Let's get moving. Let's meet up for dinner tonight…"

"I'm sorry, but I must lead a demonstration against the Left. They're planning another General Strike. I propose that we meet in your suite for lunch on Thursday. I shall have all of his documents by then. Mr. Brown should be packed and ready to leave immediately thereafter."

All of my instincts were screaming at me to back off, but my mind was focused on bringing Daphne back to her father. Afterward, I would deal with whoever was behind it all, whether it was the Count or Hambone and his Corsicans or Baby Langston.

Two hours later, I was at Mama Jane's off the Place Pigalle to meet up with Stanley for his 6:00 a.m. breakfast.

Stanley strode through the door and hurried to his table, carrying his own soprano saxophone case for a change. He looked worried, seeing my drawn face. I must have looked worse than I felt because now that the die was cast, I was looking forward to my trip to Germany—which I intended to make short—and seeing Daphne again.

Stanley studied me as he devoured his food. He pushed a plate toward me, which I refused.

"Boy, you lookin' peaked," he said. "You lookin' blue."

I shooed away Mama Jane and told Stanley everything that had happened yesterday, starting with the lunch with Daphne at La Pérouse. He got so caught up in the story that he stopped eating to listen to me.

"I was thinkin' Hambone, Baby Langston, and them Corsicans behind this for sure, 'cept for Hambone bein' so scared. I ain't never seen a man so scared. I sticks my Colt in his mouth last night and says I goin' to off him he don't give me answers, and he just cry like he beggin' me to shoot. Somethin' wrong with the man; he more scared of somethin' than dyin'."

"I'm going to go to Berlin, Germany, and bring the girl back to her daddy. Then whoever's behind it can fight over the ransom money. This one's too deep for us, Stanley. I just want to collect my fees and get on with my life."

"Yo' life be music. You gone ditch this private eye business, get back to where you belongs?"

"Yeah. The music's back. When we were playing 'Tiger Rag' and Sidney Bechet came on to buck me, the feeling came back. I haven't felt like that since Harlem."

"All right, mon petit! Time for you to re-open up 'Urby's Masked Ball,' best Creole jazz club in the whole world! Let's get her goin', 'cause I wants us to blow together again, like last Saturday night. And you tell Hannah to get back here. You needs her, not that goldilocks messin' with yo' brain."

"You know anything about Germany?"

"Used to have some high old times in Berlin eight or nine year back. Them Hitler peoples was already makin' trouble back then, but, shoot, thems was some of the best days, Berlin."

"Sounds like things have changed since Hitler took over."

"True, mon petit. But you don't look no different to them white on white folk he like so much. If you got any problems, I got people there can get you out that place lickety-split. I'm talkin' army people. My main man be a colonel. Man play piano 'most as good as Jelly Roll Morton hisself. You got somethin' to write on?"

I took out a piece of paper and a pencil, and Stanley twisted his head to and fro trying to get to grips with the complexity of his friend's name.

"Man got two name. Hold on, first one, Schultz, like that Dutch Schultz run the numbers racket in Harlem, the second Horn, like a horn."

"You mean Dieter Schulz-Horn? He was a major last I heard."

"He the man," Stanley said.

I remembered the name from the war. My Foreign Legion Corps had come up against his troops at Belloy-en-Santerre in 1916. I remembered someone saying to me, "If we get captured, I hope it's Schulz-Horn does it. He's old-school. He won't let the Boches use our white flags as a target marker to machine gun us down."

"He Colonel Schulz-Horn now," Stanley said, reading my thoughts. "You got any trouble with them Hitler folk, you look him up. You needs money?"

"No, I've got all I need."

"You protect yourself, you hear? Take that tin Homburg hat I give you. And yo' Colt."

"I'm leaving all that behind. If the Boches catch me with that stuff, I'll end up in prison, or worse. Can you let Schulz-Horn know that I might look him up?"

"No 'might' about it. You *best* look him up soon's you can. If you got to get out of Germany real fast, he be the man to help you."

We hugged each other good-bye, and then I left to cop some sleep. I woke up in the afternoon, packed, and phoned Jean Fletcher to meet up at the Coupole. What I hoped was that she'd give me the lowdown on the "new Germany." She probably had contacts who could help me and Daphne cut out of there double time, if Stanley's friend Schulz-Horn couldn't.

I didn't like the idea of going into Germany. My memories of the Great War and how they had nearly destroyed the world were still strong. I had killed too many of them to feel comfortable going into their heart-land. They were a fanatical bunch, the Boches: their new leader, Adolf

Hitler, seemed to be leading them to where the Kaiser left off less than twenty years ago.

Still, I had to go because Daphne was there, alone or with Baby Langston or the Corsicans, and I was going to bring her to her father, whatever it took. I kept remembering how good it felt to sink deep inside her body, but Daphne had gotten deep inside my mind and my heart, too, and it would be hard to get her out. Whatever happened, I had to be with her again. One more time, I said to myself, and then I can walk away from her and my life as a private eye. The music was back with me and, with Stanley's help, I would re-open my nightclub, Urby's Masked Ball, and then beg Hannah Korngold to come back to France.

Jean Fletcher and I started drinking at the Coupole in the afternoon while she filled me in on Germany. She liked Stanley's idea of my getting in touch with Colonel Dieter Schulz-Horn. She had met him in Paris at Le Grand Duc nightclub a few years ago with some of his fellow German officers, all of them in mufti. She could not believe that they were Boches, the way they joined in and appreciated the jazz music. Schulz-Horn had even asked if Urby's Masked Ball was open and was very disappointed to hear that it had just closed down. Jean told me that Schulz-Horn was probably my best bet if I got into a jam, but she knew a young journalist named Skip Oatman who knew the ropes and could use his connections to the American Ambassador to Germany, William Dodd, to help me get out in an emergency.

I told Jean that I had met up with Robinson III at his suite at the Ritz, and the Count had phoned him there to tell him that Daphne had been seen with Buster in Berlin, but that I had my reasons for believing that Buster wasn't there. I told her about Baby Langston and the Corsicans. Jean said that if Baby Langston was as big and as black as I had described him, he would have a lot of trouble with the Nazi brown shirts who went around attacking obvious "non-Aryans," unless they were celebrities who were treated like "temporary Aryans."

These celebrities were "protected" she said, because Hitler had too much riding on hosting the summer and winter Olympics in Germany in 1936 and didn't want to have his bully boys tarnishing Germany's reputation more than it already was. She assured me that I wouldn't have any problems because I was an "Aryan physical type." We both had a good laugh about that.

Then she became serious. "Tell you the truth," she said, "I don't like the setup. My gut feeling is that Robinson III and the Count are using you for something. I get it that Robinson III can't go to Germany because he's frightened that his old man will cut him off at the knees. The Count's got a good excuse for staying in France because the Left is itching for more action after the General Strike turned out to be a damp squib." She was sobering up fast and continued. "What bothers me the most is that Robinson III and the Count worship the ground that Hitler walks on, so why should they be so fussed that Daphne's in Germany? If she wants to escape from Baby Langston and/or the Corsicans, all she has to do is use her fluent German on any Boche in hailing distance of a brown shirt, and they'll lynch them on the spot." Jean was voicing many of the same qualms that I had, but I had brushed them aside because of my feelings for Daphne.

"You watch out for that girl, Urby," she said, all sobered up now. "She reminds me of the Lorelei in Heinrich Heine's poem: a beautiful blonde babe who sits naked as a jaybird on a boulder above the Rhine, brushing her wavy locks and singing the blues until sailors with their tongues hanging out smash their boats against the rocks and drown."

"Let's go home, Jean," I said, knowing that another drink would put me over the edge, too. She did something then that she'd never done before. She kissed me full on the lips. I was even more surprised when she burst into tears afterward.

"Sorry to go all emotional on you, Urby, but you're walking into a trap. I can feel it in the old bones. Maybe you've used up your nine lives."

We really got drunk after that and toasted our friendship until we could barely stand upright at the bar. Honoré, the waiter who was on the phone repeating, "Certainement, Monsieur le Comte" over and over again, put down the receiver to escort us to the chauffeured car Jean's magazine had laid on for her until the end of the taxi strike. She dropped me off at my place but didn't kiss me again.

CHAPTER 19

Paris-Berlin, Thursday, February 15, 1934

At the lunch with the Count in Robinson's suite, III showed me a telegram that he had received from Daphne a few hours ago. In it, she pleaded with her father to pay the ransom quickly and said that Buster was planning to ask for double the amount unless he got the money really fast. She begged her father to send the private investigator Urby Brown to Berlin to fetch her back to Paris, once Buster's terms had been met.

Robinson gave me a thousand dollars cash and the names of some of his Princeton buddies at the American embassy whom I could contact in an emergency. He suddenly looked panicked and then relieved when I whipped out my US passport, which I still have thanks to Tex O'Toole. I keep it valid for when the French cops check my papers. He handed me a thin leather briefcase, and I opened it to find train tickets, a reservation voucher for the Universal Hotel, and what looked like enough stacks of German dough to open up my own bank in Berlin. I put the briefcase into one of the two suitcases that I had brought with me. Robinson took one look at my battered luggage, went to his closet, and brought out two custom made Louis Vuitton suitcases. He asked me to repack my things into them because he had booked me into a swanky hotel, and I would arouse suspicion arriving with my tatty luggage. I took his blunt hint but asked him to keep my bags until I returned for them.

The Count also gave me the names of people to contact at the French embassy if I needed help. He said that, in the event that Buster was with Daphne, he would consider it a great favor if I could bring him back, too, and he would reward me handsomely.

Feigning sincerity, I told him that I would do my best. The Count filled me in on Daphne's last known whereabouts. Robinson poured some champagne; we drank toasts to the success of our "enterprise"; and then the Count and Robinson III drove me to the Gare du Nord in an Oriflamme-chauffeured car.

They put me on the afternoon train to Berlin and waved until it pulled out of the station. I had so much on my mind that the countryside passing by outside made little impression on me.

I kept thinking of my lunch with Daphne at La Pérouse on Monday and the whole stretches of time that I couldn't account for.

My brain was teeming with images and sounds like throwing a stone into water, hearing a splash, and seeing the circles lapping away from it. I fell asleep, my head against the cool window. When I awoke we were pulling into the Friedrichstrasse Train Station, and it was past ten in the evening.

I got my suitcases down from the luggage rack and walked out onto the platform with people rushing all around me shouting and gesticulating in German, a language that I hadn't heard much since the war. Immediately on leaving my carriage, I was accosted by two men in black leather trench coats demanding to see my passport. They scanned through it, and one of them said in American-accented English, "Are you Ernest Shipman?"

That really made me angry, but I held my temper in check. The man was holding my passport, so why was he asking me if I was somebody else? "No, my name's Urby Brown."

He kept asking me if I was Ernest Shipman, and I kept answering that I was Urby Brown. Finally, he walked off with my papers and conferred with another fellow wearing a black leather trench coat over his black storm trooper uniform. The man skimmed through a list in his hand, turning the pages like an opera score. The he disappeared into an office.

Jean had told me to watch out for the men in black. They were the SS black shirts, and they were rivals to the SA—the brown shirts—Hitler's original mob before he came to power. The black shirts and the brown shirts were at war, tearing at each other like gangs back in the Battlefield in New Orleans. Jean was backing the black shirts to win because they were more ruthless and polished than the brown shirts, who had done the dirtiest jobs for Hitler as he gobbled up power but were now an embarrassment, and a danger, to him.

After a nod from the black shirt who reappeared from the office, my first black trench coat returned my passport to me, saluted, and said, "Welcome to Germany, Herr Brown." They turned their attention to another passenger.

I walked to the taxi rank outside the station and handed the cabbie a card with the address of the Universal Hotel. He snarled and mumbled some words under his breath as he put my suitcases into the trunk of his cab; then he sped away from the train station. So far, Germany was turning out a lot worse than I expected.

The cabbie kept mumbling to himself angrily, and I could feel that he was enraged about something. I saw rows of headlights all around me and the bright lights of Berlin illuminating the red, white, and black swastika flags that were draped over every available space. I wondered if the cabbie hated the Nazis or their flags; each time he passed more bunting or brown shirts and black shirts walking on the sidewalks, his growling grew louder. I was still wondering about him when the cab stopped at a large, brightly lit hotel, the Universal.

The driver clammed up suddenly, climbed out of his seat, and grudgingly removed my suitcases from the trunk. The English-speaking hotel porter helped me out with paying the driver because I found the different varieties and numbers of paper money and coins bewildering, and the German script was hard to decipher. The driver looked so unhappy that I slipped a few banknotes to him without knowing their value; he smiled for the first time. He doffed his cloth cap and drove off smiling.

The hotel porter perked up, too, when he saw the tip that I'd given the cabbie. He whisked my two suitcases up to the front desk. The concierge looked at my American passport picture and then at me over and over again and then had me sign the register. He told me that I could pick up my passport first thing in the morning. I didn't like being without it for a second, in case I had to make a fast escape with Daphne, but it was the way they did things here and in France.

On the wall behind the front desk was a large photo of Adolf Hitler surrounded by swastika emblems. The expression on his face was stern. He wasn't the smiling "Cher Adolphe" posing with the Count in the photograph on his desk.

The concierge was all smiles and politeness as he scrutinized my passport, checking out my face to make sure that it matched the passport photograph. But there was something about his eagerness to spot a difference, something that could pigeonhole me into a racial or religious category that made me think I was back in the South. There, white people were so obsessed with race that they would check your cuticles to see if you had the mythical half-moon near them that "proved" you had colored blood in you, even if your skin was white and your hair was straight and blonde. It made me wonder what the jovial concierge's reaction would be if he knew that I was colored or if he saw a name like Korngold on my passport.

Finally, he smiled deferentially and gave my room key to the porter, who ferried my bags to the elevator and then up to the tenth floor and my room. I gave him some banknotes with the same portraits and numbers on them as the ones I'd given the cab driver, and he nearly snapped in two thanking me.

The Count and Robinson III had put me up in style. I had a large bedroom with its own bathroom, and everything was blue in the room, including the marble in the bathroom. There were two large armchairs facing each other across a round mahogany table. The huge window overlooked a park. A decanter of water, two glasses, and a siphon seltzer bottle sat on the table.

I held out some more banknotes and said to the porter, "If you can bring me some alcohol, they're yours."

"Schnapps? Made with ploms. Is good?"

"Ja," I said, using one of the two words I knew in German.

I handed some more money to the night porter when he returned with a fancy one-liter bottle of schnapps with purple plums on the label and a crystal schnapps glass. He opened the bottle and filled my glass, and I gestured for him to sit and have a drink with me. That surprised him, but he went to the door, peered both ways, closed it, and poured a short one for himself. The man was plainly nervous as if it was a first for him to have a drink with one of the guests.

"Down the hatch," I said. He looked puzzled. This was obviously not an expression that he'd heard before. I pointed to my open mouth and said, "Hatch, American for 'mouth.'" He smiled, obviously happy to learn some new slang.

"Hotch," he repeated.

"My name's Urby Brown. What's yours?"

He suddenly became guarded. I looked at him closely for the first time. He was around eighteen and had dark hair and a sallow complexion and dark brown eyes that moved constantly, never coming to rest. He was really nervous, and there was more to it than having a drink with a guest.

"Gunther Kalman." He seemed relieved when I didn't react.

"Can I call you Gunther?"

That floored him. I decided not to ask him to call me Urby. I needed a favor doing, and he was on edge just having a drink with me. He probably had to leave soon, or the front desk man would start asking him some questions.

"Yes, certainly, Herr Brown," he said. "You are American, is it not true?"

"Guilty," I said. He looked confused and then smiled nervously.

"I have cousin in America, in New York."

"Where abouts?"

He was puzzled by the words but continued, "At the end of Manhattan. Where many Europe immigrant live together. German, Italian, Polish."

Lower East Side, I thought.

"You planning to visit your cousin some day?"

He scanned the room as if somebody might be eavesdropping on our conversation. He made a decision then. He leaned closer and whispered, "I want go to America. I want to leave Germany schnell…fast. I am half-Hungarian. Not good place for me here now." He whispered again, scanning the walls and the furniture, "With Hitler and the brown shirts, is very hard. I am not Aryan type. The brown shirts attack me much; they think I am Gypsy," he hesitated, "or Jew."

Gunther was fleeing his country because of his background. We had a lot in common. He looked at his watch and then abruptly gulped down his schnapps and stood up. Tears rolled down his cheeks. I didn't bother to ask him what his "other half" was; whatever it was made him a marked man.

"Sorry for tears, sir, but I forget what is like to be human being," he said. "Thank you very much. Herr Brown, be careful in the streets. The brown shirts attack foreigners like hyenas."

"I want to ask you a favor, Gunther. I might have to leave Berlin very quickly…"

He looked wary again. "Are you spy for America, maybe?"

"No. I'm trying to help a friend in trouble. I might have to check out quickly without being seen with my luggage. So, after I pick up my passport tomorrow morning, I'm going to leave my suitcases packed in the closet. If I don't come back for them, an American friend will ask you for my suitcases on the way into the hotel, settle my bill, and tell the concierge I'll be back for my luggage later. I'd like you to have my suitcases waiting in back of the hotel for him so that he can pick them up without making the concierge suspicious.

"Is very dangerous. The concierge is strong Nazi. I cannot afford to have trouble; I lose my job. Maybe my life."

I doled out another big tip. The money calmed him down somewhat. I lied to cool him down some more. "Don't worry, Gunther, you may not even have to do anything, but I have to be prepared for the worst. And I'll see to it that you get a visa from the American embassy to visit your cousin in New York. Real soon."

That made him decide to take the risk. I hadn't contacted Jean's journalist friend Skip Oatman yet, but I hoped that he could spirit my luggage away from the hotel and deliver on the promised visa to boot. Gunther gave me a brave smile and slipped out the door.

I was acting on pure instinct, like a fox digging a hidey-hole in case all hell breaks loose with the hounds. Being in Berlin with the brown shirts roaming in packs was honing my instincts for survival.

Gunther was so jumpy that I didn't even bother to ask him if there were places where non-Aryans, like Baby Langston and the swarthy Corsicans, could go without fear of physical assault. I seriously doubted now that they were anywhere near Daphne.

It was eleven at night, but I put through a call to the colonel's number, without letting the concierge know who I was phoning. If the colonel was a friend of Stanley's, I reckoned that he must be a night owl, too. I grabbed the receiver from the concierge before he could hear the colonel answer, "Schulz-Horn."

"Sorry to call so late…"

"Is that Urby Brown?"

"Yes," I replied.

"Stanley told me that you would telephone me. Please take a taxi to the Hotel Adlon. I will be at a corner table in the American Bar, in a black leather coat and a Tyrolean hat. You know the hat style?" The man spoke English with a slight accent.

"Yes. I'm on my way."

"Be careful in the streets. Even around the great hotels, the SA prey on foreigners."

Gunther flagged down a taxi, gave the driver the address and I settled back in my seat looking out the window. More red and black swastika banners and ones with black bears on them hung from flagpoles, lampposts, and balconies. Suddenly, I watched in horror as a gang of brown-shirted troopers sledge-hammered the windows of a shop while others painted a Star of David and the word JUDEN over its front door. A blood-covered old man and woman scrambled about on their knees as the brown shirts rained kicks down on them with their heavy jack boots. It didn't look like the troopers would stop until they'd stomped them into a bloody pulp. I was glad that I hadn't brought my Colt; my fingers itched to pour lead into the jack-booted killers, who reminded me of the Count's Oriflamme thugs. None of the passersby looked at the couple on the killing ground.

I caught the driver staring at me in the rearview mirror.

"Iz nice place, Germany, ja?" he said, enjoying my horror.

CHAPTER 20

Berlin, Thursday-Friday, February 15-16, 1934

Just before midnight, I walked into the dimly lit American Bar and scanned the corners looking for Colonel Schulz-Horn. I saw a Tyrolean hat and a leather trench coat framing a pale white face in the darkest corner, and I walked toward it. As I edged closer to the table, a soft voice, unlike the one I had heard on the telephone, called out, "Herr Brown, over here please."

I sat down, and the man took off his Tyrolean hat, exposing a shaved head. He had a nasty-looking dueling scar on his left cheek, which made him look fierce, until he smiled. There were two full snifters on the table. He raised his and said, "Prost!" The schnapps had more bite to it than Gunther's.

Seeing Colonel Schulz-Horn in civilian clothes almost made me forget that he was one of the most decorated German officers of the war, feared—but respected—by all who fought him.

"Nice to meet you, Colonel," I said. "I was at Belloy-en-Santerre in the Somme in 1916 with the French Foreign Legion."

"I know, Mr. Brown. Stanley admires you for your war service." He barked a laugh and then went on. "Stanley said to me that you're the toughest Creole on earth."

"That distinction belongs to Stanley, Colonel."

He sipped at his schnapps and said, "The battle of Belloy-en-Santerre. A monument to the true stupidity of war. We Germans lost miserably and managed to kill an American poet in the French Foreign Legion, your Alan Seeger." He paused, then he said something about having a rendezvous with death or debt or something that sounded like that and knocked back more schnapps. He looked real emotional anyway.

"Stanley told me you play great jazz piano," I said. "Must be rare for a German officer these days."

"You may be surprised, but you have admirers among my officer friends, an Urby Brown fan club, so to speak. We used to sneak off to your nightclub in mufti or in disguise. We heard you play with Stanley, Louis Armstrong and other greats."

"Isn't jazz illegal here? I thought Hitler banned it as—"

"A Jewish-Negro conspiracy against Aryan racial purity," he said, completing the dictum. "We're not all little Hitlers," he continued. "Ja, my group of officer friends sits through Lohengrin and screams 'Bravo' at the finale with the other super patriots. But, we prefer Armstrong, Stanley Bontemps, and"—he raised his snifter—"Urby Brown with our schnapps."

Except for the two of us and the bartender, the bar was empty. Still, I had the feeling that we were being spied on. The colonel read my thoughts.

"You are right to be careful in this madhouse," Schulz-Horn whispered. "Stanley said that you are looking for Corsican bandits, a big black American poet, and a rich and fair Aryan American maiden, if I may paraphrase him."

"That about sums it up," I said.

"I have checked with some trusted friends in the Abwehr, our intelligence agency, and there is no trace of any large black American poet, such as described by Stanley, in Berlin, or indeed in Germany. That is formal."

Schulz-Horn's words confirmed my suspicions. Regardless of what Daphne said in her note, Baby wasn't likely to be involved in any ransom scheme, except out of loyalty to his Uncle Hambone. That only left the Corsicans holding Daphne in Berlin.

As if reading my thoughts, he said, "There are no recent arrivals of gaudily dressed Corsican bandits either. The only noteworthy arrival that definitely interests you is of a certain Miss Daphne Robinson. She stayed at this very hotel Monday and Tuesday night in its most luxurious suite. Her hotel bill was paid for by General Count René D'Uribé-Lebrun." He stopped and looked at me expectantly. He could see that I was surprised. He continued, "She was driven here from Paris by some puppets of our Deputy Führer and number three leader, Rudolf Hess, whom he has placed in our Paris embassy. She was chaperoned by Elsa Herbst, the head of the household of our beloved number two man, the war hero and one-man band, Hermann Goering.

"Where's Daphne now?"

"First, let me tell you that she created a sensation at a reception at the Chancellery last night. The gossip is that Hitler is smitten with her, but there is always such talk when our leader meets a nubile blonde Aryan maiden. It is the Nazi dream that Hitler will marry such a one and found a new dynasty to begin the 'Thousand Year Reich.' I'm afraid that your Daphne Robinson will have to stand in a lengthening queue. I trust that she has not come to Germany under the illusion that she will be Hitler's 'Chosen One' right away?"

"I doubt it," I said. I remembered how we had been together at LaPérouse. She wanted me, not Hitler, I was sure of that. Or else she was as great an actress as Sarah Bernhardt.

The colonel sipped more schnapps and said, "I have a secret to tell you that has been very closely guarded by the Abwehr. Daphne Robinson is not really a Robinson. She's a Hohenzollern, the illegitimate daughter of Kaiser Wilhelm II by her so-called grandmother, who is, in fact, her mother. Her so-called father— Stanley said you call him 'Robinson III'—is in fact, I think you say, her 'half-brother.'" Jean Fletcher's "sources" had been right again.

"I'm sorry to tell you, Colonel, but that secret's leaked out from your Abwehr. An American journalist in Paris told it to me." It was his turn to look astonished.

"Scheisse!" he said. I understood what he meant.

"Do you think that Daphne suspects it? I mean, that her father's her half-brother?" I asked.

Schulz-Horn laughed.

"That would be too straightforward, Mr. Brown. I don't believe that she could even imagine it. Hitler himself does not know it, at this juncture. But Robinson III has known it from the beginning and has helped his mother play a cruel masquerade. He and his—and Daphne's—mother have kept it secret from her husband. Otherwise, he would have divorced her. At least, that is what Daphne's mother claimed when she threw herself on the mercy of the Kaiser."

"Where's Daphne now?" I repeated. "I have to take her back to her father…her brother…to finish with this business. Then, I'm through as a private investigator. It's back to music for me. Stanley and I plan to reopen Urby's Masked Ball."

Schulz-Horn clapped his hands.

"Tell me when and I'll be there. I miss the old 'Urby's.'" Then he remembered my question and went on, "Daphne Hohenzollern is staying in Goering's residence, at the personal request of Herr Hitler, while he ponders whether to add her to the roster of finalists in the 'Bride of Hitler' sweepstakes. That means that the girl is under the great Goering's thumb. He can make or break her because his house führerin, Elsa Herbst, attended to Daphne's birth in the Kaiser's private clinic in Bavaria. She knows that the Kaiser fathered her." The colonel fiddled with the feather on his Tyrolean hat before going on. "Lance Corporal Hitler has a deep hatred of the Hohenzollerns, especially Kaiser Wilhelm II, whom he blames, along with the Jews, for Germany's defeat and most of Germany's current ills. If Goering lets slip that the girl is the Kaiser's daughter, she may be in great danger."

"How can I get her back to France? Fast?"

"It won't be easy, but I have a plan. It's dangerous and, if it fails, Goering and Hitler's revenge will be terrible."

"Colonel, I'm being paid good money to bring Daphne out of Germany. Thank you for offering to help, but…"

He stopped me with a wave of his hand.

"I promised Stanley that I would help you. I owe it to him. It's a long story that I will tell you some other time. But I must help you…there is only one way to save the girl and, unfortunately, it involves danger. I and my men understand that; we are soldiers. Let us say no more about it, please."

"Does Daphne's…brother know how much danger she's in?"

"Deep down, he is a great admirer of all things German, and there are many Abwehr files documenting his…cooperation…over the years. I don't believe he knows the full extent of Hitler's hatred of all things Hohenzollern."

"He would still have had to send me to bring Daphne back because he knows that his father will cut him loose if he sets foot here."

Schulz-Horn chuckled, as if at some private joke.

"What Papa Robinson doesn't know is that his son doesn't have to set foot in Germany. He has direct access to a man named Himmler who is the head of the SS, which is even more powerful than the Abwehr. He just has to go into the German consulate in New York to contact Himmler by coded telegraph. Mr. Brown, I believe that this so-called kidnapping of Miss Daphne Hohenzollern is the work of amateurs. Judging from what my sources told me about her behavior at the reception, she threw herself at the Führer as if she were on a mission to kidnap *him*. I think that the girl might be behind her own kidnapping, to extract money from her brother to pursue a fantasy of becoming Hitler's bride."

"Daphne isn't like that," I said.

Schulz-Horn said simply, "My information is that she is not being held here against her will. She was brought here by Elsa Herbst and two of Rudolf Hess's stooges, not by any black or Corsican men or other figments of her imagination. So she has been lying, which speaks for itself."

I chewed on that for a while. If Schulz-Horn was right, it threw a monkey wrench into my theories about who had masterminded Daphne's kidnapping.

"Why is Robinson in bed with the Nazis?" I asked, wondering, for the first time, if he could be involved in Daphne's kidnapping. Jean Fletcher had passed on information about his Nazi ties culled from her "sources," but I knew that Schulz-Horn would give me hard facts.

"When he met Hitler, together with his mother and Daphne at the end of the 1920s, there was a mutual 'coup-de-foudre' between him and Hitler. Hitler is attracted to his financial wizardry, even his Aryan looks, I suppose. Hitler may even, as you say, 'have a crush' on him. Anyway he once promised him that, when America falls from the tree, like a rotten apple, he will make Robinson the leader of the United States. Of course, Robinson likes the idea. He knows he has no chance of being elected president, but being appointed Führer by the Führer of Führers? Robinson craves power more than money, like so many rich men."

I was astonished at the colonel's wild-sounding claims and at his having access to such information.

"You are wondering if I am the head of the Abwehr, not so?"

"Something like that," I answered.

"If I told you, I would have to kill you."

I stared at him hard and we both laughed.

"Trust me," he said. "I know what I'm talking about."

"Colonel, from what little I've seen of Germany, it's not near as developed as America was when I left there in 1914. I don't see Hitler setting up an American Führer anytime soon."

Schulz-Horn clapped his hands, and a waiter came over to take his order for two more snifters of schnapps. Schulz-Horn leaned forward and whispered to me, "You're going to need another drink before you hear what I am going to tell you." The drinks came, and I knocked back some schnapps and waited for him to go on.

"A very persistent rumor has it that the SS leader Himmler and Robinson and Goebbels, the propaganda chief, have hatched a plot to foment an uprising of the blacks in the United States, which, of course, will be crushed by your police and, if necessary, your armed forces."

"They're lunatics if that's their plot," I said.

"Crazier things have happened," he replied. "After all, who would have believed that a failed Austrian Katzenjammer Kid would now be Reichskanzler of Germany?"

I lifted my glass. "Touché," I said.

"My sources claim that top Nazi leaders are convinced that, with the right financing and training by Nazi agents, the blacks could sustain a guerrilla war and force martial law to be imposed in America for a long time. This would stretch your armed forces and buy Germany time to make military alliances with countries like Japan, Italy, and, why not Russia and France? Once Germany has isolated the United States with an angry black guerrilla presence inside it—armed, trained, and commanded by Nazi secret agents—England will fall from the tree into our basket like a golden apple, and then we complete the conquest of Europe." Schulz-Horn looked horrified by that outcome.

"Then we enslave resources—rich lands in Asia, Africa, and elsewhere—which supply us and our allies with raw materials to build our planes and tanks with petrol to fuel them and with foodstuffs to feed our armies. Then we launch an all-out attack on the American mainland. As we speak, Goering is building up Hitler's praetorian guard, the Gestapo and, worst of all, a mighty air force, the Luftwaffe." His face reddened and he whispered urgently, "Hitler intends to wage total world war, Mr. Brown, as soon as he strangles the real Germany. It will make the last one seem like hopscotch games played during a school recess."

I was stunned at the madness of the plot. The idea of the Nazis getting colored Americans, despite Jim Crow and other sufferings inflicted on us, to take up arms against the United States was too crazy to be believed. But then, I had been away for a long time.

As Schulz-Horn talked on, the craziness of the plot did not bowl me over as much as the thought that Daphne, and her brother, might have staged her kidnapping. That slammed into my head like a blackjack.

"There's one more thing that my Abwehr friends have divulged to me as a 'rumor' to pay attention to," Schulz-Horn continued. "The story goes that there is an agent in the United States named Bruno Richard Hauptmann who, with the assistance of your Barnet Robinson III, is to channel funds to and lead the black uprising that I have described. Have you heard of the baby Lindbergh kidnapping and murder?"

I recalled my conversations with Jean and Robinson. "Yes."

"You know that Lindbergh has shown much sympathy for Germany."

"A friend has told me that, yes."

"The rumor has it that the kidnapping and murder of baby Lindbergh are a warning shot across Lindbergh's bows from the Abwehr. He must show support for the Nazi cause or his wife, Anne Morrow Lindbergh, will die next. The Abwehr and some prominent Nazi supporters in America had wanted Lindbergh to become an active opponent of Roosevelt, even a Presidential candidate in 1936. But Robinson III told the Abwehr that, a year ago, America amended its Constitution in a way to make Lindbergh too young to be eligible in 1936…by 15 days, I was told. So their aim now is for Lindbergh to be elected President in 1940. By which time Hitler's armies will be marching through Europe and Lindbergh will be using your armed forces to crush the black rebellion and round up American and foreign Jews. After President Lindbergh's programmed assassination, his Vice-President, Robinson III, becomes

Führer of the USA. I admit it must all sound crazy to you, but there are some crazy people running Germany now."

"I know that Barnet Robinson and Lindbergh are neighbors in New Jersey, near Princeton."

"Rumors from very high places indicate that Barnet Robinson was instrumental in financing the 'ransom' paid to Hauptmann and that Hauptmann killed baby Lindbergh on direct orders from the Abwehr. Robinson helped to finance the ransom because Himmler ordered him to do it."

"Barnet Robinson's making no secret of his role in funding the ransom," I said. "And I still don't see what the Abwehr stands to gain by having one of its agents murder the baby."

"As I said, it's to make Lindbergh toe the line. Have some more schnapps, Mr. Brown. Now, I will give you the 'pièce de résistance.'"

I finished my schnapps and waited.

"The key to the plot is that the Abwehr and Robinson are searching for a black man to be charged with the kidnapping and murder of the Lindbergh baby to fan the hatred already directed against black people. They also want to avoid the kind of hostility that Germany would face were Hauptmann's and the Abwehr's rumored role in the affair to come to light."

Having escaped from the race war already directed against colored people in the South, I knew that the Klan and its sympathizers would have a field day if Baby Lindbergh's murderer turned out to be colored.

Schulz-Horn said, "Robinson helped Lindbergh to pay the ransom with US gold dollar certificates, which the Abwehr had amassed to finance the black uprising. Then Roosevelt came along and made it illegal to hold such certificates." He smiled and continued, "I understand from Stanley that Robinson has paid you a part of your private investigator fees in gold dollar certificates and that you have turned them over to Stanley for safekeeping. I told Stanley to burn them right away. They have all been marked, and you could end up as the perfect scapegoat that the Nazis and their supporters, like Barnet Robinson, have been looking for."

He smiled, and the full enormity of the trap that I had nearly walked into walloped me in the face like a knockout blow from a bunch of Jack Johnsons reflected in a funhouse mirror. By nailing me, Robinson and the Abwehr would be tossing J. Edgar Hoover and the yellow press the perfect scapegoat: a part-colored jazz musician who consorts with white women and kills the baby of an all-American Aryan hero. Unless Robinson III and his buddies had originally stuffed some gold certificates in the ransom satchel and intended to make Buster the patsy all along.

Schulz-Horn studied my face and put his hand on my shoulder and said, "Well?"

"Colonel, I sure would appreciate hearing how you plan to smuggle Daphne out of Germany," I said.

"Here it is. Conveniently for us, one of my most trusted Regular Army, Reichswehr, officers is going to get married next week, and our circle of sworn 'blood brothers' and jazz lovers is going to throw a bachelor party for him Friday night, in Cologne. You and I are going to play at that party, and Daphne will be our guest. I will accompany you on piano, if you permit…"

"What if Daphne doesn't want to come along?" I asked.

"My informants at Goering's residence tell me that she's having second thoughts about her German adventure. Her fantasies of Nazi life involved a poetic, sensitive Adolf Hitler and not a swine like Goering who brings out the worst in everyone, even in a madman like Hitler. I think that if she cares for you as much as Stanley says, she will leave with you. If she resists, we have other means to bring her to Cologne as an unwilling guest. From Cologne, we can get you both safely into France."

"I'm with you, Colonel."

It was past midnight and Friday had already begun. I was excited that I'd have the chance to take Daphne back to France and settle up accounts with her, with Robinson III, and with the Count because I was growing more and more certain that they were in it together.

Schulz-Horn said, "I want you to write out a note asking her to meet you at the Tiergarten Zoo tomorrow at noon in front of the sign to the wild felines' cages. We will have a car nearby. You will meet her there and reason with her. If she won't leave with you, we will snatch her then and there and head for Cologne." He passed me a gold-colored Parker fountain pen, and I wrote down the words that he dictated on a piece of Hotel Adlon notepaper. He took the note from me, put it inside an envelope from the hotel, and stuffed it into the pocket of his trench coat.

"You will snatch her in broad daylight if she resists?" I asked, doubtfully.

He smiled. "Nothing is impossible for the Reichswehr." Schulz-Horn stood up and put his Tyrolean hat back on. He was of medium height, half a foot shorter than I was. He was a few years older than me. But there was something forceful and athletic in the way he held himself, and he had a natural air of command. He was not a man I would like to tangle with.

"I have a car waiting outside," he said. "I'll drop you off at the Universal. Try to get some sleep. Tomorrow..."—he looked at his watch—"today is going to be a very long and busy day for us."

I reckoned that neither of us would sleep much.

"I'm going to phone somebody to deliver my luggage to where we're meeting Daphne. I don't think it's a good idea to go back to that hotel after we pick her up. I'm sure I'm being watched."

"Good idea," he said. "Daphne might not want to go back to stay under that swine Goering's roof for another second. If she goes with us, she won't have a chance to go back for her luggage. I'll have my friends pick up some necessaries for her."

Back in my hotel room, I packed my suitcases. On the way there, I told Gunther to deliver my suitcases to the friend I had told him about at eleven sharp. The friend was willing to help to arrange Gunther's visa to America but wanted to look him over first before going to see the American Ambassador Dodd. I gave Gunther two hundred dollars and told him to start packing his own suitcases, in case he had to leave for America at a moment's notice.

Gunther was excited at having the American money and the chance of escape that I was offering him. I was hoping that Jean's friend or one of her acquaintances in the American diplomatic community could make Gunther's dreams come true.

Gunther told me not to worry; he would deliver my luggage to my friend at 11:00 a.m. I told Gunther to knock on my door at 8:00 a.m. to wake me up.

My plans in place, I slept soundly, until Gunther's insistent knocking on the door woke me up.

CHAPTER 21

Berlin, Friday morning, February 16, 1934

An hour later, at nine in the morning, I retrieved my passport and put in a phone call to Jean Fletcher's journalist friend, Skip Oatman. He had his own car, much to my relief, and I asked him to turn up at the Universal at 11:00 a.m. to pick up my luggage and settle my hotel bill. He was to tell the desk clerk that I had been called away on an urgent mission.

I told Oatman to look for a sallow-faced youngster named Gunther and to mention my name to him. Gunther would handle putting my luggage into his car at the hotel's rear entrance. I told him where to meet me at the Tiergarten with my bags; he knew the place. When I said goodbye to Oatman, I gave him a rundown on Gunther's situation and asked him if his American embassy contacts could get Gunther an emergency visa. Oatman sounded pretty sure that he could pull it off by calling in a favor from the ambassador's daughter, Martha Dodd.

Minister Hermann Goering had already made advances to Daphne twice since the Führer had ordered him, immediately after the reception at the Chancellery on Wednesday evening, to lodge her in his residence until further notice. Daphne was certain that a spark had passed between her and the Führer, and she had thought that being placed under the "personal protection" of his Minister Goering meant that he favored her over the others and that a marriage proposal was imminent.

Some "personal protection," Daphne reflected bitterly. Goering had shown her to her lavish bedroom, closed the door, and proceeded to slice her evening gown to shreds with his enormous hunting knife. He then stared at her contemptuously and locked her in her room, demanding that "the next time" she should show him more respect and affection. He warned her that, otherwise, it would not go well between her and the Führer. He threatened to tell him "all." When she had asked what he meant he laughed and waddled out of the room, his hips wide and old-maidish like Elsa's.

Daphne was depressed afterward. She had dreamed of a pure Germany led by a mystical, poetic Führer who loved her and would father her children and invest her with power. Instead, she had been bullied and browbeaten by Hitler's right-hand man, who was more uncouth even than Buster and certainly not of the caliber of Urby Brown. She wondered why Urby had not arrived in response to her SOS message to her father—and the Count—where she mentioned that *Buster* was holding her in Berlin.

She had slipped Buster's name in so that Urby would realize she was not playing games. It was a threat that if he did not come quickly, she would tell all to the Count, who would then probably set his men on Urby or go to the police. She did not want that to happen, but she needed Urby more than ever now that Goering had turned out to be a monster and seemed to want her for himself alone.

Out of desperation, Daphne decided to ask his sow-like Elsa to pass a message to the Count's friend Rudolf Hess, asking him to arrange an interview with Chancellor Hitler for as early as possible on Friday.

She had given the message to Elsa yesterday evening, Thursday, at eight o'clock. Three hours later, she was awakened by the pig Goering screaming at her and threatening her with physical violence unless she was nice to him. She pretended to go along with him, kissing his hand and begging him to give her a little more time and she turned her tears on full blast. She planted a kiss on his perfumed cheek and he grunted with satisfaction when he left her, muttering that he would see about arranging an interview with the Führer now that she was "cooperating."

Daphne realized that Elsa Herbst was devoted to her master and that no help would come from that quarter. As she lay tossing and turning in her bed, well past midnight, afraid that the next morning might bring another assault from Goering, there was a knock on the door. Daphne saw that a note had been slid under it. She opened it; it was written on Hotel Adlon notepaper. To her delight, it was from Urby Brown. He asked her to meet him at the sign to the wild felines' cages at the Tiergarten at noon on Friday, in exactly eleven hours.

Her heart raced. She was sure that Urby would rescue her and that he would make love to her in his room at the Hotel Adlon, with champagne and caviar, just as at La Pérouse Restaurant. That would drown out her nightmare stay under Hermann Goering's "protection." Just knowing that Urby was in Berlin calmed her fears.

Things had turned out so disastrously that Daphne was considering the abandonment of her German dream to return to New Jersey with her father. Urby would help her to decide by finding a way for her to escape from Hermann Goering.

Goering's morning visit did not happen. Elsa explained that he had a meeting with the Führer that would last all morning. But, she said, smiling demurely, Prime Minister of Prussia Goering had instructed her to put some Liebfrauenmilch wine on ice for a "tête-à-tête luncheon for two." Elsa's words nauseated Daphne, and her skin crawled at the thought of being in Goering's presence again and having to show him more affection.

At 11:00 a.m., Daphne told Fraülein Elsa Herbst that she wished to go out for a walk by herself, and the woman actually tried to stop her by force. Finally, Daphne picked up one of Goering's marble busts of himself from the piano top and menaced Elsa with it. When she left to go outside, Elsa followed her, walking with her waddling stride that was just like her master's.

Fraülein Herbst matched her stride for stride for the first three minutes, with Daphne walking faster and faster and Elsa barely keeping up, with her fat legs pumping like pistons and her breathing increasingly stertorous. She pleaded with Daphne to slow down.

When they turned the corner into a busy street, Daphne, the best white female sprinter in New Jersey, dashed away, leaving the woman far behind, weeping in frustration. Daphne flagged down a passing taxi and headed for the Berlin Zoo in the Tiergarten.

Having arrived early, Daphne sat down on a bench near the sign for the wild felines' cages. She was still very warm and excited from her narrow escape from Elsa Herbst and her emotions were running wild. She would laugh hysterically when she remembered looking back and seeing the bitch waddling faster and faster behind her, oinking at her to stop for the love of God.

Daphne's sprint had also got her sexual urges flaring up, and she was hoping that Urby and she could take a fast taxi to his hotel and make love for the rest of the afternoon.

She had decided that, as a last try at her dream, she would telephone Rudolf Hess from Urby's room and ask him to arrange an appointment with the Führer. If Hess refused or she felt that he was using delaying tactics, she would ask Urby to take her back to France. Whatever happened, she had no intention of returning to Hermann Goering's "personal protection."

Daphne knew that Urby would have a lot of questions to ask about the kidnapping, but she would make them wait until after they made love and she had him in her power. She had questions to ask him, too. She had arranged for her own kidnapping, but why were she and Buster abducted from La Belle Princesse before they could set their scheme in motion? That had not been part of her plan. Was the owner of La Belle Princesse, or the jazz musician, Stanley Bontemps, involved in the abduction?

Daphne was not afraid to tell Urby that she had planned her own kidnapping to get away from her father. And he would have to keep the story to himself because she knew that he had killed Buster, and he certainly did not want the Count to know that. There was also the problem of the man they called Baby Langston, but only he, in his last instants of consciousness, knew that she had killed him. Buster would take the fall for the killing; Urby would not dare to gainsay that.

At noon, my black Mercedes-Benz limousine stopped near the sign to the wild felines' cages. The windows were tinted, and I couldn't see out until I rolled down the window. A car pulled up behind us, and its driver opened the trunk, lifted out two suitcases, and placed them on the sidewalk. I stepped out of the Mercedes, shook Skip Oatman's hand, and the driver of my car, who wore a German officer's uniform, helped me put the suitcases into its trunk. Oatman drove off, refusing to be repaid for covering my hotel bill.

Daphne ran to me then. I could feel her heart pounding against my chest, and she clung to me, sucking me in.

"Please take me to your room, Urby." The Mercedes-Benz raced away from the Tiergarten as we held each other in the backseat of the car, an opaque window separating us from the driver.

"Daphne," I said. "I have only one chance of getting you out of Germany. Do you want to stay or go back to France? You have to decide now. I'm not going back to my room. I've checked out of my hotel;the concierge has probably already reported it."

"Let's get the hell out of here and back to France, Urby," she said. She tapped on the thick, opaque window separating us from the driver.

"Can he hear or see us through this thing?" she asked, her violet-blue eye sparkling,the other one covered by the wave of white-blonde hair. She put her hand on my thigh and squeezed it.

I said, "No, this is a general's limousine. We are bullet-proof, invisible, and sound-proof. If you want to speak to the driver, you use this thing." I picked up a kind of telephone receiver, pressed a button, and said, "To Cologne, as agreed." I told Daphne, "It's going to be a long drive, but they won't search for me in this car."

I had just flicked the phone off when Daphne kissed me hard and then settled cozily into my arms. She probably felt safe for the first time in days, so she fell asleep, a smile on her face. I watched her and then looked out to watch Germany racing by outside my window. I hummed riffs to myself, which I recognized were my own.

CHAPTER 22

Cologne, Germany, Friday evening, February 16, 1934

At a few minutes past eight o'clock in the evening, five German officers in tuxedos, and Daphne, were in the Blaue Ecke private club in Cologne, drinking champagne and listening to Colonel Schulz-Horn's piano improvisations on the Gershwins' tune, "The Lorelei." Playing a borrowed clarinet, I blew melodious backing riffs, and the colonel and I smiled at each other, enjoying the music we were making together and the applause of the officers at our back and forth.

Daphne, who was wearing a long, yellow silk evening gown with matching long gloves and a string of emeralds around her neck, had edged close to the piano and put a gloved hand on it. She picked up a microphone with her other hand and started singing, her voice sounding exactly like Billie Holiday's on "Riffin' the Scotch," the record Stanley had given me for Christmas.

When she paused, the men all leapt to their feet. "Noch einmal!" the officers shouted.

But Schulz-Horn and I, mesmerized by the beauty of her voice and phrasing, stopped playing and stared at her. Mimicking Buster's accent, she reddened with anger and spat out, "Buster told me over and over:

'girl, you got to learn to sing like a woman who loves her man, else I be gone.'"

We heard the sound of a motorcycle outside, and an officer tapped the signal on the door and was let in. He saluted Schulz-Horn and said, "Colonel, our travelers must leave now, as arranged."

The officers went into the dressing room and came back out a few minutes later, having swapped their tuxedos for military uniforms. One was wearing a German general's tunic and hat, and the others were dressed as his chauffeur and four outriders. They formed up around Daphne and me and were about to escort us out of the club when the telephone rang. Colonel Schulz-Horn answered it, listened, and said, "Ja, ja" with a grave expression on his face. Then he hung up.

"We'll wait, just for a few minutes. A friend is bringing Goebbels's *Nacht Angriff* newspaper for this evening." We heard a loud knock and footsteps running away. The colonel went to the door and came back, looking at the headlines, which he held up to the group. There was a photograph of Daphne on the front page. She looked at it and shrank back, horrified.

"This is very bad," Schulz-Horn said calmly. The headline says, 'Spy Plot of American Mata Hari unearthed by Prime Minister of Prussia, Hermann Goering.'" He spoke in a low, steady voice. "It tells Elsa Herbst's story of a young American woman who had introduced herself into the Goering residence as 'Daphne Robinson' after Chancellor Hitler's reception on Wednesday night." The colonel read from the newspaper again. "Fraülein Herbst then remembered where she had heard the name before; she had been present at the birth of a baby girl so named in 1913 when she was a nurse at Kaiser Wilhelm II's private clinic in Bavaria. The baby was the illegitimate daughter of Kaiser Wilhelm II and, thus, a Hohenzollern. She had aroused Elsa's and Minister Goering's suspicions by her constant attempts to see the Führer alone. It seems that the girl wished to assassinate the Führer, like a modern-day Charlotte Corday, no doubt a spy acting under the express instructions of the Jew Franklin Roosevelt and his Washington cabal of Jews and Negroes. All forces of order have been mobilized to capture the American Mata Hari before she escapes from the Führer's righteous wrath."

As he read out the article, Daphne went pale, and she fell to the floor, weeping, as if her whole world had been ripped apart. I ran to her and held her in my arms. She was trembling so badly that I could hardly hold onto her.

"But I *am* Daphne Robinson," she cried. Then a sudden realization seemed to come over her, and she looked first at me and then at Schulz-Horn.

"That awful Herbst woman kept calling me 'Ihre Hoheit,' Your Highness. This is all Goering's doing. The man assaulted me and he's trying to deflect blame from himself."

"Assaulted you?" Schulz-Horn thundered. "The swine!" I helped Daphne get to her feet, trying to steady her and keep her from falling again. Her heartrending sobs gripped all of us.

"It must all be lies," she wailed.

"No, my dear, I'm sorry to say it, but it's the truth," Schulz-Horn said. "You are the daughter of Kaiser Wilhelm II and a Hohenzollern. You were born in a private clinic in Bavaria. The records exist, I have seen them with my own eyes."

"But what about my mother? She died in the torpedoing of the *Lusitania* with her parents when I was a baby. And father?"

"He is, in fact, your half-brother. You have the same mother."

Startled, she said, "You mean grandmother's my *mother*?"

"I'm afraid so," he said. "You are the victim of a cruel masquerade." Daphne crumpled into my arms and wept as if she were going to go crazy.

"We must change our plans," one of the officers said. "The Fraülein and Herr Brown cannot leave by train."

"No, Georg," Schulz-Horn agreed. "They must leave Cologne under escort, and then two of the outriders will take them across the French border on motorcycles at a point where it is rarely guarded. I suggest that you head for Metz, going through Luxemburg. From there, Mr. Brown, I expect that you have friends who will help you get to Paris with Fraülein… Hohenzollern."

"We can make it," I said. "If you can get us to Metz, I'll have Mr. Robinson—"

"No!" Daphne shouted. "I refuse to see him until I've had a chance to think things through!"

"We'll find a hotel in Metz and stay there until you're ready to go to Paris, all right?" I asked. Daphne nodded her agreement, and the colonel's men sprang into action. They escorted us to the limousine. Daphne and I climbed in, and Schulz-Horn tapped on the car's opaque window. I rolled it down, and he shook hands with me.

"Good luck," Schulz-Horn said. "Daphne, you are a gifted singer. Mr. Brown, it was an honor to play…"

"We'll do it again, at Urby's Masked Ball."

"What's that?" Daphne sniffled.

"My old nightclub in Montmartre. I'll tell you about it on the way to France," I said. The other officers shook my hand and bowed over Daphne's.

"Thank you for everything," one of them said to me. "I speak for all in saying that we will never forget this evening."

The limousine, flanked by the four outriders, sped off. As it passed through Cologne, I could see, in the light from burning bonfires of books, brown-shirted mobs smashing shop windows, daubing Stars of David and swastikas on shops, and stomping on people lying on the sidewalks.

Daphne shuddered and said, "I feel like I'm inside a nightmare." She lay her head on my shoulder, and she slept until we reached the French border. I woke Daphne up and we climbed onto two of the motorcycles. One of the officers handed me a knife, and I cut off the bottom of Daphne's silk evening gown and wrapped it around her shoulders like a shawl.

I smiled at her. "It's going to get chilly on the ride."

"Thank you," she said and kissed my palm. "I love you. Whatever happens, remember that."

"I'll remember," I said. Then we roared off into the darkness. The officers turned on their headlights briefly when we saw road signs on the border, and then we hurtled along the French road toward Metz in pitch darkness.

CHAPTER 23

Paris, Saturday, February 17, 1934

They left us and our luggage at the Hotel de la Poste in Metz, saluted, and then roared off back to Germany. We booked ourselves into a simple room under the name Mr. and Mrs. John James. It was well past midnight. The hotel's owner, Monsieur Félix, sat us down at the kitchen table, made us ham and cheese omelets, and plunked a baguette and a bottle of red wine before us. We were both starving, only having had time to gulp down a glass of champagne in Cologne before we escaped to France.

After finishing off the meal with some homemade pâtés, we took the rest of the bottle to our room.

"Dormez bien, mes enfants," Monsieur Félix said. He kissed Daphne on both cheeks and shook my hand until I thought that he would yank it off. Daphne had bowled him over; he looked at her as if she were an angel on divine visitation to his small hotel.

"We'll sleep well, thanks to you," I said. He winked knowingly, and Daphne and I climbed the steps to our room.

We sat on the bed, both of us drained by the events of the day—our narrow escape from the Nazis and the long rides in the car and on motorcycles. We sat in silence, drinking the last of the wine.

We should have gone to sleep then, but we both had an urge to clear things up.

"I guess we'd better talk," I said. "We won't have much time when we get back to Paris."

"All right. More wine? It's really good, isn't it?"

"That would be nice," I said. She gave me a long, lingering kiss, and then she walked over to the table. I had to have some answers to set my mind at rest, and she did, too, I felt.

I stared at the cheap chandelier hanging from the ceiling. It was covered in the grime of days and nights and years, like I was. Daphne looked clean and shining, like newly minted gold, but I suspected that she had an old soul, and that it was even more scarred and dirty than my own. I heard her coming back to the bed, and the look on my face drove the smile from hers. She sat down next to me. We clinked glasses.

"We're alive, at least," she said, tentatively.

"Why did you do it, Daphne?"

She feigned not to understand.

"Do what specifically? I've done so many bad things in the last ten days that you have to tell me which 'it' you mean."

"Let's start with the phony kidnapping. Why did you go through all that pretense that Buster had kidnapped you?"

"When Mr. Bontemps got in touch with Buster and said he wanted him to be his drummer at the charity concert last Saturday, he was happy at first. Then he started worrying if he would be good enough, and that got him back onto his drugs. Then he got angry at everybody, but mainly Count d'Uribé-Lebrun and Mr. Bontemps. He said they had kept him down, kept him from becoming a star like Louis Armstrong or Duke Ellington. He was really going off his rocker. Only the drugs kept him on it."

"So, he needed more cash to feed his habit. Was the idea of the kidnapping his or yours?"

"He said that we could fake a kidnapping and pin it on Stanley. I saw the chance to get away from my father…" She stopped and finished her glass of wine and got up shakily to get more. I could hear her trying to stop herself from crying. She came back to the bed and continued, "Get away from my brother. Urby, now that I know the story about my grandmother and the Kaiser and that he's my brother and she's my mother, I can understand some things I didn't before. When I got older..."—she hesitated—"and prettier, he would put his hands on me, and he started threatening to cut my allowance if I didn't let him feel me up. I was going crazy until I met Buster at a nightclub in Harlem on a date with a boy from Williams College. I was a virgin, and when Buster wasn't taking drugs he was good to me."

"How did you and Buster make it to France?"

"He told me that he had come into some money from France. He didn't tell me anything else for sure, but he hinted there was more money for the taking, so I figured he was blackmailing somebody. He said that he already had enough in hand for us to book passage on the Ile de France and live the good life in Paris for a while. I told my grandmother—" She stopped and went on, "Anyway, I told her that I wanted to see what was going on in Germany firsthand and visit our relatives there. We often talked politics; she convinced me that the Nazis were a good thing. I told her what her son was trying with me, and she was horrified. She promised to give me enough money to travel around Europe while she had it out with my...brother. I had to promise her that I would go to Germany and keep it secret from...her husband. Of course, I didn't tell her about Buster, and I didn't tell her that I planned to stay in Europe and not finish my degree at Smith. So, I had money of my own, and she promised to wire me more." Daphne searched my face to see how her story was going down with me. I didn't give anything away.

She continued, "Buster's money ran out quickly, and then he joined Count d'Uribé-Lebrun's bunch out of the blue. The Count paid Buster wages like his other Oriflamme troopers. But Buster ran through his money like it was water, and whenever he found money in my purse, he stole from me, too. Then Buster came up with the idea that I should send my brother a cable asking him to come to Paris to rescue me from him.

Once he was here, Buster figured that he could fake a kidnapping and get enough ransom money to 'hit the jackpot.' That's what he called it. He didn't stop to think that my brother would hire a private eye to track us down, Urby. Sorry."

"So, the fake kidnapping and ransom ploy was Buster's idea at first, and then you filled in all the blanks."

"That's right. Now it's my turn to ask you some questions. Who kidnapped Buster and me at La Belle Princesse when Buster and I came for the rehearsal? Was it the owner of the club, Hambone Gaylord?"

"No, it was Stanley's idea, and I went along with it. But it wasn't a kidnapping. When Barnet Robinson hired me to find you and Buster, he paid me in gold dollar certificates, and President Roosevelt had taken America off the gold standard. So, trying to use those gold dollars could have gotten me into big trouble," I paused, "in more ways than one. We were going to turn you over to your brother later the same day, if he coughed up what he owed me. In real money."

"So, you and Stanley were going to hold me and Buster for a few hours, teach my brother a lesson because he tried to cheat you, and then turn me over to him the same day? Before the charity concert? When you'd use another drummer?"

"Yeah. That's it, more or less."

Daphne rocked with laughter, spilling some of her wine on the bed.

"That's rich," she said. "You and Mr. Bontemps were going to make a monkey out of Buster. You never wanted him to be the drummer at the concert. Stanley did want to keep him down. Buster was right about that all along."

"Look, Daphne. Buster was once the best jazz drummer in Harlem. But the drugs took it all away. They changed him into Doctor Jekyll and Mister Hyde."

Daphne got up and filled our glasses again. I didn't like the sound of her laughter.

"You really use a lot of big words for an old jazzbo. 'Doctor Jekyll and Mister Hyde'? What were you, a lit major?" Daphne was beginning to turn nasty, for the first time since I met her. Her angel wings were slipping.

"I like to read, yes. I'm not just a dumb private eye. Or a dumb 'old jazzbo.' That's insulting, you know."

"You killed Buster," she suddenly hissed. "Then you and that woman Redtop deep-sixed him in the Seine."

There it was. Daphne had faked being unconscious at Stanley's stables.

"He had Redtop's shotgun pointed at her head. He was going to blow her brains out."

Daphne calmed down. "I know. I heard her thanking you. I'm sorry for shouting at you, Urby. I must be getting tired. It's been a long day. I'm sorry for the stupid things I've said." She kissed me on the cheek and laid her head against my shoulder.

"What happened to Baby Langston?" I asked. She sat up and the way she answered made me think she was lying; it was all too well rehearsed.

"I don't know. I must have fainted and, when I woke up, the Count and that man of his, Pierre, were there. They took me away, and I saw Pierre set fire to the stables. Maybe he was inside."

"He wasn't inside. I talked to a fireman and checked those burned stables myself. There was no sign of human remains."

Daphne shrugged her shoulders and drank some more wine. "You'll have to ask the Count, then. Sorry, but I can't help you."

"What happened to the ransom money? You dictated the ransom note, didn't you? The one in Buster's handwriting?"

"Guilty," she said. "The Count said that he would deal with what my brother passed to him to pay the ransom. He gave me money from his own funds to get to Germany."

"But you made him think that Buster was with you?"

"No, that was his idea to lead my brother on. He and his men were going to hunt for Buster in France."

"Was going to La Pérouse his idea, too?"

She looked uncomfortable and then smiled. "It was the Count's idea for us to have lunch there, yes, but what happened at La Pérouse was real. Making love to you was real. You're the first man who's made me come alive inside. Buster made me do things that I don't want to tell you about, that I don't even want to think about. But with you, what I felt was real. I meant it."

"Real enough for you to slip a Mickey Finn into my champagne?"

She looked shocked. "I don't know what you're talking about. You passed out and I couldn't wake you up. I panicked and rang for the waiter and gave him the Count's phone number. The next thing I knew, he had arrived and one of his men hustled me down the backstairs."

"And then he arranged for you to go to Germany. And to send another SOS to your brother, mentioning that Buster was holding you."

"Yes. I wanted my brother to send you after me, and the Count thought it was a good idea for you to be there to protect me. He was right, I guess." She smiled and kissed me again. "You saved me, Urby."

"Daphne, a friend of mine in Berlin told me that you wanted to be Hitler's bride. You were driven to Berlin by two men from the German embassy and Elsa Herbst." I noticed that Daphne shivered at the name. "My friend said that Hitler's a madman. You have everything—beauty, wealth, and, I discovered, a beautiful singing voice. You can do anything you want in America, become anything. Why Hitler? If you believe in all that Aryan racial stuff he spouts, what were you doing with Buster? Or me for that matter?"

"It all has to do with what my grand…my mother told me when I was growing up. Now I realize that she was awestruck by the fact that as a German princess by birth, she had not only had an affair with the Kaiser, but had a child by him. A little Hohenzollern for a daughter. A real German royal, echt Deutsch. I would be the mother of the 'Thousand Year Reich.' Now that I've seen it up close and been manhandled by that pig Goering, I don't want any part of my mother's Grimms' fairy tale."

"Daphne, I think it's time you went back to America. You'll have to work a lot of things out with your brother and your mother, and it won't be easy for you. I hate your brother for what he's done to you."

"He's messed you up, too," Daphne said.

"I'll get over it," I said. "He gave me a job to do; we made a contract and when I take you back to him, I'll have honored it. And paid a debt I owe to a friend from the war."

"What about us, Urby? I love you. What're we going to do?"

"I think that I love you, too, Daphne. Loving you has brought my music back. I want to play jazz again, and you made my hunger for it come back. But staying together wouldn't be good for either of us. I'm too old to keep up with you."

"In Cologne, you told the German colonel that you're going to re-open Urby's Masked Ball. Do you need a singer?"

We laughed at that, and she went on. "I'm afraid that you're right, though. I've had enough of Europe to last me for a while. I'll regret it forever, but I guess we're not going to stay together."

She picked up our empty glasses. "One last one. For the long road ahead to Paris? And after?" she asked.

I nodded and she filled our glasses, while I thought about how hard it was going to be to lose her. I took my glass and looked at her beautiful face again.

"Be happy, Daphne. You've got it all. Your brother can't boss you around anymore. You should talk to your grandfather. I mean, he's not really your grandfather but your brother's father. He'll straighten him out."

She suddenly smiled. "What a great idea!" she said triumphantly. We clinked glasses, undressed, kissed once more, and fell asleep naked in each other's arms.

I woke up and the wall clock showed it was 22:00 hours (10:00 p.m.). I'd been in a drugged sleep for over twenty hours. Daphne was gone. She'd lied to me about giving me the knockout drops at La Pérouse. I'd let my guard down, and she'd promptly slipped me another Mickey Finn. Feeling like the world's biggest sucker, I wondered what else she'd lied about.

Panicking, I threw on some clothes and rushed downstairs.

"Madame James took the 11:00 a.m. train to Paris this morning, Monsieur James," Mr. Félix said. "She told me that you were very tired and not to awaken you under any circumstances." He rummaged through some papers behind his front desk. "She left this note for you," he said, passing it to me. I read it, my head spinning:

> Darling, I wanted to wait for you, but you were sleeping so peacefully that I didn't want to disturb you. I'm going to the Ritz to have it out with my brother. Don't worry, I'll tell him that you brought me back alive from Germany. After the way he cheated you with those gold certificates, I'll make sure that he gives you a bonus that will be big enough for you to re-open Urby's Masked Ball and still not have to worry about money for a long time. I'll have your treasure trove delivered to Mr. Stanley Bontemps. If my brother balks at the amount I'm going to squeeze out of him, I'll tell his father what my big brother and my fake grandmother have been up to with Kaiser Bill. That will put the fear of God in him! (Smile).
>
> Try to forget us Robinsons and, especially, me. I love you with all my heart, but I don't deserve your love. Maybe our paths will cross again someday. Don't ever hate me, please. I couldn't bear it. Your Daphne (Hohenzollern?!).

Mr. Felix was watching me as I read the letter, a smile on my face.

"There will be another train to Paris tomorrow morning at eleven," Mr. Félix said.

"I'll be on it."

"Monsieur James is hungry, perhaps? I have a nice beefsteak in the icebox, and I can make you frites. Would that suffice?"

"It would more than suffice," I said. I gave Mr. Félix a hug, and he blushed with surprise.

"Vive La France," I said, overcome with happiness for the first time since I arrived in Le Havre nearly twenty years ago, as a boy about to face a world of killing and mayhem.

"Oh my," Mr. Félix blurted out. "This calls for something special for your apéritif. A little concoction of the late Mme. Félix." He scurried away and returned with a clear liqueur.

"It is my late wife's special plum eau-de-vie."

"Schnapps?" I asked.

"It is called that on the other side of the frontier. We are in France now. Let us just say, 'eau-de-vie.'"

Then I thought of something that might spoil Daphne's homecoming to Hopewell, New Jersey, if her "ex-grandfather," Robinson II, got wind of it. I had to know tonight, so I asked Mr. Félix, "Can I make a long-distance phone call to Berlin? It's urgent and concerns my wife, Mrs. James."

"Sans problème, Monsieur," he said. He rang through to the international operator himself, and I gave him Skip Oatman's telephone number.

When Oatman came on the line, I thanked him for his help and told him that we'd reached France safely. I asked him if there'd been any diplomatic incidents between America and Germany about the "Daphne Robinson affair" and summarized the article about Daphne in the *Nacht Angriff* propaganda rag.

"That's a dead story, Mr. Brown. It didn't even appear in any morning newspapers, and there's no word of it on the radio. That one's dead as a doornail. By the way, Martha Dodd told me that Ambassador Dodd will grant that emergency visa to America for your hotel porter pal, Gunther."

I thanked him again.

I reckoned that Robinson knew too much for the Nazis to attack Daphne or himself, maybe because he had insider knowledge of the Abwehr's rumored role in the kidnap-murder of Baby Lindbergh.

I was determined to stop Robinson III and his Nazi pals from dragging colored people into that kidnapping and making things a lot worse for us than they already were in America. When I got to Paris, I knew who would help me stop them in their tracks.

CHAPTER 24

Paris, Sunday, February 18, 1934

After I arrived back at my apartment from the Gare de l'Est, I first collected my mail; anyone snooping through it would conclude, correctly, that my private eye services were not highly in demand. The only case that had come my way recently had landed in my lap because of my friend Tex O'Toole. If Daphne had returned to her brother, as she said she would in the letter she left for me in Metz, I had just closed my last case, whatever happened.

I unlocked the door of my office on the way up to my apartment and checked that nothing had been moved in my absence. I was delighted to find that the electricity and the heating were working. I had paid my bills and back rent, thanks to Robinson III. Then I went upstairs to my apartment and stowed away the suitcases Robinson had lent me. I decided to unpack them afterward, since I had a lot to do in the afternoon.

I didn't know where to start—with Stanley, Robinson III, or by catching up on Paris gossip with Jean Fletcher and then giving her some big scoops as a repayment for her getting Skip Oatman to help me out in Berlin. There was also the Count. I decided to save him for last because I felt that he was, finally, one of the masterminds behind the whole affair, and I wanted to know his motives for sending me into the lion's den of Germany from which I had only narrowly escaped.

I didn't plan to go along with his making me his heir and giving me his name, even if it smoothed my path to French nationality. Still, I wondered at his methods for making a "son and friend" of me. Blum's *Le Populaire* had an article about Hitler and his followers being inspired by some German philosopher called Nietzsche who'd said, "Whatever doesn't kill us makes us stronger." Maybe the Count was using me to test whether this Nietzsche had it right.

I got off the metro at Concorde and walked to the Ritz.

Even on a wet Sunday in February, it was great to be back in Paris, breathing its air and its familiar scents as a free man after the horrors of Berlin and Cologne. It was a particularly peaceful Sunday, and things seemed to be calming down in Paris for the first time since February 6, which now seemed months, not weeks, ago.

I walked along the rue de Rivoli on the Tuileries garden side, looking through the railings to see families walking in peace in their finery and children running free and wild, playing games. People of every color and every religion filled the gardens. There were no brown shirts or black shirts attacking people who looked different, destroying Jewish-owned shops, painting swastikas on them, or burning books in the street. Paris felt even more like home to me than usual.

At the front desk of the Ritz Hotel, a man in a black suit, wearing a white shirt and a black bow-tie sat enthroned in the lobby like Louis XIV. I asked him to call Mr. Barnet Robinson and, without looking up, he said, "I am sorry, Monsieur, but Mr. Robinson left yesterday evening. I understand that he has returned to America."

That really knocked me for a loop.

"Could you tell me if he left alone? Was there a young lady with him, a very beautiful young lady?"

He rose up on his high horse and looked down his nose at me.

"You must appreciate, Monsieur, that I am not allowed to divulge…"

I reached into my pocket and laid a fifty franc note on his desk. The lobby was practically empty. The man looked around, passed his hand over the note, and it disappeared.

"Yes, Mr. Brown, he was accompanied by a beautiful, blonde young woman. Very beautiful, indeed. His daughter, I presume."

I thanked him and left; then the memory of smelling ammonia and waking up in Robinson's suite early last Tuesday morning made me remember how he knew my name.

Stanley answered the door and gave me a French-style hug.

"Welcome back, mon petit," he said, flashing me his biggest smile. "I known you safe, 'cause my man Colonel Schultz done phone to say his friends brung you and goldilocks back into France. I nearly had Red-top drive me up to Metz to fetch you," he said. He ushered me in, and I saw that Stanley had company.

A beautiful, chocolate brown-skinned woman sat in Stanley's favorite tiger skin-covered modern chair.

There was something familiar about her, but my mind didn't stop to take it in, I was so dazzled by the woman. She wore a lavender-colored dress and had a white magnolia in her hair. Her lips were painted to match her dress; the woman gave off heat like a Bessemer furnace.

"This be Urby Brown," Stanley said clumsily. "And Urby I wants to introduce you to Miss Magnolia Swilley; she be Baby Langston mama and Hambone sister."

She held out her hand and I shook it, although I felt that she expected me to kiss it.

"Pleased to meet you, Miss Swilley," I said. I went to remove my hand but she held onto it. She was strong and I couldn't break her grip. Stanley hovered behind her nervously, gesturing for me to sit down, until she turned around to glare at him.

"I got somethin' to ax you, Mr. Brown," she said. She had the same deep voice as her brother, Hambone. She finally released her vise-like grip and I sat.

"Baby Langston," Stanley began.

"Darius," Magnolia corrected him, looking at Stanley as if he had better not use that nickname again.

"Darius be missing over a week now," Stanley continued. "Magnolia here got a wire from one of her friends in Paris and she done catch a fast boat to come look for him. Hambone done flew the coop, and they both missin'."

I knew that Magnolia wanted to hire me to track down Hambone and Baby. Just as I was getting out of the private investigation trade, new business was coming my way.

"I send my drummer boy Lonny Jones to bring that Hambone back dead or alive, and he ain't find him," Magnolia said. "I put a thousand-dollar bounty on Hambone head. He s'posed to look after my baby, Darius, while he be writin' his poetry in Paris, and now Darius missin'."

Stanley spoke up then. "Urby, Magnolia want to hire you as private eye to track Hambone down and reel him in. Where Baby at? That be what she want to know. Ain't that right, Magnolia?"

She ignored him.

I knew that this was a job too far because only three people could know what happened to Baby. One of them was Daphne, and she was on her way back to America, probably already at sea. The other two were the Count and Pierre because Daphne had told me to ask the Count about him. As for myself, I reckoned that Baby was dead because he had no reason to be alive.

"There's only one place that Hambone would go to hide and that's to Chez Red Tops," I said. "Redtop's got a big cellar, and Hambone has holed up there before when the heat's been on him."

Magnolia stared at me and then looked at Stanley without saying a word. Stanley looked cowed and went over to the telephone. He picked up the receiver and dialed a number.

"Hello, Redtop. Yeah, Stanley," he said. "Lonny Jones be there? Put him on, girl." Stanley lit up a panatela while Magnolia studied him, her jaw muscles working.

"Lonny," Stanley continued, "I hear tell that Hambone hidin' in Redtop cellar. She don't like that man, why she be hidin' him? Tell her Baby Langston…"—he looked at Magnolia and corrected himself—"Darius mama here, and she want to grill Hambone 'bout where Baby at. Sho', I'll wait." Stanley nodded toward the liquor cabinet and then toward Magnolia.

"Could I offer you a drink while you wait, ma'am?" I asked.

"Rye whiskey, straight, no chaser," she answered without taking her eyes off Stanley.

I went to get our drinks, and we waited for a few minutes. Finally, Stanley said, "Magnolia, it be Hambone." She leapt to her feet and snatched the receiver.

"Rawlston," she screamed. "What has you done with Darius? Don't you lie to me that you don't know. I can hear it in your voice you lyin'. I be your sister, you remember? I know you lyin' now so 'fess up. Else I'm goin' to tell Lonny Jones to yank out yo' fingernails one by one, make you chew them up, and then shoot you in yo' big fat head, you hear? You tell me the truth and I spare you yo' life, I swear on our mama head."

Magnolia Swilley was a terrible sight to behold in her rage. A beautiful woman transformed into a killer who would make some of the brown shirt and black shirt thugs I had just seen in Berlin quake in their jackboots. Suddenly, her face became a tragic mask.

"You say what? He dead? You find him dead in the cellar of my club and then you bury him 'cause you scared of me? Don't you lie to me, Rawlston. It's you done kill him. Don't you go tellin' me he be dead when you find him in my cellar. You done kill him to get at me. Now you wants to save yo' hide. You gone show Lonny where you done buried him, right now. Put Lonny back on the phone, Rawlston."

While she waited, she tossed down half a tumbler of neat rye, and then her face, hands, and body started trembling as if struck by the Saint Vitus Dance. She put down the tumbler and gripped the receiver with both hands, the tears running down her cheeks. We could hear a squawking at the other end of the line.

"You go find Darius, Lonny. Say what? Hambone say his head all bash in when he find him?" She ran her hand through her hair, and then she turned her face to us and stared at us coldly before saying, "Lonny, you listen to me. I wants you to get that nigger to dig Darius up, and then you gone shoot Hambone dead and put the same dirt back over him. I'm goin' back to my hotel. You know the place. Yeah. You phone me there when you done finish, and then we gone find us a funeral parlor to bury my baby Darius right and proper here in France. Then I be goin' back to Harlem."

Magnolia put down the receiver and threw Stanley's crystal tumbler against the wall, sending shards of glass flying around the room. She stormed out, a killer's look in her eyes.

Stanley and I really needed some booze after that, and we sat, drinking in silence, our hands trembling.

"Lord have mercy," Stanley finally said.

I told Stanley about what had happened in Berlin, although I was sure that Colonel Schulz-Horn had already filled him in. Then Stanley went into his bedroom, and I heard the clinking of the combination lock on his safe. Stanley came back into the room hardly able to drag along the floor the brown leather satchel I had last seen when I stowed it in a locker in the Gare du Nord.

"This be yours, Urby. Goldilocks got my address at La Belle Princesse and had a chauffeur deliver the satchel here yesterday evening. It's locked, but there's an envelope here with a key inside it."

I opened the envelope and took out the note and the key. The note said,

Contribution to Urby's Masked Ball's re-opening fund, as promised, and payment of final investigation fees. Love always, Daphne Hohenzollern-Robinson

Robinson III had scribbled,

Many thanks for a job well done, Mr. Brown. I will tell Mr. O'Toole how helpful you've been. Best regards, Barnet Robinson III

I opened the satchel with the key and found inside a mixture of greenback dollar bills, gold francs, and three heavy gold ingots. There were no US dollar gold certificates. Stanley counted the bills, hefted the gold ingots, and scraped at one with his switchblade. He brought a small bottle with a dropper in it, squeezed the liquid on the scratch, and checked its color.

"This be real gold, Urby. Times three bars with that paper money, there be nigh on to one hundred grand of value in this satchel."

"Can you hold onto it for me, Stanley? Until we decide what to do with it?"

I dragged it back to his safe and hefted it in.

"Ain't no 'we,' Urby. This be yours, to the penny. I be glad to hold onto it for you, but goldilocks right about somethin' this time. You can buy you a club and re-open Urby's Masked Ball. They sho' be space openin' up. Magnolia told me she own La Belle Princesse, and it don't look likely to me that Hambone be gladhandin' nobody there no time soon."

"Thanks, Stanley. I need to think things over a while. But my private eye days are done forever. I need to play some music."

"Now you talkin' righteous, mon petit. And you get Hannah back here, tout de suite." He was really excited, and there we were, two ageing Creole waifs from St. Vincent's Colored Waifs' Home in New Orleans, Louisiana, hugging each other like real Frenchmen, in Paris.

I asked Stanley if I could use his telephone to phone Jean Fletcher. We made a rendezvous to meet in the La Coupole bar in a half-hour.

She promised to pay for drinks on her "expense account" when I told her I had some big scoops for her "Paris Diary."

I told Jean what Colonel Schulz-Horn had said to me about the rumors of a plot that Robinson III, the Abwehr, Goebbels, and Himmler had cooked up to fan the race hatred in America into a full-scale race war by pinning the kidnapping and murder of the Lindbergh baby on a colored man. Jean got so angry that she knocked her whiskey glass over, and the waiter had to bring her a fresh one. I told her about the belief held by some high-level Nazi officials that there was an Abwehr agent named Bruno Richard Hauptmann who had committed the kidnapping and murder of Baby Lindbergh and was going to fund and lead an uprising of the colored people against Uncle Sam on behalf of Adolf Hitler. I also told her how Robinson III had nearly nailed me as a potential Lindbergh baby killer by paying me with marked gold certificates.

"I'll get the word about this Bruno Richard Hauptmann to a contact of mine who works with J. Edgar Hoover. I'm sure that, by now, Hoover will be satisfied with a white German kidnapper. Congressmen are beginning to grumble about how long it's taking his famous G-men to catch the perpetrator."

Jean was very interested to learn that Daphne was definitely the illegitimate daughter of Kaiser Bill and that the story had already appeared in a German newspaper. She said that she could do Skip Oatman a favor by giving him some ideas on how to break the story for his own American newspaper. She would also use it, but she wanted to break it in a way that more heat would fall on Robinson III and his mother than on Daphne. She felt that Robinson III's days were numbered. If the Germans or Hoover didn't get him, then Robinson II would. As for Daphne, I told Jean that Robinson III had started molesting her when she was a kid. Jean, to my surprise, was totally unsympathetic.

"Do you believe her?" Jean asked skeptically. "I don't trust that bitch, pardon my French, any further than I can throw her. I guess *you* believe her?"

"I don't know," I answered, suddenly doubtful.

"Let's put a hold on that story about III molesting her," Jean said. "I don't have a lot of faith in her word."

I gave Jean my impressions of what it was like to be in Nazi-run Berlin and of the civil war between the brown shirts and the black shirts that Colonel Schulz-Horn had told me about.

"He thinks there'll be a big bust-up by the summer," I said.

"I can use that," she said. "That dovetails with the stuff that's going on in Paris and Rome and the growth of extremism in Europe. That's my next 'Paris Diary.' Thanks a bunch."

"I think I'd better move on, Jean. I have one more visit today. I'm going to see the Count."

"How's your old man?" she asked.

"Up to his neck in stuff that's so nasty that you can't imagine it."

"Give him the regards of freedom-loving peoples everywhere."

"Will do, Jean. By the way, one last scoop. I'm closing my private eye agency. I'm going to re-open my nightclub."

"That's great news. I'll start drumming up publicity for the re-opening."

I told her that I wasn't planning to re-open right away and thanked her again for putting me onto Skip Oatman. Then I went to Honoré and asked him if he could get me a line so that I could make a phone call. He was all smiles as he handed the telephone to me. He waited for a beat longer than usual; I got the message and tipped him lavishly. He walked off whistling, as if sunlight had burst into the dim interior of La Coupole.

I left Jean to pay the bill and phoned the Count. We arranged to meet at his office in an hour. In the meantime, I started writing in my head the letters that I was going to send to Hannah, begging her to come back. I started throwing in words like "loving her" and "needing her" and "marriage" and "starting a new life together." I whiled away the time brain-writing the love letters in the calm, peace, and freedom of a Paris Sunday.

I couldn't concentrate, though. I kept seeing Buster dead in Stanley's stables, my bullet taking his life away. I thought about the rage inside me and in the world that had brought me to France, and then to its killing fields in the Great War. War had not killed the Beast of Rage anywhere, though. Rage was flaming up again everywhere, not dying down. Maybe, with my music, I could calm that rage. But I doubted that anything would ever slake it, not even another war or the war after that.

CHAPTER 25

The Count listened to my Berlin stories carefully at times, as if learning something new, and, at other times, I sensed that Daphne, or Robinson III, had already told him parts of the story. I left out any mention of how Daphne and I managed to escape from Germany and the role played by Colonel Schulz-Horn and his officer friends because that would be like signing their death sentences. I sensed that Daphne had left that part of the story out, too.

"I know that you and Daphne and maybe Mr. Robinson were somehow involved in her fake kidnapping and the ransom demand. You will deny it, of course, and nothing can be proved one way or the other. Anyway, I've stopped working as a private eye."

"That's very good; it's a vulgar job for a Count of the d'Uribé-Lebrun lineage."

"Then you'll be even happier to hear that I'm going to re-open my nightclub, Urby's Masked Ball. That's even more vulgar in your eyes. Don't worry. I'm not planning to call it 'Count Urby's Masked Ball.'"

"You may call it what you like. I very much enjoyed hearing you play at the charity concert Saturday before last. I may even say I was proud of you that night. You are gifted, my son."

That really amazed me; and he seemed sincere when he said, "If you need any financial help, please let me know." Then he leaned forward and, with a wry smile on his face and his blue eye boring into mine, he said, "But then, I understand that you have been amply rewarded for your work on the kidnap and ransom affair of my colleague Bartholomew Thigpen and Miss Daphne Hohenzollern. One hundred thousand dollars, was it not? Curious how certain dollar figures repeat themselves in ransoms and fees. Pure coincidence, no doubt."

The ransom from a bogus kidnapping had been returned to its rightful owner, Robinson III, who had Daphne turn it over to Stanley to "pay my fees." Robinson III was perfectly within his rights to do so. It was, theoretically, his money. Daphne had blackmailed him into giving it to me, of that I had no doubt. I felt that I had earned the money, wherever it really came from, and I planned to hold onto it.

The Count got up from his chair, went to his bar, and poured us two snifters of Domfront calvados.

"Let us toast the successful conclusion of your investigation. I await the re-opening of your nightclub. Please invite me."

I didn't know what to say, so I waited.

"One day, you will see the light and I, like any father, hope that we can grow closer over the years. Especially because I am now the only family that you have."

I waited, playing his words back again in my head. "What do you mean by you are 'now the only family that I have'?"

He feigned surprise. "Did you not know that Bartholomew Lincoln Thigpen Junior was your brother? You had the same mother, my beloved Josephine Dubois. I understand that Bartholomew now lies buried on the floor of the Seine. Near Argenteuil." He sighed and spun around in his chair to smile at me. I put the snifter of calvados on his desk and walked out of his office, with the Count close on my heels.

Daphne had given me a "poisoned gift." The Count would want his cut of the "ransom", which he could now demand thanks to Redtop, his eyewitness to Buster's death and burial.

I saw Redtop's frightened face again in my mind's eye. She had sold me out to the Count in exchange for freedom from her greatest fear, being forced to leave France and return to America and Jim Crow. Once again, I saw Buster sink to the ground with my bullet in his brain and then, like a mariner buried at sea, into the icy waters of the Seine. My brother. Bartholomew.

"I need you, my son," the Count cried out suddenly, as I hurried away. "You must tie your destiny to mine and to our lineage. Now!"

I remember brushing past Pierre on my way out, the Count's plea ringing in my ears. Pierre and some other Oriflamme stood at attention like a guard of honor as I hurried out the door.

Outside, the air had grown colder as the winter night fell over Paris. I started sprinting down rue Boissy d'Anglas toward the Seine, but I knew that its waters would never mean freedom to me as they had before. I had killed one man too many.

The thing I most wanted to do was to get rid of my weapons for killing and maiming: my guns and my saps and, above all, my rage. I vowed then and there never to kill or harm anyone again. Ever. I was going to deep-six my Colt in the Seine.

The Count, Pierre, and two other Oriflamme had followed Urby out onto the street and watched him racing toward the Seine. The Count nodded to Pierre and his two colleagues.

"Follow him and make sure that he doesn't do anything rash," the Count ordered. "There are already enough of our cadavers in that river."

CHAPTER 26

Le Havre, France, Saturday, 11 April 1936

Hannah Korngold strained her eyes to see if she could spot Urby in the crowd waiting on the dock as her ship headed for its berth at Le Havre. His last of many letters had finally convinced her to start her life with him all over again. She loved him and he loved her and it had been that way for a long time. As a Jew, she feared the terrible events that were occurring in Europe, especially in Germany, but she knew that life without Urby would have no meaning for her.

She saw Urby and waved excitedly, happier than she had been for a long time. He was waving at her with his clarinet, so she opened her violin case and waved at him with her violin.

EPILOGUE

Related Events of 1934–1936

"THE NIGHT OF THE LONG KNIVES"

Between June 30 and July 2, 1934, Adolf Hitler ordered a purge of the brown shirts of the Sturmabteilung (SA) and of its leader, the Führer's former comrade in arms, Ernst Röhm. Hitler realized that the continuing recourse to violent street actions by his former comrades, who had supplied the muscle behind his rise to power in Germany, was incompatible with the image of respectability, which, at that juncture, he wanted to cultivate among bourgeois German conservatives. Above all, Hitler wished to mollify the regular army apparatus of the Reichswehr, who found the brown shirts and their leader, Röhm, repellent.

The death toll from the purge, which has come to be known as the "Night of the Long Knives," may never be known with exactitude. The number of those killed, wounded, and summarily arrested no doubt ran into thousands.

The majority of the killings and arrests were carried out by the black-shirts(SS) and the Gestapo, or secret police. The purge helped Hitler to build support for his regime among the Reichswehr and provided a basis for it to carry out other extra-legal activities in the future, as long as these were deemed by the Führer to be in the interests of the German Reich.

Urby Brown received a telephone call from Colonel Schulz-Horn on July 4, 1934, Urby's thirty-ninth birthday. After wishing him a happy birthday, the colonel told him that he and all of the members of his circle of "blood brother" officers had survived the purge. The colonel once again promised to be present for the re-opening of Urby's Masked Ball nightclub come hell or high water. Urby told him that he had not yet decided when to re-open the nightclub. It depended on the reply that he received to a letter that he had sent to a friend in America.

THE LINDBERGH KIDNAPPING AND ITS AFTERMATH

Acting on a tipoff, law enforcement agencies were on the lookout for expenditures in dollar gold certificates, a number of which had been marked and included in the ransom demanded and paid over for the safe return of the kidnapped and murdered baby, Charles Lindbergh Junior. In September 1934, a ten-dollar gold certificate was used as payment in a gas station, and the pump attendant noted the New York license plate number of the Dodge sedan concerned and turned it in to the police. The car was traced to one Bruno Richard Hauptmann, who was put under surveillance and captured in New York City after a high-speed car chase by the police.

During his trial, which lasted from January 2 to February 13, 1935, Hauptmann, a carpenter by profession, became "The Most Hated Man in the World." Hauptmann maintained to the end that he was innocent of the kidnapping and murder of Charles Lindbergh Junior, but he had no satisfactory explanations for the presence of a shoebox containing $15,000 of the ransom money, partly in gold certificates, which had been found in his garage. It later transpired that Hauptmann had been sighted near Hopewell, New Jersey, where the Lindberghs resided, on the day of the kidnapping. He was also positively identified as the person who had collected the ransom money, and incriminating testimony was given by other witnesses who had seen him spending gold certificates on various items.

While the defense argued that, on balance, the evidence against Hauptmann was mainly circumstantial, and, even the governor of New Jersey had doubts as to whether Hauptmann had acted alone, he was finally electrocuted in New Jersey State Prison on April 3, 1936.

MURDER AND SCANDAL IN THE BARNET ROBINSON FAMILY

On April 4, 1936, the day after Bruno Richard Hauptmann's execution, a homeless man was found strangled to death on a park bench in Battery Park, facing the Statue of Liberty. The victim was identified as Barnet Robinson III. He had once been a prominent businessman, educated at Princeton University. Notorious for his pro-Nazi sympathies, he had been forced to step down from the Board of Trustees of Smith College. His father, Barnet Robinson II, had fired him from his role as CEO of Barnet Industries in March 1934 and also disinherited him. His father had also divorced the mother of Barnet Robinson III in March 1934, after it came to light that she had had an affair with Kaiser Wilhelm II before the outbreak of the First World War which resulted in the birth of an illegitimate daughter by the Kaiser in 1913. She committed suicide one year to the day after her divorce, in March 1935.

According to informed sources, the suicide occurred two days after her former husband had re-married, this time to her illegitimate daughter by Kaiser Wilhelm II, known as Daphne Hohenzollern-Robinson. Among the controversies swirling around the marriage was the age gap of forty-two years between Barnet Robinson II and his erstwhile granddaughter: he was sixty-four years old and she was not yet twenty-two years old at the time of their marriage in March 1935.

Family members and associates of Barnet Robinson III cited his firing as CEO of Barnet Industries and his mother's divorce from his father in March 1934, as well as his father's re-marriage to his half-sister Daphne Hohenzollern-Robinson a year later followed almost immediately by his mother's suicide, as the major factors that led to a total breakdown in his character and moral fiber and, finally, sent him spiraling into dissolution and vagrancy. The police have determined that the cause of his death was intentional homicide but have provided no leads regarding the motives behind the murder of Barnet Robinson III.

Barnet Robinson II, who had enjoyed robust good health all of his life and had been captain of Princeton's undefeated national champion football team of 1893, died of a heart attack, on April 18, 1936, two weeks after his son was found murdered. He had specified in his will that, upon his death, his entire estate and full control of the management of Barnet Industries were to devolve upon his grieving young widow, Daphne Hohenzollern-Robinson. She thus became one of the richest and most powerful women in America before her twenty-third birthday.

ATTEMPTED ASSASSINATION OF LÉON BLUM

On February 13, 1936, Léon Blum, leader of the Socialist coalition, was in a car on the Boulevard Saint-Germain-des-Près, returning home from the National Assembly with friends, when, according to newspaper accounts, he was set upon by a large band of extremist youths belonging to various royalist, Fascist, and anti-Semitic groups. After smashing the car windows with blackjacks and iron bars, they dragged Blum from the car and nearly beat him to death as he lay prostrate on the sidewalk. He was saved from death by the timely intervention of workers from a nearby building and several policemen who came to his rescue.

Blum's Socialist coalition won the legislative elections of May 1936, and he became the first Socialist and Jewish Prime Minister of France, leading the Popular Front Government from June 1936 to June 1937. During that period, the Popular Front initiated major reforms in France's social and labor systems, such as the introduction of a forty-hour week, paid vacations for workers, and the widening of their bargaining rights.

During his time in government, Blum was showered with abuse by right-wing extremists and anti-Semites, the leader of the Oriflamme du Roi, Count René d'Uribé-Lebrun, being the most virulent of Blum's detractors.

STORY ON FRONT PAGE OF THE PARIS-PANAME SOIR EDITION OF JULY 4, 1936

The renowned American clarinetist and long-time Paris resident, Urby Brown, will re-open his once-popular Montmartre nightclub Urby's Masked Ball tonight on the occasion of his birthday. A stellar audience of American and French musicians, as well as international celebrities from the worlds of the stage, the screen, and the plastic and literary arts, are expected to be present for the re-opening. It is already being whispered that Louis Armstrong, Sidney Bechet, Stanley Bontemps, and Josephine Baker will be on hand to pay homage to the great New Orleans Creole clarinetist, Urby Brown.

Brown left America as a young man of nineteen at the start of the Great War to rally to the colors of his "adopted" country, France. His musical career is matched only by his military career. Serving at the rank of sergeant in the French Foreign Legion by the end of the war, he had beforehand been an ace in the volunteer American air unit of the French Air Force, the Lafayette Flying Corps, with six confirmed kills to his credit. He had been decorated with a Croix de Guerre with Palm.

The re-opening of Urby's Masked Ball will take place two months after the announcement of Mr. Brown's engagement to Hannah Korngold, a distinguished classical violin soloist and, like Mr. Brown, a native of New Orleans, Louisiana.

The End